Murder,
My Dear Watson

Murder,
My Dear Watson

New Tales of Sherlock Holmes

EDITED BY

Martin H. Greenberg • Jon Lellenberg • Daniel Stashower

CARROLL & GRAF PUBLISHERS
NEW YORK

Murder, My Dear Watson
New Tales of Sherlock Holmes

Carroll & Graf Publishers
An Imprint of Avalon Publishing Group Inc.
161 William Street, 16th Floor
New York, NY 10038

First Carroll & Graf edition 2002

Library of Congress Cataloging-in-Publication Data is available.

ISBN: 0-7867-1081-0

Printed in the United States of America
Distributed by Publishers Group West

CONTENTS

FOREWORD

Jon Lellenberg

SHERLOCK HOLMES IMITATIONS have been appearing in print —and, later, on stage and screen—almost from the moment that the original short stories began running in *The Strand Magazine* in 1891. So striking and eccentric a character as Sherlock Holmes, with such pronounced attributes and manner of speech, could hardly fail to prompt considerable lighthearted parody. And the fact that everyone seemed to be reading Sherlock Holmes guaranteed A. Conan Doyle's imitators that everyone would recognize and understand their parodies as well. Many were done by writers whose status, then and forever, was minor, but others, such as A. A. Milne and P. G. Wodehouse, cut their literary teeth on Sherlock Holmes parody when they were young, and writers of the stature of Bret Harte, James Barrie, Mark Twain, and O. Henry did not hesitate to write Sherlock Holmes parodies in those early days as well.

Sherlock Holmes was on stage quickly as well, but it was 1899 when he first attained theatrical stardom in the person of William Gillette, America's greatest actor and playwright of that day. Writing with the blessing of Conan Doyle, Gillette turned elements of various Sherlock Holmes stories into a superior melodrama that became a Broadway hit and then a nationwide sensation. Similar success followed when Gillette took the play to England, where, after its London run, traveling companies performed it throughout the British Isles and on the Continent. In time there would be a motion picture (now lost, alas!), and then a Farewell Tour, which began touring America in 1928 and only ended in 1932. Gillette even played the role the first time that Sherlock Holmes was dramatized on radio, in 1930.

Gillette's impact upon the public conception of Sherlock Holmes was second only to Conan Doyle's: the actor became the model for the American illustrations of the stories when Conan Doyle brought Holmes back to life in 1903; he was imitated for decades by subsequent portrayers of Sherlock Holmes on stage and screen; Orson Welles adapted Gillette's play for radio in his *Mercury Theater of the Air*, and the play continues to be performed to this day—sometimes by companies as august as the Royal Shakespeare Company, whose 1973 revival of it in England and America triggered a new Holmes craze not over yet.

Gillette drew upon the actual Sherlock Holmes stories for his play's situations and plot, which pitted Holmes and Watson against Professor Moriarty, but he did not hesitate to invent new characters and situations as well. One new character was the detective's ingenue client Alice Faulkner. When Gillette's writing of the playscript had reached a certain impasse, he cabled Conan Doyle diffidently: "May I marry Holmes?" The answer from the character's creator gave license to uncounted liberties taken with Sherlock Holmes ever since. "You may marry him or murder him or do what you want with him," ran Conan Doyle's reply—and Gillette ended his play with Alice Faulkner in Sherlock Holmes's arms.

So, in a sense, if we take liberties with Sherlock Holmes today, in our admiring way, Sir Arthur Conan Doyle has no one but himself to blame. Once again we present a new set of tales about the Great Detective, by writers who know him well but not too worshipfully; plus some nonfiction contributions that survey the cultural phenomenon of Sherlock Holmes, from the cold type of *Beeton's Christmas Annual* in 1887 and *The Strand Magazine* in the 1890s to the computers and Internet of today.

Murder,
My Dear Watson

THE ADVENTURE OF THE DYING DOCTOR

Colin Bruce

Ｔ HE MOST SPECTACULAR natural event of our times was of
course the Great Comet of 1882. Despite the excellence of modern astronomy, the sight probably inspired as much superstitious awe as it did scientific fascination, and during its closest approach in the month of September, the talk in London—and no doubt in almost all other parts of the world—was of little else. My regular readers may have wondered that it is mentioned nowhere in my memoirs. I can now reveal that there was indeed a Sherlock Holmes case involving this strange period. I have not written of it until now because the story is tangled up with another which shows me up in a very bad light. But now I feel the tale must be told, and in full, if only as a warning to future generations against more than one kind of folly.

I HAD SLEPT very badly, and came down early for breakfast. Yet I was not looking forward to the meal, for I had decided that this was the occasion when I must break the news to Sherlock Holmes that I could no longer serve as his companion and assistant. I must throw myself wholly into my medical work, putting in the longest possible hours with no side distractions; and furthermore I must move to wherever the best fees were to be earned.

So I was somewhat relieved, as well as surprised, to find that my colleague had breakfasted already, and was donning his coat and gloves. I was able to deduce from the suitcase by his side that he was setting off on a substantial journey.

"Good morning, Holmes. I thought you were currently detained in town by the Threadneedle Street affair?"

He shook his head. "No, Watson, that has progressed to the point where it can be handed over to Lestrade with reasonable certainty that it will not come unstuck. I am off to the South Coast, I am not sure for how long. I will see you possibly tonight, but more likely not for a few days." And with that he was gone.

I found myself once again alone with my troubled conscience. And now I must tell you the cause. You may recall that after being invalided out of the Afghan war with a bullet in the leg, I was evacuated to a hospital in Peshawar. That conflict is often described as part of The Great Game: the slow unending struggle between Imperial Russia to the north and Imperial Britain to the south to control the centre of gravity of the Asian continent. But I was there, and I can assure you it was no game: indeed I returned scarred as much in my soul as on my body. This may partly explain, though it certainly does not excuse, what followed.

Due to the flood of war wounded, there was an acute shortage of nurses in Peshawar, and their efforts were supplemented by female volunteers from the British families there. One such—I will call her Sarah, though that is not her real name—was herself the daughter of a surgeon at the hospital. By then I was in a recuperative ward, awaiting passage back to Britain. Although in very black spirits, my medical needs were slight, and the regular staff quite understandably neglected me in favour of those with more immediate needs. But Sarah overlooked no-one. She always delayed for a chat at the beginning and end of her shift, and my spirits were always lightened as much by looking forward to those talks as for their brief duration. When I was transferred to a small cottage within the hospital grounds, it was natural that she should volunteer to be my daily visitor and housekeeper. Our feelings grew for one another, but of course I could not speak my wishes. How could I ask such a girl to marry a cripple with no means of support beyond a small war pension? For at the time, it still looked as though I would end up on crutches at best, in a wheelchair at worst. In the end I am sure that the unexpected completeness of my recovery owed as much to her nursing as to any surgery.

Then suddenly came the news that there would be a spare berth on the *Orontes*, sailing for England the next day. That last evening together, our tenderness for one another overcame our scruples. I take full responsibility for what followed. I never saw her again, and though I wrote to her from London at increasing intervals, my letters went unanswered.

Until a week ago. Then had come a letter from Eastbourne, unstamped, so the postman had asked whether I wished to receive it, and was prepared to pay the postage. Thankfully, I had decided to do so, even though he would not permit me to see the envelope first. (Apparently this is because some people try to communicate free of charge, by the way they space the address on the envelope: for example soldiers who merely wish to reassure their family at home that all is well with them. Rather ingenious!)

But I digress. The letter was from Sarah, but written in a bitter tone quite unlike that of the sweet girl I once had loved—and no wonder. She had paid the price for our folly: it had left her with child. She had written to me several times, but with no certain address to write to, and receiving no reply, had been too proud to try to contact me again, despite the horror that followed. For her family had taken the sternest view possible, buying her a third-class ticket home, giving her a small amount of money, and telling her that they never wished to see or hear from her again.

She had struggled to bring up the boy as a "widow," working as a seamstress in a town where no-one knew her, but times had become desperately hard. Her landlord was about to evict her. If I had no feelings for her, had I none even for my son? She had at last found my address from the Medical Register, and with no pride left, she was begging for my help. My financial help, that is, for she was unwilling to see me under any circumstances.

At first I almost disbelieved the letter was from her: her personality seemed to have changed so completely. Then I reflected how sustained hardship can transform the strongest character, and the realisation that any such change was entirely my fault was almost too much for me. Of course I sent what money I could afford at once. But

I realised that my own future must now be very different. No longer could I be a part-time doctor who spent much of his energy playing at detective work. I must leave Baker Street, bid Sherlock Holmes find another assistant, and devote myself to a life of hard work to support the good woman and the even more innocent child for whose predicament I was responsible.

Napoleon famously remarked that an army marches upon its stomach, and with this maxim he led France to capture much of Europe. If so, it is surely upon the traditional English breakfast that the backbone of our Empire depends. For after a long night wrestling with my guilty thoughts, Mrs Hudson's generous breakfast table, with its usual spread of scrambled eggs, bacon, mushrooms, deviled kidneys, and fried bread, all served by the lady herself, did more to restore my spirits than I would have believed possible. No wonder the Continentals struggle to keep up with us, starting the day as they do with a scrap of croissant and a cup of coffee. I arrived at my surgery if not cheerful, then at least confident that I had the strength to deal with whatever life's caprices should set before me.

Alas for such confidence! Perhaps the cruellest of the many tricks that the Fates play upon us is their unfair habit of dealing not one but two blows in quick succession, like a boxer who first sets his opponent reeling from a head blow, then delivers a low punch with even greater force.

Two letters rested on the mat. The first was one of those unsolicited commercial letters which have become such a pest in the mails recently: I now receive as many as one or two every week! It contained an offer of life insurance from a company I had never heard of. The payment offered in the event of early death was generous, but the premiums payable were outrageous even in proportion, and I consigned the thing to the wastebasket without a second thought.

The second item was more interesting. It came from a Dr. Nagel at an address in Harley Street. Although the letter was printed, it was written in a frank and engaging way that warmed me as though I was being addressed personally. It opened with a reminder of the old saw that we doctors know full well that half the medicines we prescribe are ineffective—the problem is that we do not know *which* half! Dr. Nagel proposed to set up a reporting system whereby well-respected general practitioners (here I felt a glow of pride at being so chosen) would report honestly, in confidence, on the success or failure of each course of treatment they performed. As the reports came in, so medicine would gradually be transformed from an intuitive art into an exact science.

This was obviously a project I should become involved in, now that I was committing myself fully to doctoring. Dr. Nagel had an initial request for those taking part. Had I seen a recent article in *The Lancet* describing a diagnostic test for Marchant's syndrome that could be performed overnight, using no more than a drop of blood and common chemicals available in every surgery? If so, I probably remembered that the test seemed pretty much infallible in detecting the disease in its earliest stages. It was also claimed that the test would rarely give false positives: that is to say, only one time in a hundred would it wrongly indicate that someone who was in fact *not* suffering from Marchant's had the disease. Dr. Nagel wanted all the doctors taking part in his scheme to help verify the latter claim, by performing the test on themselves and reporting the results. I mixed the required chemicals immediately. The task occupied me until my first patient of the morning arrived. Then I placed the test-tube to one side, to give the reaction time to complete.

I did not have a chance to examine it again until the lunch hour. Indeed, I had been out to visit the pie-seller on the corner, and was consuming his wares, before I remembered the experiment. I retrieved the test-tube and held it up to the window. For several seconds, my mind simply refused to accept the implications of the bright blue colour that was evident. Not until I had leafed through *The Lancet* with trembling fingers to confirm what I already knew, that the colour showed proof—or to be exact, a 99 percent chance, which is surely proof for all practical purposes—of the presence of Marchant's, did the awfulness of my situation hit me.

I would die within a year. Within a year at the most. My hopes and plans, my guilts and worries: soon all would be equally irrelevant. It is not the first time I have faced death: it came close to me in Afghanistan, and several times since I have willingly followed Sherlock Holmes into great danger. But I now realised that my courage in those situations had sprung from the fact that I had stood a sporting chance—indeed, a better than even chance—of survival. Now hope must be abandoned.

I got through my early afternoon surgery somehow, though five minutes after each patient had left I could not have told you who each was, or what malady they were suffering from. Tea-time found me motionless in my chair, staring at the wastebasket. Somehow I had the feeling of something forgotten, something urgent to be done.

The other letter! Not the one from Dr. Nagel, but the offer of life insurance I had so contemptuously cast aside. If there was nothing I could do for myself, I could still help Sarah, and the child whose name she had not even told me. I retrieved the crumpled sheets, and read the document more carefully. The monthly instalments were indeed substantial, but I would not be paying them for long. And the payment on my death in a year's time would be sufficient to pay for a good education for my son, and still keep Sarah in comfort if not luxury for the rest of her life.

There was of course the usual declaration that to the best of my knowledge, I did not suffer from any illness of a life-threatening nature. I signed without a qualm. After all, I was not doing this for myself. Surely the welfare of my once beloved and her son were more important than the profits of a life insurance company? No-one could ever know that I had by the wildest of coincidences tested myself for Marchant's syndrome that same day: there had been no witnesses. Thus I rationalised a fraudulent act involving more money than I had ever seen, or indeed would now ever see, in my whole life. I went out to the waiting-room and had two patients who knew me personally witness and date the document as required.

My homecoming that evening was somewhat unusual. I was met in the hallway by Mrs. Hudson.

"Doctor! Is your colleague not with you?"

"I am afraid not. I doubt he will be back before tomorrow at the earliest. Has a client come with urgent business?"

"Not a client, sir, but Mr. Mycroft Holmes. He gave me a sealed note that he made me promise to hand to his brother by six-o-clock tonight, and there is less than an hour left. He stressed that the matter was most important."

I raised my eyebrows. Mycroft was a rare visitor: we saw him once a year if that, not because of any lack of cordiality between the brothers, but rather because his work was so important, and his habits so fixed, that rarely did he venture farther than the little zone encompassing his residence, his club, and his desk at the Foreign Office. It took something very serious to fetch him further afield. I persuaded Mrs Hudson that in the circumstances she could give the envelope to me, and tore open the seal. The contents were something of an anticlimax. A strip of paper bore the message: "Stock market down ten points. Gold up tuppence an ounce. Use the enclosed."

The other item was a ticket for an unspecified performance at the Royal Albert Hall at seven o'clock that evening.

I hastened to reassure Mrs. Hudson that even the likes of Sherlock and Mycroft Holmes sometimes leave quite trivial communications for one another. Having soothed her down, it occurred to me that in his absence, I would be doing Sherlock Holmes a favour if I used the ticket myself, and reimbursed him for it when he returned. I had no wish to spend another evening moping alone in our rooms, and the last event I had attended at the Albert Hall had been most enjoyable, one of the famous Promenade Concerts.

The walk across Hyde Park to the Hall was rewarding in itself. There was no moon, but the whole landscape was lit by the ethereal glow from the great comet which hung low in the southern sky like a vast candle flame. At a casual glance you might have mistaken it for a cloud, but as you looked more closely your eye was drawn to the pattern of fine lines of glowing gas which arced out from an invisible centre point, with a hint of further colour and structure beyond that which you could discern. All around I heard the murmur of awed voices and saw upturned faces, for a large crowd of people were strolling in the same direction as myself. By the time I was near enough to the Hall for the comet to become hidden behind its great bulk, I had to slow as the crowd thickened into a queue heading up the steps of the nearest entrance. It edged forward gradually: tonight's performance was evidently a sell-out.

When I finally reached my seat, however, after wending my way through that maze of cramped little corridors and stairways that make the Promenade-goer feel like a rat in a warren, albeit helpfully directed at every turn by an usher inspecting the seat number on his ticket, I gazed about the Hall in some bafflement. It was obviously not a concert we were expecting, for there was not a musical instrument in sight. The few props visible on the stage floor below (for my seat had turned out to be high up in the Gods) reminded me more of a conjurer's set.

Before I could speculate further, the electric chandeliers above us dimmed, the audience quietened, and a figure in evening dress took the podium and bowed briefly. I say figure because the young man (as he turned out to be) had long blond hair, and his voice, when he spoke, was so high-pitched that it could equally have been a girl's.

"Ladies and gentlemen, I am Mr. James Moriarty. Perhaps you are surprised at being addressed by one so young, but I can assure you I am a qualified mathematical physicist. I replace your expected speaker, Professor Morrison because—as you can imagine—my seniors in the department of astronomy are fully occupied at present, in the study of the comet which is at this moment lighting the sky outside. Yet I think I will not disappoint you, for my nominal superiors are perhaps a little set in their ways, a little unimaginative in their teaching methods. I will endeavour not merely to inform you, but to keep you awake."

There came a titter from the young students who occupied the standing-room on the floor of the hall. I did not approve—even if his words were partly in jest, I believe that one's elders should be treated with respect—but as he continued, I could not help being impressed by his skill.

He described first how the bodies of the solar system revolve not around the Earth, as the ancients thought, but around the gigantic ball of flaming gases that is the Sun, for the Sun's mass is a million times greater then the Earth's—if the latter was represented by a mouse, then the Sun would mass as much as an elephant! As he spoke, one of the electric chandeliers brightened tremendously to represent the Sun, and the others went out altogether.

Then he called the planets into existence one by one. And as he did so, each appeared in the air above us, seemingly hanging in space, and slowly orbiting the chandelier at the appropriate distance. Of course I could guess it was all done with wires, but it was impressive nevertheless. First came a charred little ball representing Mercury, then a larger milky-white one for Venus. Earth herself was represented by a slowly spinning globe: with the opera-glasses provided by every seat, you could clearly make out the continents and oceans. Red Mars was followed by a huge sphere representing Jupiter, and similar ones for the great, cold planets beyond. As each body was revealed, Moriarty described what astronomers had been able to deduce about it. When all were in view, his tones became soft and hypnotic as he described the great age of the solar system, the billions of years for which each planet had followed the same constant, near-circular path.

So could we rest assured that celestial mechanics was always benign, predictable, all but eternal, he almost purred? He implored us to watch carefully. Seemingly from far away, a trumpet note sounded. Then came a hissing sound, growing ever louder, nervously reminiscent of a boiler about to explode. And down from the edge of the ceiling swooped the comet!

It seemed a ball of ice, but it evaporated furiously even as we watched, trailing a cloud of steam very much like a comet's tail. And it wove a desperately unpredictable path which ever and again took it close to members of the audience. At one point it seemed to head straight for me at incredible speed. I am not a nervous man, yet I could not prevent myself flinging my hands up to protect my face. But whoever was operating the hidden wires was very skillful: again and again, it seemed that the thing must hit some person, but it never did. It would have caused a nasty burn, for it must in reality be a lump of dry ice, solid carbon dioxide whose intense cold can scald skin as badly as boiling water. But in the end, it was against the hanging sphere representing the Earth that the thing collided and stuck. The last of the ice quickly evaporated, leaving a large blemish on the affected globe.

Mr. Moriarty seemed most taken aback at the mishap. He hastened to explain that the chances of a comet striking the Earth in reality were remote—very remote indeed. But the spell had been broken, and the audience were no longer inclined to accept his word without question. For the first time hands were raised, and questions put.

Perhaps one individual comet was unlikely to hit Earth, but how many comets lurked out in the depths beyond Neptune? No-one knew, Moriarty replied, for they were beyond detection by current telescopes at such distances. But some estimates put their number in the millions, or even billions.

This answer left an uncomfortable impression. Someone had the boldness to ask the obvious: was the great comet currently visible in the skies going to hit the Earth? Its course had been measured with great accuracy, Moriarty replied, and it was expected to miss us by some three-quarters of a million miles. Yet there was some hesitation in his manner as he said this. Clearly honesty forced him to say more, and he admitted that because the gas evaporating from the surface had a rocketlike propulsive effect, comets were the only known celestial bodies which did not always follow a predictable path.

What would be the effect if the comet did hit Earth? After all, although a comet's tail is so spectacular, it is composed of gas so tenuous as to be almost a vacuum. The solid nucleus is only a few miles across. Surely the damage would be localised.

Not so, said Moriarty. Although the nucleus was small compared to the Earth, its kinetic energy was enormous due to its great relative speed. Even if the comet struck in a remote ocean region, the tidal wave caused would destroy coastal areas right around the world. This would have an immense effect on civilisation, for the vast majority of the human race, and almost all of its factories and industries, are situated close to sea level. But he begged the audience to remember that the chance of impact was very remote. He looked at his watch and announced with obvious relief that there was time for only one further question. A forest of hands went up, and he seemed to hesitate before pointing to a man not far from myself.

"I would like to know, Mr. Moriarty, where you yourself plan to be in one month's time, when I understand the comet will be at its point of closest approach? Will you be at your post at one of the observatories?"

"I was unable to obtain observing time on any telescope large enough to be of use: they are all booked up. I shall be on holiday in Switzerland." He said the last words almost in a mumble, as if he did not wish to be heard.

"Indeed." His questioner rose and pointed accusingly. "You have told us not to worry, sir. Yet what a coincidence that you will be visiting the only European nation which is situated entirely on high ground remote from the sea."

Moriarty appeared quite at a loss. He muttered an unconvincing denial before returning to his script and bringing the proceedings to a close. It was a silent and thoughtful audience that filed out of the Hall shortly afterward.

I RETURNED TO Baker Street to the sight of a roaring fire just started in the grate. Sherlock Holmes knelt before it with his back to me, prodding logs into position with the poker.

"Watson, at last! What has kept you so late? I have just returned to find our living room cold as ice."

"I was at a science lecture. Mycroft had left you a ticket and—"

"Yes, yes, I know all about it. He is dropping by here later. He claims to have discovered a mathematician who commits crimes that are not crimes, and has generously announced he will use our rooms as the scene for his grand *denouement*. He says I will find it an educational experience. But first I have some news that may cheer you."

He rose from the hearth and took his usual chair. "Watson, it has not escaped my attention that you have not been your usual self of late."

"I did not think you had noticed."

"Most assuredly I have, but I did not wish to arouse false hopes until I had got to the bottom of the matter. Would I be correct in assuming that your troubles were not unconnected with events that took place some years ago, in the town of Peshawar?"

"Holmes, how on earth—?"

"I therefore went down to Eastbourne today to interview one Margaret Blackstock."

I gazed at him, baffled. Then I remembered the name as that of the formidable ward sister who had made life a terror for both the regular nurses and the volunteers.

"Good lord, Holmes, you have got completely the wrong woman! I would hardly—"

He cut me off again. "No, I had the right woman. In a hospital replete with male war heroes and young female volunteers, you and Sarah were not the only pair between whom romance was obviously blossoming.

"On retiring to the south coast on a modest pension, it occurred to Sister Blackstock, who was very much a woman of the world, that although few such affairs lead to marriage, a much higher proportion lead to physical intimacy. She had the brilliant idea of writing to each of the men whose address she could trace a reproachful letter that appeared to come from their former lover. I believe you have seen a sample."

I gazed at him in amazement. "So it was all a hoax! Holmes, I am once again indebted to you." But then I hesitated. "I wonder what became of the real Sarah, though. My conscience has been disturbed. Do you think I should seek her out?"

"I thought you might feel that way, Watson. I have already done so, but with more discretion than you might have employed. She is happily married to a chemist in Hove. They have two children, both born well into their marriage. She sends her regards, and bears you no ill-will whatsoever, but under the circumstances you will understand she wishes no further meeting between you."

"How did you guess that the letter was likely to be a fake?"

"There were several factors, Watson. But the main point was that a single indiscretion rarely creates a baby: the chance is roughly five percent, or one in twenty. On the occasion of a woman's first experience, it is lower still, no doubt because her body has had no prior warning that it is to prepare for pregnancy. So I investigated."

I sat back, feeling the burden of guilt lift from me. Then I remembered the far worse news that I had received that morning.

"Holmes, I am unspeakably grateful. But I must tell you nevertheless that I will be able to stay with you only for a limited time." My voice almost broke on the final words.

My friend looked at me more intently than I could ever remember him doing. When he spoke, his voice was as gentle as when addressing a client in great distress.

"Tell me why, Watson."

With far less dignity than I had intended, I poured out my story: Dr. Nagel's letter, the test for Marchant's, the result. I left out nothing, not even my foolish attempt to claim the now irrelevant insurance for Sarah's benefit. As he listened, my friend's face grew ever graver. He questioned me intently on several points. I could see what he was driving at, but there were no loopholes to be found. The test had been described repeatedly in the medical literature: There was no question of its ninety-nine percent reliability. The chemicals I had used could not have been tampered with. This was a problem beyond even my friend's power—indeed, beyond any mortal power—to ameliorate. Eventually the doorbell rang. Sherlock Holmes sprang up.

"That will be Mycroft. I will tell him to take his business elsewhere. Excuse me just one moment, my dear fellow. Then we will turn our attention to finding you the best specialist in London."

"No, Holmes, please do not send him away. I assure you, what I need more than anything at this moment is distraction. Your brother's problems are always entertaining. Pray show him up."

My friend hesitated, then nodded. No sooner had Mycroft installed his ample bulk in our largest armchair than the bell rang again. The next guest astonished me: he was none other than the astronomy lecturer, the girlish Mr. Moriarty. As he was seated, the brothers gazed at him intently, but more with the air of scientists inspecting a specimen than men greeting a fellow human being.

Mycroft spoke first: "I must congratulate you upon a most effective lecture tonight. I was in the audience; I believe the doctor here was also present."

"Thank you. I believe the public should be correctly informed about scientific matters."

"Oh, I did not say that you did that. Rather the reverse, in fact. I believe that you inspired the audience with a wholly excessive fear of the comet which is currently in our skies, just as you intended."

This was so unreasonable that I sprang to the young man's defence.

"On the contrary, Mr. Moriarty was doing his best to reassure the audience," I cried.

Mycroft smiled. "'The best way to tell a lie effectively is to tell the truth badly,'" he quoted. "With the help of a few stooges planted in the audience, and a little misdirection, he has sown the seeds of a real panic."

The young man hunched in on himself. "Every word I uttered was the truth," he said defensively.

Mycroft nodded. "That is just what is so diabolically clever about your methods. Tell me, doctor, speaking as a typical member of that audience, what is your impression of the chance that any given comet will hit the Earth?"

I recalled the demonstration I had seen. It had certainly looked very likely that the ice puck would collide with one of the globes suspended in its path, as indeed it had done before long. But perhaps the models had not been to scale? I decided to err on the conservative side.

"I suppose perhaps one in a thousand." I said

"And what would you say is the chance that the great comet now passing will hit us?"

This time I hesitated for longer. "I know it is predicted to miss us by a good margin. But then given that the motion of comets is unpredictable, as Mr. Moriarty convincingly explained, I suppose there must still be some chance. Say, one in ten thousand?"

"Wonderful. Quite wonderful!"

"I have guessed accurately, then?"

"No. Utterly wrongly. Just as Mr. Moriarty intended." Mycroft held his arms wide. "Let us consider a comet which is plunging in from the outer reaches, passing close to the Sun before retreating again. If we draw a spherical shell centred on the Sun, whose radius is that of the earth's orbit, the comet will pass through it as it approaches. What is the area of that sphere?"

"I have not the faintest idea," I replied coldly.

"The distance from the Earth to the Sun is about ninety million miles, so the area is about one hundred million billion square miles. Now the Earth looks to the comet like a circular target eight thousand miles across, inscribed on the sphere. That target's area is only some fifty million square miles. The chance the comet will hit it in transit is therefore the first number divided by the second: of the order of one in two billion. Of course the comet has two chances: one coming in, and one coming out, so the actual odds are one in a billion. Still quite absurdly small."

"But if there are millions of comets out there?" I said.

"The question is not how many there are in the depths of space, but how many large enough to be really dangerous approach the Sun each year. That is only a dozen or so, so an impact with globally catastrophic effects is to be expected only about once per hundred million years.

"As to the chance that the comet now passing will hit us: the evaporation of gases from the surface does measurably affect the course of comets, but that is only because our measuring instruments are very accurate. The magnitude of the acceleration is tiny: about one-millionth that of an object falling under gravity here on Earth. The probability that this particular comet will hit us is zero, and was known to be so almost from the moment it was first discovered. It will be three-quarters of a million miles away at closest approach: three times the distance of the Moon."

Moriarty was sneering openly, but Mycroft merely inclined his head toward him and continued: "Of course, the author of the justly celebrated paper, 'On the Dynamics of an Asteroid,' knows better than any of us how absurd it is to visualise a comet zigzagging about the sky like a malfunctioning firework."

"But what on Earth—or indeed in the solar system—has Mr. Moriarty to gain by alarming everybody so?" I asked. I could tell from Sherlock Holmes's intent expression that he, too, would like to know this.

Mycroft smiled. "Money. Manipulation of the stock market."

"But how?"

"Stockbrokers understand little of the companies whose shares they deal in. They prosper mainly by imitating one another. If you see your neighbour buy a stock, he probably thinks it is about to go up; if he sells, it is probably going down. Usually this rule of thumb works well, but sometimes you get a runaway effect, where company shares shoot upwards quite out of relation to their reasonably possible earnings. The Americans tell the story of a man who starts a rumour that they have struck oil in Hell. After everyone else has gone there, he begins to think there must after all be something in the story, and follows them."

"No doubt inspired by the true history of the South Sea Bubble," I said. "My grandfather lost all his money. But that was a hundred years ago. We are more sensible now, and also more rapidly and accurately informed, thanks to the electric telegraph."

Mycroft snorted. "You are an optimist, Doctor. I anticipate men will still be as gullible a hundred years in the future. I wonder what kind of illusory real estate will then be the focus of their deluded hopes? At present, however, Mr. Moriarty is trying to create the opposite of the South Sea Bubble: a stock market depression, as nervous investors lose confidence in the future, and follow one another into a panic of selling."

"But how can anyone profit from such a crash?"

"In this case, by buying gold. In times of crisis, gold soars in value: it is the safe investment of last resort, guaranteed to retain its worth even when all the world's stocks and currencies are so much waste paper. Mr. Moriarty has little money of his own, but he has unsavoury business associates with plenty. His friends have been stockpiling gold."

The young man had turned quite white. "I have done nothing illegal!" he cried. "I have said not one word that is untrue."

Mycroft frowned.

"That is arguable," he said. "But now let us turn to your second, still more ingenious, scheme. I refer to the letters which I believe you have sent out to all ten thousand of the doctors currently listed in the Medical Register, inviting them to test themselves for Marchant's syndrome, and the letters that they also received, apparently from a quite unrelated source, inviting them to buy life insurance. Doubtless Dr. Watson has seen examples."

He glanced at me. As he took in my expression, I succeeded, for the first and only time in my life, in startling Mycroft Holmes.

"Good heavens, doctor, were you one of those unlucky ones who tested yourself positive? Have no fear: the chances are a hundred to one against your death."

"A hundred to one in favour of death, you mean!"

"Not so. Tell me, is Marchant's syndrome common?"

"No, it is fortunately rare."

"Indeed it is. In fact, at any given time, only about one individual in ten thousand is in the early, symptomless stages of the disease. Of the ten thousand doctors who did the test, only one is really likely to have it. But the test gives a false positive result one time in a hundred— so one hundred of the ten thousand doctors got a positive result, and are now convinced that they almost certainly have the disease, just as you were!"

I felt my head reel. "That is completely paradoxical." I said. I looked across at Sherlock Holmes. "Surely there is a contradiction. The test is known to be reliable."

My friend was shaking his head, and smiling wryly. "Mycroft is correct, Watson, and there is no paradox. When you gave yourself the test, there was indeed only one chance in a hundred it would give a false positive. But unlikely as that was, it was still more unlikely—by a further factor of a hundred—that you really had Marchant's. My dear fellow, I am gladder than I can say. If I had thought more clearly earlier this evening, I could have saved you an hour of needless worry."

Gradually, I felt the dreadful fear ebb within me, bringing such a feeling of relief that I almost cried out in joy. Mycroft coughed to regain our attention, and pointed accusingly at Moriarty.

"Most or all of those one hundred doctors convinced they have Marchant's will no doubt hasten to buy your unreasonably expensive life insurance. You will probably have to pay out in only one case. You have put a hundred men and women in terror of their lives in order to make some fast money."

The young man shrugged. "That is not my fault," he said. "You cannot blame me if they are all so stupid that they have jumped to false conclusions. I repeat, I have done nothing illegal, nor indeed in my own eyes even immoral, for I have told no falsehoods. There is nothing to prosecute me for." He looked scornfully at me, then across at the two brothers. "You are both intelligent men. Surely you will sympathise with the maxim that a fool and his money are soon parted." Suddenly, he giggled. "In fact, the felons are those who have signed a declaration that they are healthy while under the impression that they almost certainly have Marchant's syndrome. Doubtless including yourself, Doctor."

Sherlock Holmes sprang to his feet. He picked up a horsewhip which some visitor had left propped by the fireside.

"Get out," he shouted. "Never let me set eyes on you again."

Our unwelcome guest sprang to his feet with a squeak of terror. Clearly he had been unprepared for such direct action. He scuttled to the door, but paused a moment to look back at us from the threshold.

"Good-bye, gentlemen. But you have not seen the last of me. I shall remember this!"

"I THOUGHT YOU let Moriarty off very lightly," I said to Sherlock Holmes, as we sat before the still-glowing fire later that evening.

My friend shook his head. "He was right: the law could not touch him," he said. "Mycroft has put an end to his present schemes, for he has ensured articles will appear in tomorrow's papers explaining to the general public why they need have no fear of the comet, and also in the medical press to reassure doctors on the subject of Marchant's syndrome. At least we have put enough of a scare into the young man that I fancy it will be quite some years before he dares to cross our paths again."

"I am most glad to hear it. It has been a trying day for me."

My colleague extended his slippered feet toward the fire with a sigh. Suddenly he smiled.

"Really, Watson, I feel that I should congratulate you."

"Congratulate me? My dear Holmes, I feel that I have made an utter ass of myself, in several ways."

"Precisely, Watson. How many men can say that they got themselves into such a bind that it took the efforts of not merely one, but both of the Holmes brothers to extricate them from it? You really have been busy. But I trust the moral of the day's alarms has not been lost on you?"

I cast my thoughts over comets, disease, insurance, and deception.

"Perhaps I am dense, Holmes, but I really cannot perceive any factor in common."

"The moral, Watson, is that while life contains its hazards, it is the man who does not know how to calculate the risks who is in real danger."

His gaze strayed to the window. "The comet is particularly fine tonight. Let us enjoy it at our leisure, and without the slightest fear that it may come crashing down upon our heads."

THE ADVENTURE OF THE
YOUNG BRITISH SOLDIER

Bill Crider

I HAVE WRITTEN previously about the three massive manuscript volumes containing the record of Sherlock Holmes's exploits of the
year 1894, a remarkable year indeed, not only for Holmes's return to
Baker Street but for both the number of cases in which he involved
himself and of their curious nature. The adventure of the golden
pince-nez, for example, admirably displays the singular powers of my
friend, while the nauseating tale of the red leech gives an idea of the
depths of depravity to which some men will sink to attain their ends.
But there is one case that is not recorded in those three volumes
because at the time of its occurrence it seemed far too personal for
inclusion. Never before had my own life and affairs intruded into the
realm of Holmes's detective work, and the result when they did so was
far from happy. I have decided, however, now that the passage of years
has eased the sting, to commit the events to paper in the hope that
they might prove of interest to my readers.

IT WAS A BITTERLY cold winter's night near the beginning of Decem-
ber. There was no snow or ice outside, and the wind did not blow, but
the cold was so intense that it seemed to settle on the city with a weight
of its own, a weight so heavy that it almost cracked the paving stones.

Holmes and I sat secure in our Baker Street rooms, he attempting to organize some of the clippings that he kept relating to criminous activities of all sorts, and I leafing through a book of Mr. Kipling's poems, pausing now and then to read one of them. I was particularly affected by one entitled "The Young British Soldier."

The fire had burned down to the last log, which was glowing, though hardly alight at all, and while the room was beginning to cool, I felt quite warm. My face was flushed, and I limped to the window to stare out at the freezing darkness, though what I saw in my mind's eye was neither dark nor freezing. Far from it, indeed, and I pressed my hot, damp palms against the cold glass.

"It must come to you strongly, now and then," said Holmes.

Startled, I turned to stare at him. "Whatever do you mean?"

"The memory of your service," said he, "and of the time the Jezail bullet struck you down."

I was surprised, but not astonished. This was not the first time that Holmes had seemed to read my mind. I said, "But how could you know what I was thinking? It seems impossible."

"Hardly impossible," said Holmes. "First there is the matter of the book you are reading, the one by Mr. Kipling. I wager that I could tell you the exact words you came across when the blood rushed to your face and you began to perspire as if you were still on the Afghan plain. And then there is the matter of your limp."

"Ah."

"Indeed. Your wound has hardly troubled you in recent days, even in the cold, yet when you crossed the room it might have been only a few months ago rather than fourteen years that you had a bullet through your leg."

"Now that you explain it, I can see that it was rather easy for you to discover my thoughts. But one thing still puzzles me."

"And what might that be?"

"Your comment about the poem. I can hardly believe you could quote the exact lines. I will grant that no man in England, or the world for that matter, can approach your knowledge of crime and criminals. I hold it as an article of faith that there is no one who knows more about tobacco ash or poison or the criminal mind than you. As for poetry, however, I have never known you to read a line of it."

Holmes rose from his chair and walked to the mantel, where he filled a briar pipe with tobacco from one of the pouches there. He lit the pipe and puffed on it for a few moments until the tobacco was burning to his satisfaction. Then he removed it from his mouth and said, "'When you're wounded and left on Afghanistan's plains, / And the women come out to cut up what remains, / Just roll to your rifle and blow out your brains, / And go to your Gawd like a soldier.'"

I had not been astonished earlier, but now I confess that my mouth fell open. It was not so much that Holmes had discovered the exact verse, for more times than once Holmes had amazed me with his deductive powers. But in all our acquaintance I had never heard him quote four lines of poetry from memory.

"You see, Watson," he said with a thin smile, "I have hidden depths."

"You do, indeed," said I. "But why?"

"Why memorize a bit of verse? Do you not recall that you have read that poem to me previously?"

"Yes," I admitted. "But that was a year ago, and I never thought that you would commit it to memory."

"The subject matter has its own grisly interest," said Holmes. "And I remembered those particular lines because they seemed to have a great deal of meaning for you."

The last log fell apart on the grate and sparked into coals. I shivered, though not from the cold.

"They remind me of things that I would prefer not to recall with any clarity," I said. "Had it not been for my orderly that day at Maiwand, I might have been the young British soldier of that poem."

"Your orderly," said Holmes. "Murray."

"Yes. Had he not slung me across a packhorse and taken me from the field, I would have been left to the mercy of the foe, though mercy was not something much heard of on that field."

"And what of Murray?" Holmes asked. "I do not believe you ever told me of his fate."

"Only because I do not know it. He returned to the fighting after I was safe in Peshwar, and after that I lost all touch with him. Perhaps he, too, returned to England."

"Or died in battle in some foreign land," said Holmes.

"Perhaps," said I. "But I suppose we shall never know."

After that, I set Kipling's book aside and Holmes went back to his clippings. We spoke no more of Murray until seven days later when a carriage arrived outside our window early one morning.

The weather had gone from unbearably cold to merely seasonable, and the sun shone dimly through our windows. Holmes was examining something or other through his microscope, and I was leafing through a medical journal when I heard the long scrape of a wheel against the curb below in the street.

Holmes heard it as well. He raised his head and said, "I believe we are about to have a visitor, Watson. Be so good as to get the door."

I went downstairs and admitted a woman of about my own age. She looked around distractedly and said, "Mr. Sherlock Holmes?"

"No," I replied. "He is upstairs. Follow me, and I will take you to him."

I led the way upward, and she followed me into the room, where Holmes sat as if engrossed in whatever he saw through the lenses of the microscope.

"Holmes," I said, "you have a visitor."

He turned to face us, and the woman at my back said, "Oh, no. It is not Mr. Holmes that I have come to see. It is someone else, a Dr. Watson."

"I am Dr. Watson," I said, a bit taken aback. Seldom did anyone come seeking me at Baker Street.

"Do not be so surprised, Watson," said Holmes. "The woman is clearly in need of your help." He rose and walked to her. "Please be seated," he said, and cleared a space on the couch for her.

She sat as if grateful for the opportunity, and I saw for the first time that her face was flushed and that her eyes were sunken. No doubt Holmes, keen observer that he was, had noticed these symptoms immediately and known that the woman was in need of my medical attention. But he said to her, "Who is it that needs the services of Dr. Watson?"

"My husband," she replied.

Holmes looked at me. "Worry, Watson, worry produces the lack of sleep that darkens the skin under the eyes. Anxiety reddens the skin as much as any fever."

"So I see," I said.

"And who is your husband?" Holmes asked the woman.

"He is known to Dr. Watson," she said. "His name is Edward Murray."

"The man who saved your life, Watson," Holmes observed.

"Yes," said Mrs. Murray, turning to me. "And now, Dr. Watson, he needs you to save his."

MRS. MURRAY EXPLAINED that her husband was quite ill, "And he says that you, Dr. Watson, are the only one who can save him."

"I am afraid that he might have an exaggerated idea of my skills," I said.

"Nonsense," said Holmes. "You are a fine physician, Watson, as any of your patients would attest."

"But how did he hear of me?" I asked.

"You have recorded the cases of Mr. Holmes," Mrs. Murray said. "And Edward has read them all eagerly. He often speaks of the time he carried you off the battlefield to safety, and he was delighted to see an account of it when you published the first of Mr. Holmes's adventures."

"It was no more than he deserved," I said. "Had it not been for him, I would surely have died in Afghanistan."

"Many did," said she. "Edward could not save them all."

"Nor could anyone have done more than he," said I. "What are your husband's symptoms?"

"He fears that they are the result of some illness that lingers from his years of service, which is the main reason he has asked for Dr. Watson. None of the doctors we have consulted has been able to give a satisfactory diagnosis, and his condition worsens day by day, slowly but inevitably."

"But the symptoms?" Holmes asked, to bring her back to my question.

"At first we believed Edward suffered from jaundice, but the doctors have said that is not the case. Now he has difficulty balancing himself, so much so that he is confined to his bed. He seems to weaken with every passing hour." She touched the corners of her eyes with a handkerchief she removed from her reticule. "I fear that he is dying, Dr. Watson. Please. You must help him."

I was about to say that I hoped her husband had not placed too much faith in my powers, but Holmes raised a hand to silence me.

"Dr. Watson will be glad to be of assistance," he said. "In fact, we are ready to see your husband immediately if you will be so good as to provide us transporation."

"You would come, too?"

"Perhaps I can provide Dr. Watson with a bit of assistance, as he has so ably done for me in the past."

"I am sure my husband will be honored to meet you. There is a coach waiting for me below. You are welcome to share it with me."

"Very well," said Holmes, with rather more enthusiasm that I would have expected. "Watson, get your bag."

I did as I was bidden, though a bit puzzled by Holmes's interest in the matter. His curiosity about medical matters was usually restricted to those relating to crimes of one sort or another, preferably gruesome. But I did not question him, as I believed that a trip in the open air would be beneficial for him. He had been growing restless lately, and to see him take an interest in anything at all was a pleasant surprise.

WHEN WE WERE in the coach and on our way, Holmes asked me to tell him more about my experience in Afghanistan.

"You have never spoken of it in detail," said he.

"Nor has Edward," said Mrs. Murray. "He does not like to speak of those days."

I shifted uncomfortably, whether from the throbbing of my leg where the musket bullet had passed through or from the sting of memory, I cannot say.

"Many soldiers prefer not to recall battlefield experiences," I told them. "Rather unpleasant, for the most part."

"But instructive, at times," said Holmes. "How did you come to be wounded?"

My mind turned back to that day at Maiwand.

"Our troops left Kandahar on 3 July," I said. "It was a blistering day, as indeed the entire summer had been. There were nearly three thousand men, marching off to support six thousand tribesmen engaged in fighting against one Ayub Khan. Ayub was in rebellion against the Amir, who had reportedly immured himself in Kabul. We had hardly gone any distance at all before we learned that the tribesmen we were going to aid had changed sides and were now supporting Ayub Khan.

So the odds against, overwhelming to begin with, had become much worse. And later on the situation worsened even more."

"But switching sides?" said Mrs. Edwards. "Surely the tribesmen would not ally themselves with their enemy?"

"That is the way of things in Afghanistan," I replied, thinking of Kipling's poem. "And there were other problems. Among the three thousand of us, many were raw recruits, hardly trained in fighting at all. Besides that, when we received orders to engage the enemy at Maiwand late on 26 July, we had already spent much of the night breaking up our camp. So it was a group of tired, untrained men who faced a force so large that it seemed a veritable moving forest, like the one in *Macbeth*."

"A bloody tale, indeed, that one," said Holmes.

As I have remarked elsewhere, Holmes's knowledge of literature was limited, but it did not surprise me that he knew something of one of the bard's gorier tales.

"It was a bloody tale that played out that day in Afghanistan, as well," I said. "The temperature had climbed to well over one hundred degrees, perhaps to as much as one hundred and twenty. The enemy forces had increased to more than twenty-five thousand men, more than eight times our own strength. The only cover to be had was dry ravines and watercourses. The battle was, of course, a disaster."

"But you survived," said Mrs. Murray.

"Thanks only to your husband. There were thirty cannon ranged against us, and though the enemy fell by the score under the fire of the Martini-Henry rifles of our troops, there were far too many of them for us to overcome. Our casualties mounted nearly as swiftly as did theirs, and there were far, far fewer of us."

"How did you come to be shot?" asked Holmes.

Remembering, I wiped my face and felt yet another twinge in my old wound.

"I was ministering to a wounded man," I said, "though there was little I could do for him. He had been shot through the lungs, of that there was no doubt. I could hear the air whistle in the wound as he tried to breathe. In any case, I was doing what I could when someone else called for me. I looked and saw another wounded man, not more than twenty feet away. Mind you, he was not the only one calling.

There were wounded and dying all around me, and many of them were crying or screaming their need for help or water, for their wives and sweethearts."

I shook my head to rid it of the picture that had formed in my brain, but the picture persisted. I could remember the cries of the men, the smell of blood and fear.

"In any case," I said after a moment, "there was one man quite nearby. The pleading in his eyes was terrible to see. I stood up to go to him, and at that very moment I was struck by a musket shot. There was no pain, just the sudden shock, but when I tried to take a step, I fell on my face. I lay there for a while, how long I do not know. There was a strange buzzing in my ears, but I could still hear the wounded man calling for my help. I tried to call back to him, but no sound came from my lips. I must have lost consciousness then, for the next thing I was aware of was the motion of the horse that was carrying me to safety."

I stopped my narrative and looked at Mrs. Murray.

"I never think of that day without thinking of your husband," I told her. "His courage and devotion saved me, and I will do whatever is in my power to return that favor."

"Edward is counting on you," she said. "He has great faith in your medical skills."

I opened my mouth to protest, but Holmes said, "As well he should have. Dr. Watson will soon set him right."

"I appreciate your confidence, Holmes," said I, wishing that I shared it.

OUR DESTINATION WAS a sizable house at the end of a blind street. The houses on either side of the street were small but neat. While the Murrays' home was on a grander scale, it was in ill repair. As we left the coach, I could hear the muffled sounds of hammering from inside it.

"When did you begin work on your house?" Holmes asked.

"Shortly before Edward became ill," Mrs. Murray said. "We have only recently moved here from a much smaller place. One of my aunts died almost a year ago, and this house was my inheritance."

"It is often hard to find good workmen these days," said Holmes. "Reliable men, I mean, who will stick to a job until it is finished."

"The men who are working here came highly recommended. They were quite busy, and at first I did not think they would take the job, but when they met Edward, they were convinced to do it."

We entered the house, where the sound of the workmen was louder. Our coats were taken by a tall sallow man with thin lips and a shiny bald head.

"Thank you, Oliver," said Mrs. Murray. When he had departed, she added, "Oliver and his wife worked for my aunt, she as cook and he as butler. They have stayed on to help me and Edward."

"I suppose they knew him before his illness," Holmes said.

"Oh, no. We never visited here. In fact, the inheritance was quite unexpected. Please, follow me, and I will take you to Edward's room."

We went down a dim hallway and ascended the stairs to the second floor, where the noise of hammers and saws was louder than ever. There were men building a bookcase in the room from which the noise emanated, and as we followed Mrs. Murray past a second open room, Holmes paused to look inside. The old wallpaper and backing had been peeled away to expose the wood, and a man was getting ready to apply fresh paper.

"That is Mr. Gordon," said Mrs. Murray, joining Holmes at the door.

The man turned at the sound of her voice. He had a thicket of beard from which two dark eyes peered at us. He set the glue pot he was holding on the floor and said, "Good morning, ma'am." He limped slightly as he stepped toward us and raised his hand to touch his forehead. "And how is the mister today?"

"As well as could be expected, Mr. Gordon," Mrs. Murray replied in a voice that indicated that was not very well at all. She indicated me. "This is Dr. Watson, who has come to examine him, and this is Dr. Watson's friend, Mr. Sherlock Holmes."

Gordon saluted us, muttered a greeting of some sort, and immediately turned away to get back to his work.

Mrs. Murray started to speak again, but she refrained and took us down the hall to her husband's room.

I confess that I hardly recognized Edward Murray. I had known him but briefly those fourteen years ago, and then he had been young and hale, strong enough to lift a man of my size across the back of a horse. Now, however, he was shrunken and jaundiced, his cheeks hollow, his neck thin and wrinkled. He sat with his back braced by several pillows as he stared blankly out a window.

"Edward," his wife said, "I have brought Dr. Watson."

He turned his dark and sunken eyes in our direction.

"Dr. Watson," he said. His voice was weak. "You have not changed."

"Hello, Murray," I said. "It is good to see you again."

"You know me, then?"

"I do, indeed."

"It is a wonder. Until recently, I looked much the same as ever, or so it pleased me to think, but now . . . "

"You have changed," said I, stepping forward. "But I know you nevertheless. Let me introduce my friend Sherlock Holmes."

He raised a hand and made a feeble wave. "I have read of your adventures, Mr. Holmes, and you have told them ably, Dr. Watson."

"Please call me John," I told him. "We are old friends, after all."

"And will my old friend be able to help me?" he asked.

"I am sure he will," said Holmes, once again expressing his confidence in me.

"Then he will be the first. I have almost despaired of any cure. And that is odd indeed, for until recently I was always the healthiest of men."

I walked to the bedside and cleared a space for my medical bag. Then I took Murray's sticklike wrist in my hand and felt for his pulse. Its beat was feeble at best beneath the hot, papery skin, flakes of which lay on the bedclothes, and I knew that Murray was in dire straits indeed.

"We have come a long way since Afghanistan," he said.

"Indeed we have, and I have come thanks entirely to you," I said. "Had you not put me on that horse, I would never have survived Maiwand."

"I am glad I was able to help," said Murray. "It was all that I could do that day."

"But it was enough," said Holmes. "I do not know how I would cope without Watson's help."

There was no response to that, and I went about my examination. When it was completed, I had deduced no more about Murray's disease than his wife had confided to us earlier.

"Have you an appetite?" I asked, taking in his wasted frame.

"I eat very little," said he. "Mrs. Oliver prepares my meals, but they are meager indeed. Bread and soup, though the soup does not taste as soup should. A consequence of my disease, no doubt."

"I have great confidence that Watson will have you in good appetite again, and quite soon," said Holmes. "I have no doubt of it. Is that not right, Watson?"

"Of course," said I, wishing that I believed it, for the case seemed quite beyond me. I had, in fact, seen nothing like it in my career as a medical man, and I was not at all certain that there was anything I could do.

"I knew I could count on you," Murray said. "It is not that I believed you owe me a debt, you understand."

"But I do. Had it not been for your efforts, I would be long since dead on the Afghan plains. And I will do all that I can to aid you."

I did not add that I thought the *all* I promised was little enough, and Murray seemed satisfied with my assurance. He sank back into the pillows and closed his eyes.

"Thank you, Dr. Watson," said his wife. "He does not often rest well, but your presence here has given him hope. What will you prescribe?"

"I must think about that," said I.

The noise of the carpenters, which I had forgotten, came to my ears again, and Holmes said, "You must be very proud of your new home. Did the Olivers feel that you were intruding when you moved here?"

Mrs. Murray smiled. "No, they did not. I believe they were quite pleased, as our coming meant they did not have to seek other employment."

I hardly saw what this exchange had to do with Murray's medical problem, but I did not interrupt.

"And are they pleased with the changes you are making in the house?"

"Oh, I am sure they must be. My aunt had let it fall into a sad state of disrepair, but soon we will have things set to rights."

"I can see that you will," said Holmes. "Well, Watson, shall we have a look around the place?"

"Whatever for?" I asked.

"Why, so Mrs. Murray can sit with her husband while you mull over his treatment, of course."

"Of course," I said, though I had no idea why.

Holmes turned, and I followed him from the room. When we were outside, I asked where we were going.

"To the kitchen," said he, "to meet Mrs. Oliver."

MRS. OLIVER WAS her husband's opposite: round, smiling, and cheerful. She welcomed us to the kitchen where a pot of savory-smelling soup bubbled on the stove.

"Poor Mr. Murray does not eat much, but he must keep up his strength," she said, and invited us to share some of the meal she was preparing as there was plenty for all.

"All?" said Holmes.

"Yes, sir. The carpenters often share a meal with us here."

"I am not surprised," said Holmes. "I am sure they enjoy your cooking."

Mrs. Oliver laughed. "Oh, go along with you, sir. But it is true, nevertheless."

"Do they ever help you out?" Holmes asked. "By way of repaying your hospitality?"

"How do you mean?"

"Do they, for example, ever take Mr. Murray his meals?"

"Why, yes, they sometimes do."

"All of them, or only Mr. Gordon?"

"Indeed, Mr. Gordon is the very one. How did you know that?"

"He knows a great deal more than anyone would suspect," I said. "Where is all this leading us, Holmes?"

"To a diagnosis, my dear Watson. Come along."

We returned to Murray's room. He was lying back on the pillows, his eyes closed, with his wife watching over him. She looked up when we entered, and Holmes said to her, "Dr. Watson will soon have your husband on the way to recovery. We have discovered that he is being slowly poisoned."

Murray struggled to sit up in his surprise, and I confess that I was no less amazed than he. His wife said, "But how can that be?"

"Oh, it is quite easy if one has access to arsenic," said Holmes. "And arsenic is indeed the poison being used. I thought as much when I first heard your description of Mr. Murray's symptoms, and my observation of him has confirmed my opinion."

As I have often said, Holmes has no peer when it comes to knowledge of poisons, and I had no doubt that he was correct in this case. No wonder that I, and the other doctors whom Murray had consulted, had been unable to determine what was afflicting him. Arsenic poisoning is notoriously difficult to diagnose. Once a diagnosis has been made, however, a cure can be effected, especially if the source of the poison is removed. Now I knew why Holmes was so confident that I would be able to help Murray.

"Who would want to poison Edward?" Mrs. Murray asked.

"There were a number of possibilities," said Holmes, "including yourself." At the look on her face, he added, "But I eliminated you at once, for you said that you and your husband knew of me. No guilty person who had read Watson's somewhat exaggerated accounts of my cases would be likely to come to him for help for fear of my involvement."

Mrs. Murray did not appear much mollified by this remark, so I said, "Who were the other possibilities?"

"The Olivers, of course, came to mind," said Holmes, "but they harbor no resentments against their new employers, and Mrs. Murray has assured us that they are happy to have new tenants in the house."

"But there is no one else here," I protested.

"There are the workmen," said Holmes.

"The workmen?" I said.

"Consider this," said Holmes. "You were once a wounded man, rescued by your orderly, Edward Murray. But there was another wounded man. What might he have felt to see the two of you leaving the field while he lay there awaiting his fate, and no rifle to roll on, as Kipling so charmingly put it."

Murray's voice came quaveringly from the bed. "He would have felt a hate deep and lasting. I could see it in his eyes that day. But my duty was to Dr. Watson."

"True," said Holmes, walking to the bedside, "and you performed it admirably. But suppose that man lived and managed to escape the battlefield before the women came to cut up what remained of him. And suppose that eventually he returned to England. He might have tried to put the incident out of his mind, but every twinge of his wound would remind him of it. As it does you, Watson."

I nodded my agreement.

"And suppose, then, that years later the man saw face to face the very person who had left him there that day so long ago and realizing that the person did not recognize him, might he not be tempted to extract a bit of revenge?"

I remembered a heavily bearded face, a limp, and a half-conscious salute and said, "Gordon?"

"Very good, Watson," said Holmes. "As you are probably not aware, the dyes in wallpaper in houses of this age often contain arsenic. I am sure that Gordon scraped and pulverized a quantity of the old paper he removed from the wall. This he added to Mrs. Oliver's soup that he so helpfully brought to Murray. Seeing the slow death of the man he believed had deserted him must have brought him a great measure of satisfaction."

"It did, indeed," said Gordon from the doorway. "I am sorry that you have put an end to my game, Mr. Sherlock Holmes. Now I will have to take a more direct approach." He pulled a pistol from beneath the canvas apron he was wearing. "Please step back from the bed, Mr. Holmes."

"Very well," said Holmes. "I . . ."

His voice seemed to stick in his throat, and his face contorted horribly as he began to stumble forward.

Gordon was momentarily distracted, but I, being better acquainted with Holmes than he, was not. As Gordon stared, I turned and grabbed the arm that held the pistol, jerking it downward and causing it to discharge a bullet into the floor. I twisted Gordon's wrist with both hands, and he dropped the pistol just as Holmes reached us.

"Hold him, Watson!" said Holmes, and I secured both Gordon's arms. Though he struggled, he could not escape me.

"Good old Watson," said Holmes. "I knew you would not be fooled by my ruse. Now if Mrs. Murray will be so kind as to send for the police, we will turn Mr. Gordon over to them. After that, you can begin caring for your former orderly."

Mrs. Murray, who had been somewhat shocked at the gunshot and the brief struggle, recovered herself and dashed from the room to summon the law. Her husband said, "I would never have left anyone on that field had I been able to help."

Gordon struggled in my grip.

"Swine," he said.

"You should read more Kipling," Holmes said to him.

Gordon glared at him but did not deign to respond, so I said, "Whatever do you mean, Holmes?"

"That poem you are fond of had some advice for people like Gordon," said Holmes. "'Be thankful you're livin', and trust to your luck, and march to your jail like a soldier.'"

I smiled in spite of myself. "I do not believe that Kipling said *jail*, Holmes."

"Perhaps not," said he. "But it fits the case."

As usual, he was correct.

THE VALE OF THE WHITE HORSE

Sharyn McCrumb

G RISEL ROUNTREE was the first to see that something was strange
about the white chalk horse.

As she stood on the summit of the high down, in the ruins of the
hill fort that overlooked the dry chalk valley, she squinted at the white
shape on the hillside below, wondering for a moment or two what was
altered. Carved into the steep slope across the valley, the primitive outline of a white horse shone in the sunshine of a June morning.
Although Grisel Rountree had lived in the valley all seven decades of
her life, she never tired of the sight of the ancient symbol, large as a
hayfield, shining like polished ivory in the long grass of early summer.

The white horse had been old two thousand years ago when the
Romans arrived in Britain and the people in the valley had long ago
forgotten the reason for its existence, but there were stories about its
magic. Some said that King Arthur had fought his last battle on that
hill, and others claimed that the horse was the symbol for the nearby
Wayland smithy, the local name for a stone chamber where folks said
that a pagan god had been condemned to shoe the horses of mortals
for all eternity.

Whatever the truth of its origins, the village took a quiet pride in
its proximity to the great horse. Every year when the weather broke,
folks would make an excursion up the slope to clean the chalk form

of the great beast, and to pull any encroaching weeds that threatened to blur the symmetry of its outline. They made a day of it, taking picnic lunches and bottles of ale, and the children played tag in the long grass while their elders worked. When Grisel was a young girl, her father had told her that the chalk figure was a dragon whose imprint had been burned into the hill where it had been killed by St. George himself. When she became old enough to go to the village dances, the laughing young men had insisted that the white beast was a unicorn, and that if a virgin should let herself be kissed within the eye of the chalk figure, the unicorn would come to life and gallop away. It was a great jest to invite the unmarried lasses up to the hill "to make the unicorn run," though of course it never did.

Nowadays everyone simply said the creature was a horse, though they did allow that whoever drew it hadn't made much of a job of it. It was too stretched and skinny to look like a proper horse, but given its enormous size, perhaps the marvel was that the figure looked like anything at all.

The hill fort provided the best view of the great white horse. Anyone standing beside the chalk ramparts of the ancient ruins could look down across the valley and see the entire figure of the horse sprawled out below like the scribble of some infant giant. Grisel Rountree did not believe in giants, but she did believe in tansy leaves, which was why she was up at the hill fort so early that morning. A few leaves of tansy put in each shoe prevented the wearer from coming down with ague. Although she seldom had the ague, Grisel Rountree considered it prudent to stock up on the remedy as a precaution anyhow. Besides, half the village came to her at one time or another to cure their aches and pains, and it was just as well to be ready with a good supply before winter set in.

She had got up at first light, fed the hens and did the morning chores around her cottage, and then set off with a clean feed sack to gather herbs for her remedies and potions. She had been up at the ruins when the clouds broke, and a shaft of sunlight seemed to shine right down on the chalk horse. She had stopped looking for plants then, and when she stood up to admire the sight, she noticed it.

The eye of the great white horse was red.

"Now, there's a thing," she said to herself.

She shaded her eyes from the sun and squinted to get a clearer image of the patch of red but she still couldn't make it out. The eye did not appear to have been painted. It was more like something red had been put more or less in the space where the horse's eye ought to be, but at this distance, she couldn't quite make out what it was. She picked up the basket of herbs and made her way down the slope. No use hurrying—it would take her at least half an hour to cross the valley and climb the hill to the eye of the white horse. Besides, since whatever-it-was in the eye was not moving, it would probably be there whenever she reached it.

"It'll be goings-on, I'll warrant," she muttered to herself, picturing a courting couple fallen asleep in their trysting place. Grisel Rountree did not hold with "goings-on," certainly not in broad daylight at the top of a great hill before God and everybody. She tried to think of who in the village might be up to such shenanigans these days, but no likely couple came to mind. They were all either past the point of outdoor courting or still working up to it.

Out of ideas, she plodded on. "Knowing is better than guessing," she muttered, resolving to ignore the twinge of rheumatism that bedeviled her joints with every step she took. The walk would do her good, she thought, and if it didn't, there was always some willow tea back in the cottage waiting to be brewed.

Half an hour later, the old woman had crossed the valley and reached the summit where the chalk horse lay. Now that she was nearer she could see that the splash of red she had spotted from afar was a bit of cloth, but it wasn't lying flat against the ground like a proper cape or blanket should. She felt a shiver of cold along her backbone, knowing what she was to find.

In the eye of the white horse, Grisel knelt beside the scarlet cloak spread open the ground. She wore a look of grim determination, but she would not be shocked. She had been midwife to the village these forty years, and she laid out the dead as well, so she'd seen the worst, taken all round. She lifted the edge of the blanket and found herself staring into the sightless eyes of a stranger. A moment's examination told her that the man was a gentleman—the cut of his bloodstained clothes would have told her that, but besides his wardrobe, the man had the smooth hand and the well-kept look of one who has been waited on all his life. She noted this without any resentment of the differences in their stations: such things just were.

The man was alive, but only just.

"Can you tell me who did this to you?" she said, knowing that this was all the help he could be given, and that if there were time for only one question, it should be that. The rest could be found out later, one way or another.

The man's eyes seemed to focus on her for a moment, and in a calm, wondering voice he said clearly, *"Not* a maiden . . ."

And then he died. Grisel Rountree did not stay to examine him further, because the short blade sticking out of the dead man's stomach told her that this was not a matter for the layer-out of the dead but for the village constable.

"Rest in peace, my lad," said the old woman, laying the blanket back into place. "I'll bring back someone directly to fetch you down."

"MISSUS ROUNTREE!" YOUNG Tom Cowper stood under the apple tree beside the old woman's cottage, gasping for breath from his run from the village, but too big with news to wait for composure. "They're bringing a gentleman down from London on account of the murder!"

Grisel Rountree swirled the wooden paddle around the sides of the steaming black kettle, fishing a bit of bedsheet out of the froth and examining it for dirt. Not clean yet. "From London?" she grunted. "I shouldn't wonder. Our PC Waller is out of his depth, and so I told him when I took him up to the white horse."

"Yes'm," said Tom, mindful of the sixpence he had been given to deliver the message. "The London gentleman—he's staying at the White Horse, him and a friend—at the inn, I mean."

Grisel snorted. "I didn't suppose you meant the white horse on the hill, lad."

"No. Well, he's asking to see you, missus. On account of you finding the body. They say I'm to take you to the village."

The old woman stopped stirring the wash pot and fixed the boy with a baleful eye. "Oh, I'm to come to the village, am I? Look here, Tom Cowper, you go back to the inn and tell the gentleman that anybody can tell him the way to my cottage, and if he wants a word with me, here I'll be."

"But missus . . ."

"Go!"

For a moment Tom gaped at the tall white-haired figure, pointing imperiously at him. People roundabouts said she were a witch, and of course he didn't hold with such foolishness, but there was a limit to what sixpence would buy a gentleman in the way of his services as a messenger. Choosing the better part of valor, he turned and ran.

"Who is this London fellow?" Grisel called after the boy.

Without breaking stride Tom called back to her, "Mis-terr Sher-lock Holmes!"

GRISEL ROUNTREE FINISHED her washing, swept the cottage again, and set to work making a batch of scones in case the gentleman from London should arrive at tea time, which, if he had any sense, he would, because anybody hereabouts could tell him that Grisel Rountree's baking was far better than the alternately scorched and floury efforts of the cook at the village inn.

The old woman was not surprised that London had taken an interest in the case, considering that the dead man had turned out to be from London himself, and a society doctor to boot. James Dacre, his name was, and he was one of the Hampshire Dacres, and the brother of the young earl over at Ramsmeade. The wonder of it was that the doctor should be visiting here, for he had never done so before, though they saw his brother the baronet often enough.

A few months back, the young baronet had been a guest of the local hunt, and during the course of the visit he had met Miss Evelyn Ambry, the daughter of the local squire and the beauty of the county. She was a tall, spirited young woman, much more beautiful than her sisters and by far the best rider. People said she was as fearless as she was flawless, but among the villagers there was a hint of reserve in their voices when they spoke of her. There was a local tradition about the Ambrys, people didn't speak of it in these enlightened times, but they never quite forgot it either. Miss Evelyn was one of the Ambry Changelings, right enough. There was one along in nearly every generation.

By all accounts Miss Evelyn Ambry had made a conquest of the noble guest, and the baronet's visits to the district became so frequent that people began to talk of a match being made between the pair of them. Some folk said they would been betrothed already if Miss Evelyn's aunt had not suddenly taken ill and died two weeks back, so that Miss Evelyn had to observe mourning for the next several months. And now there was more mourning to keep them apart—his lordship's own brother.

Grisel was sorry about the young man's untimely death, but it's an ill wind that blows nobody good, she told herself, and if the doctor's passing kept his brother from wedding the Ambry Changeling, it might be a blessing after all. Whenever a silly woman sighed at the prospect of a wedding between Miss Evelyn and the baronet, Grisel always held her peace on the subject, but she'd not be drinking the health of the handsome couple if the wedding day ever came. It boded ill for the bridegroom, she thought. It always had done when a besotted suitor wed an Ambry Changeling, and so Grisel had been expecting a tragedy in the offing—but not this particular tragedy. The baronet's younger brother dying in the eye of the white horse. She didn't know what it meant, and that worried her. And his last words—"*Not* a maiden"—put her in mind of the village lads' old jest about the unicorn, but how could a gentleman doctor from London know about that? It was a puzzle, right enough, and she could not see the sense of it yet, but one thing she did know for certain: death comes in threes.

She was just dusting the top of the oak cupboard for the second time when she heard voices in the garden.

"Do let me handle this, Holmes," came the voice of a London gentleman. "You may frighten the poor old creature out of her wits with your abrupt ways."

"Nonsense!" said a sharper voice. "I am the soul of tact, always!"

She had flung open the cottage door before they could knock. "Good afternoon, good sirs," she said, addressing her remarks to the tall, saturnine gentleman in the cape and the deerstalker hat. Just from the look of him, you could tell that he was the one in charge.

The short, sandy-haired fellow with the bushy mustache and kind eyes gave her a reassuring smile. "It's Mistress Rountree, is it not? I am Dr. John Watson. Allow me to introduce my companion, Mr. Sherlock Holmes, the eminent detective from London. We are indeed hoping for a word with you. May we come in?"

She nodded and stepped aside to let them pass. "You're wanting to talk about young Dacre's death," she said. "It was me that found him. But you needn't be afraid of upsetting me, young man. I may not have seen the horrors you did with the army in Afghanistan, but I'll warrant I've seen my share in forty years of birthing and burying folk in these parts."

The sandy-haired man took a step backward and stared at her. "But how did you know that I had been in Afghanistan?"

"Really, Watson!" said his companion. "Will you never cease to be amazed by parlor tricks? Shall I tell you how the good lady ferreted out your secret? I did it myself at our first meeting, you may recall."

"Yes, yes," said Watson with a nervous laugh. "I remember. I was a bit startled because the innkeeper said that Mistress Rountree had a bit of reputation hereabouts as a witch. I thought this might be a sample of it."

"I expect it is," said Holmes. "People are always spinning tales to explain that which they do not understand. No doubt they'll be coming out with some outlandish nonsense about the body of Mr. Dacre being found in the eye of the white horse. I believe you found him, madam?"

Grisel Rountree motioned for them to sit down. "I've laid the tea on, and there are scones on the table. You can be getting on with that while I'm telling you." In a few words she gave the visitors a concise account of her actions on the morning of James Dacre's murder.

"You'll be in the employ of his lordship the baronet," she said, giving Holmes an appraising look.

He nodded. "Indeed, that gentleman is most anxious to discover the circumstances surrounding his brother's murder. And you tell me that Dr. Dacre was in fact alive when you found him?"

"Only just, sir. He had been stabbed in the stomach, and he had bled like a stuck pig. Must have lay there a good hour or more, judging by all the blood on the grass thereabouts."

"And you saw no one? There are very few trees on those downs. Did you scan the distance for a retreating figure?"

She nodded. "Even before I knew what had happened, I looked. I was on the opposite hill, mind, when I first noticed the red on the horse's eye, so I could see for miles, and there were nothing moving, not so much as a cow, sir, much less a man."

"No. You'd have told the constable if it had been otherwise. And the poor man's final words to you were—"

"Just like I told you. He opened his eyes and said clear as day. *Not a maiden.* Then he lay back and died."

"*Not a maiden.* He was not addressing you, I take it?"

"He were not," snapped the old woman. "And he would have been wrong if he had been."

"Did the phrase convey anything to you at the time?"

"Only the old tale about the white horse. The village lads used to say that if anyone were to kiss a proper maiden standing upon the chalk horse, the beast would get up and walk away. So perhaps he had been kissing a lady? But that's not what I thought. The poor man was stabbed with a woman's weapon—a seam ripper, it were, from a lady's sewing kit—and I think he was saying that the one who used it was not a woman, despite the look of it."

Holmes nodded. "Let's leave that for a bit. I find it curious that the doctor was walking on the downs at such an odd hour. In fact, why was he here at all? The family estate, Ramsmeade, is some distance from here."

"The doctor's brother is engaged to a squire's daughter here-abouts," said the old woman.

"So I am told. I believe the Dacres had come to attend a funeral at the Hall."

"T'were the squire's younger sister. Christabel, her name was. Fan-ciful name for a flighty sort of woman, if you ask me. Ill for a long while, she was, and her not thirty-five yet, even. Young Dacre were a doctor, you know. So when the squire's sister took sick, the family asked Dr. Dacre to do what he could for the poor lady, on account of the family connection, you see. The doctor's brother affianced to the niece of the sick woman."

"Ah! Mr. Dacre often visited here to treat his patient then?"

"Not he. He has a fine clinic up in London. She went up there to be looked after. Out of her head with worry, she was, poor lamb. Even came here once to see if I had any kind of a tonic that might set her to rights. *Now, Mistress Rountree,* she says to me, *I've got such a pain in my tummy that I don't care if I live or die, only I must make it stop. Is there anything you can give me for it?* But I told her there were nought I could do for her, excepting to pray. There never has been for such as she. An Ambry Changeling, she was. Know it to look at her, though I kept still about that. So up she went to London, and died upon the operating table up at the Dacre clinic."

"It was not, by any chance, a childbirth?" said Watson.

Grisel gave him a scornful look. "Childbirth? Not she! I told you: an Ambry Changeling she was. Not that I believe all the tales that are bandied hereabouts, but call it what you will, there is a mark on that family."

"Now that is interesting," said Holmes. He had left off eating scones now, and was pacing the length of the cottage while he listened. "What do people say about the Ambrys? A family curse?"

"Not a curse. That could be lifted, maybe. This is in the blood and there's no getting away from it. The Ambrys are an old family. They've been living at the Hall since the time of the Crusades, that I do know. Churchyard will tell you that much. But folk in these parts say that one of the Ambry lords, a long time back, married one of the fair folk . . ." She hesitated, choosing her words carefully. "One of the lords and ladies . . ."

"He married into the nobility, you mean?" asked Watson.

"Stranger than that, I think," said Holmes still pacing. "I think Mistress Rountree is using the countryman's polite—and wary—circumlocution to tell us that an Ambry ancestor took a bride from among the Shining Folk. In short, a fairy wife."

The old woman nodded. "Just so. They do say that she stayed for all of twenty years and twenty days with her mortal husband, and she bore him children, but then she slipped away in the night and went back to her own people. She was never seen again, but her bloodline carries on in the Ambrys to this day. Their union was blessed with five children—or blessed with four, perhaps. The fifth one took after the mother. And ever since that time there has been in nearly every generation that one daughter who takes after the fairy side of the family—a changeling."

"Fascinating," said Holmes.

"But hardly germane to an ordinary stabbing death," said Watson.

"One never knows, Watson. Let us hear a bit more. By what signs do you know that an Ambry boy or girl is the family changeling?"

"It's always a girl," said the old woman. "The prettiest one of the bunch, for one thing. Tall and slender, with beautiful dark hair and what some might call an elf face—big eyes and sharp cheek bones—not your chocolate box pretty girl, but a beauty all the same."

"A lovely girl in every generation?" Dr. Watson laughed. "That sounds like the sort of curse any family would envy."

"But that's not the whole of it," said Grisel. "That's only the good part."

"I suppose they were high-tempered ladies," Watson said, smiling. "The pretty ones often are, I find. Still, I hardly think that fairy stories would deter a modern gentleman."

"There is a good deal of sense wrapped in country fables," said Holmes. "He might do well to heed them. However, I don't quite see its connection to the death of the good doctor. Was the Ambry family angry that Christabel Ambry had died in the doctor's care?"

"No. She were in a bad way, and they knew there was little hope for her. They didn't suppose anybody could have done any more than what he did."

"I wonder what was the matter with her?" mused Watson.

"That is your province, Watson," said Holmes. "You might call in at the clinic and ask. I shall pursue my present line of inquiry. We know that Dacre arrived here on the Friday. The funeral then was on Saturday, and he was found dying within the white horse in the early hours of Sunday morning. He had been stabbed with a silver seam ripper from a sewing kit, but his last words—presumably on the subject of his murderer—were 'not a maiden.'"

"Is there a tailor in these parts?"

"Watson, I hardly think that James Dacre would be taking an evening stroll across the downs with the village tailor."

"Nor do I," said Grisel Rountree. "Anyhow, we don't have one. So you do think the person up on the hill was a lady after all?"

"We must not theorize ahead of the facts," said Holmes. "This seems to be a country of riddles, and the meaning of the doctor's words is still not clear."

A FEW DAYS later Sir Henry Dacre, Bart., received his distinguished London visitors in his oak-paneled study at Ramsmeade. He was an amiable young man with watery blue eyes and a diffident smile. At his side was a dark-haired woman whose imperious nature made her seem more the aristocrat than he. She was nearly as tall as Sir Henry, and her sharp features and glowing white skin were accentuated by the black of her mourning clothes.

"Good morning, Mr. Holmes, Dr. Watson," Sir Henry said. "May I present my fiancée, Miss Evelyn Ambry. My dear, these are the gentlemen I told you about. They are looking into the circumstances surrounding the death of poor James."

She inclined her head regally towards them. "Do sit down, gentlemen. We are so anxious to hear of your progress."

Dr. Watson raised his eyebrows, glancing first at Holmes and then at their host. "The matters we have to discuss are somewhat delicate for a lady's ears," he said. "Perhaps Miss Ambry would prefer not to be present."

Evelyn Ambry gave him a cool stare. "If the matter concerns my family, I shall insist on being present."

Sir Henry gave them a tentative smile. "There you have it, gentlemen. She will have her way. If Miss Ambry wishes to be present, I'm sure she has every right to do so."

With a curt nod, Sherlock Holmes settled himself in an armchair near the fire. "As you wish," he said. "I have never been squeamish about medical matters myself. By all means let us proceed. As to the physical facts concerning the death of your late brother, we have done little more than confirm what was already known: that he died in the early hours of twelve June as the result of a stab wound inflicted in his upper abdomen. The weapon was a seam ripper, but it was not of the professional grade used by tailors. Rather it seemed more appropriate to the sewing of a woman."

"I have not the patience for sewing," said Miss Ambry. "Such an idle past-time. Grouse shooting is rather more in my line."

"Yet the instrument was of silver, which seems to preclude the villagers from ownership. Does anyone in your household possess such an item?"

She shrugged. "Not to my knowledge. Did you ask the household staff?"

"Yes. They could not be certain either way. Leaving that aside, we know that the doctor came to the village to attend the funeral of his patient, Christabel Ambry, that he stayed at the inn, and after seven in the evening, when he had a pint in the residents' lounge, he was not seen until the next morning, when his body was found in the vale of the White Horse. This much we knew. So we turned our attention to London."

Sir Henry nodded. "You think some enemy may have followed my brother down from London and quarreled with him?"

"I thought it most unlikely," Holmes replied. "In any event we were unable to discover any enemies."

"No, indeed," said Watson. "Dr. Dacre was highly esteemed in the medical profession. His colleagues liked him, and his patients are quite distressed that he has been taken from them."

"He was the clever one of the family," said Sir Henry. "But a dear fellow all the same."

"Are you quite sure that James had no enemies?" asked Evelyn Ambry. "Surely you did not interview every one of his patients? What about the relatives of the deceased ones?"

"Indeed we have not yet spoken with you," said Holmes. "I believe you would be included in the latter category. Had your family any resentment toward Dr. Dacre as a physician?"

"Certainly not!" Her cheeks reddened and she pursed her lips in annoyance. "Christabel was very ill. We had long feared the worst. I never go to doctors myself, but I thought James was an exceptional physician. He was tireless on Christabel's behalf. He fought even after we all had given up hope."

"Had the doctor ever mentioned any unhappy patients?" asked Watson, addressing Sir Henry.

"Never," said Sir Henry. "He seemed quite content in his relations with mankind, taken all round."

"Which brings us to *womankind*," murmured Holmes. "I am thinking of the doctor's final words: *Not a maiden*. Had your brother any romantic attachments, Sir Henry?"

"Yes. James was engaged to an American heiress. She was in New York at the time of his death, and as she was unable to return for the funeral, she has remained in America with her family. She is quite distraught. They were devoted to one another."

"I see. So there is no question then of a dalliance with a village maiden?" He glanced at Miss Ambry to see if the question called for an apology, but she had managed a taut smile.

"James was not at all that sort of man," she said. "Anyone can tell you that. He lived for his work, and he was quite happy to allocate the rest of his attention to Anne. She is a charming girl."

Dr. Watson cleared his throat. "I have been examining the medical records of Dr. Dacre's patients. They all seem straightforward enough. He specialized in cancer—a sad duty most of the time. I did wonder about your aunt, though, Miss Ambry. The records on her case were missing. There was only an empty folder with her name on it, and a scribbled note: *'No hope! Orchids?'*"

"Do you know what Christabel Ambry died of?'

"Cancer, of course," said Evelyn. "We knew that. I'm afraid we did not press for details. Christabel seemed not to want inquiry on the subject."

"In that case, why did Dacre destroy the records?" said Watson. "He seems to have discussed the case with no one. And what of the notation on the folder?"

"Orchids? Well, perhaps he was thinking of sending flowers for the funeral," Sir Henry suggested.

"Orchids would be most unsuitable, Henry," said his fiancée.

"Well, I suppose they would be. At any rate I know he sent a wreath, but I'm dashed if I know what it was. White flowers, I think. I confess it is all Greek to me, gentlemen."

Sherlock Holmes stared. "I wonder if . . ." He stood up and began pacing before the hearth. After a few more moments of muttering, during which he ignored their questions, Holmes held up his hand for silence. "Well, we must know. Watson, again your medical skills will be called upon. Let us go and see the Squire. I fear that we must discover a buried secret."

"I will not give you a love potion, Millie Hopgood, and that's *final,*" said Grisel Rountree to the rabbit of a girl in her cottage door. "That young man of yours is a Wilberforce, and everybody knows the Wilberforces are mortally shy. He's the undertaker's boy, and he don't know how to talk to live people, I reckon."

"Yes, but—"

"All he wants is a bit of plain speaking from you, and if you won't make up your mind to that, all the potions in the world won't help you."

"Oh, I couldn't, I'm sure, Missus Rountree!" gasped the girl. "But as you'll be seeing him up to the Hall today, I was thinking you might have a word with him yourself"

"Me going to the Hall? First I've heard of it."

The girl pulled an envelope out of her apron pocket, holding it out to the old woman so that she could see the wax seal crest of the Ambrys sealing the flap. "I'm just bringing it now. The two gentlemen from London are back, and they'd like a word with you."

"Well? And what has your young Wilberforce to do with it?"

"Please, missus, they're going into the vault—after Miss Christabel."

"I am coming then," said the old woman. "See you tell Miss Evelyn that I am coming straight away."

GRISEL ROUNTREE FOUND Sherlock Holmes walking in the grounds of Old Hall within sight of the Ambry family vault. It was a warm June afternoon, but she felt a chill on seeing him pacing the lawn, oblivious to the riot of colors in the flower beds or the beauty of the ancient oaks. As single minded as Death, he was. And as inevitable.

"So you've gone and dug up Miss Christabel, then?" she said. "Well, I don't suppose dug up is the right term, as she were in a vault."

He nodded. "It all seemed to come down to that. Dr. Watson is in the scullery there, performing an autopsy, but I think we both know what he will find."

"The lady died of cancer," said Grisel Rountree, looking away.

"Cristabel Ambry died of cancer, yes," said Holmes.

"Ah," said the old woman. "So you do know something about it."

"I fancy I do, yes." He turned in response to a shout from the door of the scullery. "Here he is now. Shall we hear his report or will you speak now?"

"Does Miss Evelyn know what you are doing?"

"She has gone out with a shooting party," said Holmes. "We are quite alone, except for the undertaker's boy."

"Wilberforce," she said with a dismissive sigh. "He hasn't the sense to grasp what to gossip about, so that's safe. Let the doctor tell you what he makes of it."

Watson reached them then, rolling down his sleeves, his forearms still damp from washing up after the procedure. "Well, it's done, Holmes," he said. "Shall I tell you in private?"

Holmes shook his head. "Miss Rountree here is a midwife and local herbalist. I rather fancy that makes her a colleague of yours. In any case she has always known what you have just been at pains to discover. Do tell us, Watson. Of what did Christabel Ambry die?"

Watson reddened. "Cancer, right enough," he said gruffly. "Testicular cancer."

"You must have been surprised."

"I've heard of such cases," said Watson. "They are mercifully rare. It is a defect in the development of the foetus before birth, apparently. When I opened up the abdomen, I found that the deceased had the . . . er . . . the reproductive organs of a male. The testes, which had become cancerous, were inside the abdomen, and there was no womb. The deceased's vagina, only a few inches long, ended at nothing. I must conclude that the patient was—technically—male."

"An Ambry Changeling," said Holmes.

"But how did you know, Holmes?"

"It was only a guess, but I knew, you see, that orchis is the Greek word for testis, and I was still thinking about the changeling story. It was an old country attempt to describe a real occurrence, is it not so, madam?"

Grisel Rountree nodded. "We midwives never knew what their insides were like, of course, but the thing about the Ambry Changelings is that they were barren. Always. Oh, they might marry, right enough, especially to an outsider who didn't know the story about the Ambrys, but there was never a child born to one of them. Some of them were good wives, and some were bad, and more than a few died young, like Christabel Ambry, rest her soul, but there was never an Ambry changeling that bore a child. That could be curse enough to a landed family with the property entailed, don't you reckon?"

"Indeed," said Holmes." And the doctor knew of this?"

"He did not," said Grisel Rountree. "None of us were like to tell him—no business of his, anyhow. And when Miss Christabel came to see me, she said she might be going up to London to the clinic. *'But I'll not be airing the family linen for Dr. Dacre, Grisel,'* she says to me. *'Not*

with Evelyn engaged to his brother.' Miss Christabel put off going to a doctor for the longest time, afraid he'd find out too much as it was."

"And Miss Evelyn stated that she never consults physicians."

Watson gasped. "Holmes! You don't suppose that Evelyn Ambry
is . . . is . . . well, a man?"

"I suppose so, in the strictest sense of the definition, but the salient
thing here, Watson, is that Evelyn Ambry cannot bear children. Since
she is engaged to the possessor of an entailed estate, that is surely
a matter of concern. I fear that when Dr. James Dacre discovered
the truth of the matter, he conveyed his concerns to Evelyn Ambry—
probably at the funeral. They arranged to meet that night to discuss
the matter."

"Why did he not tell his brother straight away?"

"Out of some concern for the feelings of both parties, I should
think," said Holmes. "Far better to allow the lady—let us call her a lady
still; it is too confusing to do otherwise—to allow the lady to end it on
some pretext."

Grisel Rountree nodded. "He mistook his . . . person," she said. "Miss
Evelyn was not one to give up anything without a fight. I'll warrant she
took that weapon with her in case the worse came to the worst."

"Not a maiden," murmured Watson. "Well, that is true enough, I
fear. But the scandal will be ruinous! Not just the murder, but the
cause . . . Poor Sir Henry! What happens now?"

From the downs above the Old Hall the sound of a single shot rang
out, echoing in the clear summer air.

"It has already happened," said Grisel Rountree, turning to go. "It's
best if I see to the laying out myself."

"Now there's a thing," said Sherlock Holmes.

THE ADVENTURE
OF THE MOONING SENTRY

Jon L. Breen

DESPITE THE IMPLIED finality of "His Last Bow," and the elegiac note that concluded that tale, few of my readers have been willing to believe that Sherlock Holmes, with his mental powers and patriotic enthusiasm at their peak, would retreat into permanent retirement at his country's darkest hour. When that east wind blew across England, he did not wither before its blast. Indeed, he undertook several more investigations in his country's service before the world war had finished energizing, glorifying, decimating, and mutilating a generation of young men.

Early in the autumn of 1917, I received a surprising invitation to a weekend house party at the country holding of Sir Eldridge Masters, a wealthy baronet best known as an amateur historian—or, less politely, a dilettante. The gathering was to be in honor of a visiting American cinematograph director, and would include a special showing of one of the fellow's films. It all sounded very jolly, to be sure. However, not feeling particularly festive in those dark days, and finding weekend house parties a somewhat frivolous activity with the country at war, I was about to decline. But a second message in the next day's post changed my mind: "My dear Watson, / Do please join me in accepting Sir Eldridge's hospitality. Come alone, bring your sidearm, and withhold recognition of an old friend. Your country needs you, and so do I. / Holmes." Loyalty to friend and to king made a negative response unthinkable.

Everything about the Masters estate, from the long winding carriageway lined with lime trees to the venerable oaks framing the great ivy-covered house itself, bespoke wealth and tradition. When I arrived by pony cart from the station that evening in early October, the other guests had already assembled. From my room, I was shown to what the butler characterized as the "small ballroom," a chamber quite large enough for most purposes in which a score of men in white ties and women in stunning gowns posed in the light of a crystal chandelier with a grand staircase behind them. Spirits flowed freely, with only the lack of young male servants to suggest the country was at war. I was immediately greeted and taken aside by my host, an erect man of around sixty with an impressive grey moustache and a hesitant manner of speech that contrasted with his military bearing.

"Dr. Watson, isn't it? So good of you to come, so, ah, very good of you." With a hand on my sleeve, he lowered his voice conspiratorially. "Now, ah, when we come upon our mutual friend, you know, ah, that is, you have been apprised . . ."

"Certainly, Sir Eldridge. I understand fully." In truth, I understood nothing, except that our host was aware of Holmes's mission, whatever it was, and that I was to take the cue for my behavior from Holmes.

A young woman of about thirty approached us from across the ballroom. She was ethereally lovely, but the grandness of her gown only served to accentuate her frailty and fragility. She had the air of someone doggedly performing an unavoidable duty. A spinster daughter of the house, I concluded, but my surmise proved incorrect.

"My dear," Sir Eldridge said, "may I present Dr. Watson. Doctor, my wife, Lady Miranda Masters."

"Welcome, Dr. Watson," she said, her voice little more than a whisper. Sir Eldridge watched her with a keen eye and obvious concern as we exchanged the traditional comments of hostess and guest. Her words were perfect, but her manner nervous and distracted. Even as we spoke her eyes, looking troubled, even haunted, darted about as if searching corners of the room for someone or something. Looking at her lovely face, I was certain I had seen her before.

Courtesy forbids questioning a man about his wife's past, but as Lady Miranda moved on to mingle with other guests, Sir Eldridge seemed to read my mind. "My wife was on the, ah, stage before our marriage, Dr. Watson. She enjoyed, ah, quite a popular following before consenting to, shall we say, cast her lot with me. She was known then as Miranda Delacorte."

I did not comment on my difficulty in believing this wispy wraith could command a stage, but again my expression apparently made the comment for me.

"My wife has, ah, not been well, I fear. Her health is a matter of grave concern to me. Grave concern, indeed."

I feared I was on the brink of being consulted in my professional capacity, but the subject was closed by the weaving approach of a portly man who had clearly been imbibing copiously of his host's generosity.

"Sir Eldridge, my congratulations on your book. A superb overview of the Etruscans in all their merry malefaction and malfeasance, eh?"

"Ah, thank you, Mr. Barrows. I, of course, value your opinion most highly indeed. Do you, ah, know Dr. Watson? This is Mr. Conrad Barrows, someone rather in your line."

"Oh? Medical man?" I ventured.

"More your, ah, literary line. Mr. Barrows is a book critic, who was, ah, most kind to my rather amateurish tome on the Etruscans. A hobbyist's scribbling, I fear."

"You are much too modest, Sir Eldridge," Barrows protested. "You made those mad Italians come to life more vividly than a battalion of professors!" He turned to me. "And what sort of writing do you do, Dr. Watson?"

Our host looked rather embarrassed. "Surely you're aware of Dr. Watson's accounts of his cases with Mr. Sherlock Holmes."

"Oh, *that* Dr. Watson. But you see, I never review fiction."

I suspected the fellow was being deliberately offensive, but I did not rise to the bait, merely muttering something polite. In truth, I'd been accused before of writing fiction—by Holmes himself, in fact!

"Well, now, Sir Eldridge," Barrows went on, "when will we be so honored that we may give honor to our guest of honor, eh?"

"Mr. Griffith has been, ah, resting in his room. His schedule has been, ah, rather taxing of his energies, I fear. You see, he, ah, only recently returned from filming at the front in France. But, ah, he will be down to introduce the showing of his film for us, and after that he will be pleased to, ah, mingle with all the guests."

Barrows looked around the room with comic exaggeration. "Well, the poor fellow. You know what he wants, Sir Eldridge. Money. Investors for his next project, whatever it is. My understanding is that his latest production, *Intolerance,* has done disappointing business in the States."

"Really? But, ah, I believe it has attracted large audiences here—"

"Certainly. Where it had the good fortune of opening at the Drury Lane on the very next day after President Wilson announced America's entry into the War. But now the chap once again needs money. And when he descends from his cloister, makes his dramatic entrance, what will he find? A room full of actors and society ladies who long to pose for the cinematographs, eh?"

Sir Eldridge seemed flustered. "Well, ah, really, I hardly think—"

A tall, saturnine figure with a commanding presence, which was only intensified by the stunningly beautiful woman on his arm, came to our host's rescue. "You malign Sir Eldridge, Mr. Barrows," the newcomer intoned, in a rich theatrical voice. "I do believe that I, apart from our distinguished hostess who has retired from the stage, am the only professional thespian in the room. My companion, Lady Veronica Travers, surely has the beauty to shine on the cinema screen but has to my knowledge no such ambitions."

The humorous sidelong glance the magnificent Lady Veronica gave her companion suggested ambitions beyond his knowledge.

"And these guests," the actor went on, his rolling delivery now commanding the attention of the entire room, "are here neither to flaunt their wealth nor to seek immortality on film but rather to appreciate the greatest artistic advance of our young century. For *The Birth of a Nation* has revolutionized the cinema, raising a commercial novelty to the stature of an art that may stand beside painting, sculpture, and drama in the pantheon of human aesthetic endeavor. And any viewing of great art is enhanced by the presence of the artist. Thus, I long to sit at the feet of Mr. David Wark Griffith, not for any employment he might afford this poor and aging player but for the enlightenment that can come from any association, however brief, with a genius." He paused for a moment, possibly allowing an opportunity for applause. "But I must apologize for my rudeness in interrupting your conversation, gentlemen."

"Not at all, Hope, ah, not at all," Sir Eldridge said. After formally presenting us to Lady Veronica, he introduced the actor as Sherrington Hope, but I knew him by another name. On some past occasions, my friend had so transformed himself with wigs and false whiskers as to fool even me. This time, however, the disguise was more one of speech and manner. I had known from first glance that this preening, posing ham was none other than Sherlock Holmes.

Another guest joined our circle then, a tall and well-built American, with a sensitive, long-jawed face, but loud and brash as his countrymen so often are. Sir Eldridge introduced him merely as Ernest Wheeler.

"Say, Dr. Watson, this is a pleasure. We're in this thing with you now, and about time, too. We'll take care of the kaiser for you."

"Yanks come to crown or kill the kaiser," Barrows slurred, having armed himself with another glass from a servant's passing tray. "Jolly big of you, big of you indeed. We're probably in for some dreadful American films about the war now, eh?"

"Isn't that exactly why Mr. Griffith has come to our shores?" Lady Veronica, speaking for the first time, revealed a melodious voice that complemented her visual beauty. "I understand he's been asked by the government to make a film to aid the war effort."

"It won't be dreadful, though, I can assure you of that," Holmes said.

"As I heard it," Barrows said, "the whole idea was to convince the Yanks to come in with us." Addressing the American, he added, "And now that you lot are in with all your colonial superiority, the war won't last past Tuesday, so who needs the film?"

"Well, I guess morale is still important," Wheeler replied, choosing as I had to ignore the critic's offensiveness.

"Some of us," Lady Veronica went on pointedly, "appreciate your country's entry on the side of righteousness, Mr. Wheeler, even if our friend Mr. Barrows takes it as an opportunity for derision."

Barrows seemed instantly abashed, saying with inebriated dignity, "I do apologize to one and all for my flippantly habitual manner, that is to say, my habitually—well, you take my meaning, I'm sure. We should all be grateful, as Lady Veronica so rightly asserts, to our colonial allies. I abase myself, Mr. Wheeler."

"No apology necessary," the American replied briskly.

"But, Mr. Wheeler, we don't see many American travelers these days," the critic went on. "Are you by chance of Mr. Griffith's battlefield-touring troupe of cinematographic artistes?"

"Oh, no, no, indeed. Rarely even attend the flickers, to tell you the truth. I owe my presence here to an interest in common with Sir Eldridge, whose hospitality I have been enjoying for nearly a week. I'm a professor of Etruscan literature, you see, at the University of California."

"A rare specialty, sir," Holmes remarked.

"A criminally undervalued body of literature, Mr. Hope. I have done my best to give it the serious study it deserves."

"Well, then, you and Sir Eldridge will have a lot to talk about, won't you?" I said, doing my bit to sooth the uneasy atmosphere. I was relieved when Wheeler drifted away. He seemed a pleasant enough fellow, but Americans can be wearing at times.

A group of unobtrusive servants—mostly women even for this technically demanding job—had begun to prepare an area of the "small ballroom" for the film viewing, hanging a screen on one wall, carrying in a projector, arranging the seating. The chairs looked to be antiques, and it struck me as ironic we would be sitting on such venerable objects while enjoying such modern entertainment. A half dozen musicians, apparently employed to accompany the film, were unveiling their instruments and setting up their stands.

It was at this point that the guest of honor, the celebrated D. W. Griffith, made his entrance down the staircase at the other end of the room. He was a tall and commanding figure, his most prominent features a hawkish nose and a receding hairline. My impulse, in common with the other guests, was to draw toward the guest of honor, but Holmes took the opportunity to pull me aside for a quiet word.

"I must be quick, old fellow. We are here at the behest of my brother Mycroft. Put simply, Griffith is to make a film to help the war effort, and a German spy is believed to be among our fellow guests, possibly with the intent of assassinating Griffith. We must not let that happen." He laughed loudly, as if I had made some great joke, then added,

"Lady Miranda has reported seeing a sinister stranger, both in the garden and in the house, oddly dressed and able to vanish as suddenly as he appears. No one else has seen this person, however, and Sir Eldridge fears she may be unbalanced, losing her reason."

"And is she?"

"It's too soon to say. We must be alert to anything." To this point, Holmes had spoken quietly and almost without moving his lips. Now he raised his voice for the benefit of those guests nearest us. "Come, Doctor. Let us hear what the great man has to say."

But in fact, as we approached the circle around Griffith, another guest was doing most of the talking. It was the American, Ernest Wheeler, who apparently had chosen to provide an excessively complete answer to a polite question about his academic specialty.

"You know, Mr. Griffith, the Etruscans were a happy, fun-loving people, much more so than the Romans who eventually overran them. Though they were a religious people, they had liberal attitudes to merrymaking and, shall we say, romance."

"My sort of people," the director murmured humorously.

"Yes, indeed your sort. I often think it would be enjoyable to be an Etruscan. But then I remember that not all Etruscans had a life of pleasure, that many of their celebrations included the beating of their slaves. Slavery is an ugly stain on human history. I am embarrassed that our country was so slow to rid itself of that deplorable institution."

"But so we did, sir, and painfully."

"Some of our countrymen who have seen *The Birth of a Nation* believe you regret the abolition of slavery."

Griffith drew himself up, but his tone remained civil. "That is a gross and I think deliberate misunderstanding of my film. I am a Southerner, through and through, but I am no champion of slavery. The themes of my film were the effects of war on the individual and the human hunger for power and exploitation, not a brief for the subjugation of one race by another."

The tension in the air was palpable, and Sir Eldridge looked speechless with embarrassment at seeing one American guest insulting another. Though controlling his emotions, the courtly Griffith appeared old-fashioned enough to demand satisfaction at dawn. Once again, it was Lady Veronica who came forward to calm the waters.

"Surely, Mr. Wheeler, we needn't refight the American Civil War here in Sir Eldridge's ballroom, when shortly we can watch it unfold most vividly and brilliantly on the screen."

As Griffith smiled her way, I imagined a degree of lust mingled with the gratitude in his regard. If Lady Veronica does long to pose for cinematographs, I reflected, she might get her chance.

"You are very kind, m'lady," Griffith said. "But I must offer one small correction. In my part of the world, we prefer to call it the War between the States."

"I understand some of your actors and technicians accompanied you to our shores, Mr. Griffith," Lady Veronica went on. "Will none of them be joining us this weekend?"

Griffith smiled. "I fear I have been keeping them much too busy for that, m'lady, but they have found their stay as memorable as I. Miss Lillian Gish, a most brave lady, accompanied me to the front. We were, I hasten to assure you, well chaperoned by others of my company. And Miss Dorothy Gish made her contribution to the war effort during her crossing by coaching General Pershing for his newsreel appearances— but perhaps I am telling secrets."

"Ah, ladies and gentleman," said our host, finding his voice at last, "if you will kindly take your seats, Mr. Griffith has agreed to say a few words to us before we view his wonderful and, ah, might I say, historic film."

As the guests moved to the other end of the room, Holmes attached himself to Griffith, very convincingly suggesting an actor seeking a role. But the director, understandably, appeared more intrigued by Lady Veronica on his other arm.

I took a seat in the back row, where I could observe the entire gathering. To my surprise, the American professor sat down next to me, looking rather more pleased with himself than embarrassed at the tension he had caused.

"Don't think I'm too popular at the moment, Dr. Watson," he said. "The way some of these folks were looking at me, I could figure in one of your stories before the night is out. 'The Adventure of the Murdered Professor,' eh? But where I come from, that war isn't really over yet, and I don't know if it ever will be. Have you seen this film before?"

"Can't say that I have. Don't get out to the cinema much. Busy practice, you know."

"Certainly. Mr. Griffith's presentation of American history purports to be scholarly—he even provides occasional pretentious footnotes. But his memory is selective, owing to his background, I guess. When they stop to change reels, I'll try to give you a more truthful view of the facts."

"That will be splendid," I replied, with an utter lack of sincerity.

When we all were seated, D. W. Griffith, standing in front of the white screen, assured us how welcome he had been made in England, how enthusiastically he and President Wilson supported our great cause, and how he chose to let his film speak for itself. Then he proceeded to orate at such length, I began to doubt we'd see the film at all. He praised Lord Beaverbrook, the head of the government's cinematograph office who had invited him to Britain, and Minister of Munitions Winston Churchill, who had suggested to him many promising ideas for scenarios. He spoke of being under fire during his time at the front in France. He movingly described the impact of observing the war first hand on this side of the channel. He and his company were staying at the Savoy, and from their rooms they could watch the German aeroplanes flying up the Thames to their targets. He remarked on his British ancestry, his Kentucky boyhood, his father's heroism in the War between the States, his family poverty, his early films for a company called Biograph, and finally some details on the making of the film that would soon speak for itself. He made no reference to the controversy that apparently had attended its release in the States, but my American companion whispered in my ear accounts of the negative reaction of Negroes to their depiction (sometimes inflammatory, other times merely patronizing) by white actors in the film, and of the story's origin in a vicious novel championing white supremacy, Thomas Dixon's *The Clansman*.

At last, the lights were dimmed and the film itself began. All thought of political issues and questions of historical accuracy were banished. *The Birth of a Nation* proved as extraordinary as had been promised. The period leading to the war was depicted in historical tableaux. A prosperous southern family, the Camerons, and their northern visitors, the Stonemans, were introduced. The ties of friendship and romance forged among the younger generation would soon be tested. The acting in these scenes, particularly by the young women of the two families, was remarkably subtle and natural, free of exaggerated gestures and excessive emotions.

The attention of the audience was rapt throughout these early scenes. Then, about one hour into the film, came one of its few humorous moments. In a Northern hospital, the magnificent Lillian Gish, in the role of Elsie Stoneman, the daughter of Northern abolitionist Austin Stoneman, has been working as a nurse, serenading on the banjo the Southern hero, Benjamin Cameron, played by Henry B. Walthall. At one point, Miss Stoneman passes a Union sentry, leaning on his rifle, who sighs and looks longingly at this beautiful woman. It was a memorable human moment, but its effect was broken by a loud scream.

Someone turned on the electric lights, and all the assembled guests turned to see Lady Miranda, on her feet with her fists to her cheeks, sobbing uncontrollably, a terror-stricken look in her eyes. Sir Eldridge reached out to support her. The projector stopped.

"My dear, ah, my dear," was all the baronet could say.

"It's him! It's him! He's the one! He's the one, I tell you."

"Come, my dear," Sir Eldridge said, and with the help of Holmes and Lady Veronica, he guided her out of the room. As the only medical man present, I followed to give what aid I could.

"My wife is, ah, somewhat upset," Sir Eldridge said. "Can you, ah, give her something to help her rest?"

Before I could suggest a sedative, Holmes gently asked the stricken woman, "Whom did you see, Lady Miranda?"

"He's a murderer, I know it. The man on the screen. The man who looks at her in that terrible way."

"He's an actor," Lady Veronica said reasonably. "He's admiring her beauty and daydreaming. It's only a play."

Lady Miranda tried to take this in, her features troubled. "An actor? But I never played with him. Have you, Mr. Hope?"

Holmes shook his head. "But he's an American actor, Lady Miranda. One of Mr. Griffith's company. Where had you seen him before?"

"In the garden. Three nights ago. He appeared out of the shadows, looking at me, just as in the film. And then he was gone, as suddenly as he had come." She turned to Sir Eldridge, imploring him. "I told you to look for him, dear."

"I did look, my dear," said Sir Eldridge sadly and gently. "I looked, and all the servants looked. We looked everywhere. There was no one."

"Then last night. I saw him again. In my bedroom. He was there, and then he wasn't. He might have murdered me. He might have murdered us all. I told you I saw him, dear. I told you. But you said there was no one."

"And there was no one, my dear."

"But there was. You thought I imagined him. I knew I had seen him, but I came to believe he was a ghost, one only I could see. Yet there he was on the screen tonight, so that proves he exists, doesn't it? If I imagined him or if he was a ghost, he couldn't appear in Mr. Griffith's film, could he? He's here to do some evil, I know it, I can feel it."

Sir Eldridge shook his head sadly. With a nod from Holmes, I carried out my professional duty and administered a sedative. Lady Miranda was delivered to the charge of her lady's maid, and the rest of us returned to the small ballroom, where D. W. Griffith was again speaking to the other guests, noting that while his film had been controversial, audiences had usually found that particular scene more amusing than disturbing. When he saw the four of us return, he fell silent and looked enquiringly at our host. Sir Eldridge, with a halting reference to his wife's delicate health, insisted the screening continue.

As the film went on, even the genius of Griffith and the amazingly natural performances of his actors could not keep at bay the many thoughts that passed through my mind. Among them was the question of whether Holmes's masquerade was in danger of exposure. Some of the guests had looked at him suspiciously, and I could imagine what they might be thinking. It was natural that Sir Eldridge, her husband, or Lady Veronica, another woman, or I, a doctor, should have attended to the stricken lady. But why this flamboyant actor?

When the screening had finished and the assembled guests retired, Holmes and I visited the great cinematograph director in his bedroom. Immediately, Holmes dropped the "Sherrington Hope" masquerade and revealed to Griffith his true identity.

"It is an honor, sir, to meet someone so preeminent in his chosen profession," the director declaimed.

"No more so than you are in yours," Holmes replied handsomely, but somewhat impatiently, eager to move past the customary civilities.

"Mr. Griffith, what was the name of the actor who played the mooning sentry that so frightened Lady Miranda?"

"Many have asked me, but I have to confess I don't know," Griffith replied. "He was a day player, an extra. We employed hundreds of them on that picture. Quite often, I would pick one out of the crowd and give him a bit of business to do. That particular idea proved a great success, but of course, we didn't know that at the time. At the end of the day, the fellow presumably picked up his wages and we never saw him again. Miss Gish might recall his name, I suppose, but I cannot."

"So," I ventured, "this fellow was not among the actors who came with you here or went with you to France?"

"Certainly not. I only brought a few of my most important players."

"Might he have sailed here on his own?"

"I should think that very unlikely, Watson," Holmes said, before Griffith could answer.

"Quite so," I said. "You are probably quite right to believe that Lady Miranda was imagining things. She is certainly in a perilous state of mental health and could be subject to hallucinations."

"No, in fact, I believe the mooning sentry that appeared to her was quite real and of sinister origin. But it need not have been the same man who portrayed the sentry in the film. All it would take was the blue cap and jacket, belt and sword of a Union Army sentry plus a long face, a mustache, a tilt of the head, and a comical expression of longing. In her emotional state, Lady Miranda would be unlikely to notice subtle differences in the face of the person on the screen."

"But why?" I demanded.

"Mr. Griffith, did any of the costumes from your film accompany you to England?"

"No," the director answered. "Why would they, unless it were for a museum exhibit of some sort?"

"Still, the sentry uniform would be easy enough to copy," Holmes mused.

"But why?" I asked again.

Ignoring me, Holmes told the director, "We shall be outside your door throughout the night, Mr. Griffith. We are armed and prepared for any eventuality. If anything unusual occurs, call on us."

"Yes, certainly," the puzzled American said.

And so we remained. After two hours, at about the point I had decided our efforts were unnecessary, we heard sounds of a struggle in Griffith's room. I drew my pistol as we burst through the door. Out-lined in the moonlight from the window, we saw a figure in a Union sentry uniform, arms outstretched, hands encircling the throat of D. W. Griffith, who gripped his assailant's wrists in desperate defense.

"Raise your hands!" Holmes shouted.

The attacker emitted a mad growl and continued his assault. I fired, striking the attacker in the shoulder. With a howl of pain, he released Griffith's throat and surged toward the open window by which he had undoubtedly entered the room. For only an instant I saw his maddened, ravaged face, just long enough to recognize the American professor, Ernest Wheeler. As he climbed through the window, his wounded arm betrayed him, he lost his grip and fell with an anguished cry.

"Quick, Watson!" Holmes cried. "He must not escape." Holmes could still move quickly when the occasion demanded it. I followed my friend's reckless descent of the stairs, barely conscious of doors opening, lights going on, and querulous voices.

When I bent over the body of the man who had called himself Ernest Wheeler, lying where he fell under Griffith's second story win-dow, I quickly saw there was nothing I could do for him. The broken ivy clutched in his hand told the tale. He had been fatally injured, his neck broken in his fall.

We heard Sir Eldridge's voice imploring his guests not to leave the house. Then the baronet, in his dressing gown, rushed to join us under the window.

"What has happened? My God, what has happened?" he demanded, looking down at the body. I quickly recounted the attack and its dra-matic conclusion.

"He must have climbed from his window to enter Griffith's," the baronet said, looking upward. "They aren't far apart, and there are, ah, sufficient hand and footholds to give purchase. Still, it would have required considerable, ah, agility and indifference to danger."

"And a touch of madness, if you ask me," I said.

Sir Eldridge shook his head disbelievingly. "So that's the end of it. And he can never tell his tale. But, ah, I would say it's better this way."

"I daresay you would," Holmes replied.

"Well, that is to say, your brother's information was that a German spy was among my guests, and, ah, there he is, isn't he?"

"There he is indeed. In his Union sentry's uniform from the American Civil War. Not standard issue for German spies, I shouldn't think."

"I believe he was a bit of a lunatic," I offered. "He certainly appeared to have a genuine hostility toward Griffith, even when they were introduced in the ballroom. Perhaps that was why he was given the job, eh?"

"But that leaves unexplained the ghostly appearances by which Wheeler terrorized your wife, Sir Eldridge."

"Oh, yes, I see," the baronet nodded. "Now at last I see. She really did see someone in the garden and in her room, and I was convinced it was, ah, part of her illness. I never suspected Wheeler."

"I suspected him at once," Holmes said. "Why do you suppose it became part of this assassin's mission to drive your wife mad?"

Sir Eldridge shook his head sadly. "I cannot think. She has, ah, suffered so much, my poor dear, and I have done her an injustice. Perhaps now things will become brighter for her."

"So they may if she gets away from here as quickly as possible," Holmes said sharply.

"Sir, ah, what are you suggesting?"

"Why is it, Sir Eldridge, you haven't even inquired how I came to suspect Ernest Wheeler, how I knew he was an impostor? I am accustomed to imprecations to explain my deductions. My vanity is wounded by your indifference."

The baronet essayed an unconvincing laugh. "Ah, Mr. Holmes, I do apologize for my failure. Tell us now, if you please."

"Wheeler claimed to be a professor of Etruscan literature. You know as well as I, Sir Eldridge, that there is no Etruscan literature to profess. Unlike the writings of the Greeks and Romans, whatever literature your Etruscans produced failed to survive their civilization. The average uninformed person might take Wheeler's claim at face value. But he could never have fooled an Etruscan expert like you with that absurd story. Could he?"

"And so I told the fool when he had already adopted it," Sir Eldridge said softly. "Go on, then. What else do you have to say?"

"The rest is surmise, but with a foundation of logic. The assassin stayed under your roof. You knew he was an impostor, so you must have been in league with him. You, sir, are the German agent my brother warned me about. Either your wife had begun to suspect your activities, or information she had been exposed to made you believe she might come to know the truth. You feared she might use this week-end event to expose you. You had for some time isolated her and essayed to ruin her health, physical and mental. The physical part of it, through what poisons I do not know, but the mental part consisted in ghostly appearances by Wheeler during the past week in his disguise as the mooning sentry. You hoped, as proved the case, that your wife would react hysterically to the sight of the mooning sentry on the screen, that whatever babbling she might do to me or to any other guest would be ignored in view of her obvious madness. Can you deny this, sir?"

Sir Eldridge's vague manner had disappeared. When he dropped the mask, his cultured accent was the same, but his clipped tones sounded subtly Germanic. I gripped my revolver warily.

"You were right, Dr. Watson. Wheeler was quite mad. He is actually an American as he claimed, an assassin for hire to the highest bidder. He had an ancestor who performed such services for the Union Army, and he had an unbalanced hatred of the American South and, for whatever reason, of D. W. Griffith. When he appeared here with that ridiculous Union Army uniform and his litany of grievances against Griffith and the Confederacy, I could have cursed my superiors for their administrative failures, but instead I chose to use what they had provided me in as creative a manner as I could." The baronet's body tensed subtly, and a look in his eye suggested he was poised for action, but he went on speaking in the same even, clipped tones. "If you had not been here, Holmes, I might have succeeded. How many of my guests had any idea if the Etruscans had a literature or not?"

With that he sprang at Holmes, a dagger clutched in his hand. Before my friend could test his joints with a defensive move, my pistol spoke for me. The wound to Sir Eldridge Masters was enough to stop him, but he would live to stand trial for treason.

The next day, as Holmes and I shared a pony cart to the railway station, I remarked, "I ought to have known that Wheeler chap was up to no good when he suggested that dreadful title, 'The Adventure of the Murdered Professor.' Deplorable taste. I wouldn't dream of putting a tale before the public with an unpleasant word like murder or death in the title. My literary agent would never approve."

"I do recall you made one exception to that rule, Watson, or nearly. Wasn't there a story called 'The Dying Detective'?"

"Yes, yes, so there was. But you'll never die, Holmes."

"You'll never let me, my dear fellow."

The Adventure of the *Rara Avis*

Carolyn Wheat

A CLUB WITHOUT a bow window is no club at all. This reflection absorbed me as I sat in the comfortable leather chair that constituted the premier place of honor in the Strangers' Room at the Diogenes Club. Beyond the panes of the gently curving window stepped, or so it seemed, all of London, high born and low, gentlemen and pickpockets, men in frock coats and ladies in velvet cloaks, high-stepping horses and mangy curs.

Carriages rattled past, some the crowded omnibuses of the great city, others bearing lozenge crests denoting rank and birth. Deliverymen shouted at coachmen, vendors cried their wares, and ladies whose cheeks showed perhaps a touch too much color smiled at passing gentlemen in a most unseemly manner.

I fancied myself something of a student of humanity—or at least I did so before I made the acquaintance of my remarkable friend Sherlock Holmes and his even more remarkable brother Mycroft.

"The man risked a fine just to speak to me," Mycroft Holmes said, helping himself to a liberal bite of cucumber sandwich. "Indeed, we shall probably both be brought to the attention of the committee in a most embarrassing fashion." It was the custom of the Diogenes, quite the most eccentric club in England, for members to address not a word to one another in the private rooms. Conversation was permitted in the Strangers' Room alone (and, indeed, that sobriquet served notice upon those who in any other club would have been referred to as "guests" that, at the Diogenes, they were a sort of infection to be quarantined).

"I can only conclude that his business is a matter of the utmost importance."

"Important to him, my dear Mycroft," Sherlock Holmes replied. "Not necessarily important to me." He contented himself with a sip of tea, ignoring the feast of sandwiches and scones brought by the ancient club waiter. "But tell me, what do you know of your fellow club member?"

"He is but lately retired from the academic profession," Mycroft replied. "Not a fellow of Oxford or Cambridge but of a lesser institution somewhere in the north. He is an archaeologist, not by profession but by passion."

"An amateur," Holmes said with a brisk nod. "Which means he is either a genius or a dilettante. There is no in-between in such cases."

"His particular passion is early British pottery, and to that end he has participated in several 'digs' in various parts of the country." Mycroft wiped his fleshy lips on a snow-white napkin. He reached into the pocket of his silk waistcoat and pulled out a neatly folded note, which he handed to his brother with an air of one conferring a great favor.

My friend lifted the paper to the light and said in a low murmur, "Fine cream laid, watermark from Brewster and Sons, deckle edges— quite the dandy as far as writing is concerned, your friend—written in a plain hand by a man capable of much more decorative lettering, no smudges, no blots, no—I revise my earlier estimate. The man is a genius and not a dilettante."

"What does the note say?" I tried in vain to keep the impatience out of my voice; Holmes and his brother could discuss the missive for half an hour without actually reading it, but as a lesser mortal I wanted to know the contents.

" 'I must consult your celebrated brother regarding the singular contents of an ancient British barrow.' Signed, Wilfred Patchford, M.A."

"A barrow?" I glanced out of the window; a passing flower-seller having brought an image of Covent Garden to my mind. "What could possibly—" I broke off with a blush, realizing my mistake. As an archaeologist, Patchford no doubt meant "barrow" to signify an ancient collective burial site, not a container for fruits and vegetables.

"Singular contents? Whatever can the man mean?"

"There is but one way to find out," Holmes replied. "Have the waiter invite Mr. Patchford to join us in the Strangers' Room."

"IT APPEARED TO be—but of course I know nothing of such matters —but it did have the appearance of the Horus figure in the British Museum, the Elgin rooms, you know, but of course I am no Egyptologist, only that it did look so very like." Patchford at last ran out of breath and slowed down like an exhausted horse.

Reading between the lines of the man's breathless, disjointed manner of speech, it appeared that his ancient British barrow had contained, not relics from the seventh century as he had hoped, but a small figure of a bird, made of some black stone, and belonging to no period of British history.

"It is surely very valuable and quite old," the antiquarian continued, "but it is not British in any way and it has no business turning up in Sir Cadogan's burial place." The little man sounded quite indignant, as if the black bird had flown into his tumulus just to annoy him.

He was a woolly little man, with tufts of white hair shooting from his pink scalp as if he'd been electrified. Watery blue eyes peered through silver pince-nez and knobby fingers made invisible cats' cradles in the air as he spoke. I pitied the students who had sat through his lectures if his colloquial speech was anything to go by; they must have had quite a job to stay awake.

"It certainly does look Egyptian," Mycroft Holmes said. He lifted the bird from the tea table where Patchford had placed it. "Basalt, I think," he murmured as he stroked the smooth dull black sides of the little statue.

"A funerary object, do you think?" I was surprised at Holmes; normally his knowledge extends to matters of criminology and no further. "I believe statues of this size were often placed inside pyramids as guardians over the mummies."

"But what was it doing in Sir Cadogan's barrow?" The professor's face wore an expression of petulant outrage.

"Was the late Sir Cadogan a Crusader, by any chance?" I picked up the last cucumber sandwich. "He might have brought the statue back as a souvenir from the Holy Land."

"He might indeed," Patchford said with an irritating smile, "if he hadn't died four hundred years before the first Crusade."

"Professor Patchford," Holmes asked, steepling his fingers, "do you have any opinion regarding how long the bird had been in the barrow? Could it have been put there, say, within the year, or had it lain in place a long time?"

"An excellent question, sir." The little man beamed. "I can see I was quite right to appeal to you, quite right. When I first opened the tumulus, I would have staked my oath that I was the first person to have done so. Often, you know," he went on, his hands twisting in his lap, "we archaeologists come to the site after everyone else has already ransacked it—grave robbers, curiosity seekers, carrion beasts."

"But this time the site appeared undisturbed," Holmes prompted.

"It appeared," the little man lowered his voice and giggled, "virgin. So undefiled was it that I had a momentary lapse in reason and thought I might release a ghost upon the world. That's the local legend, you know, that barrows are occupied by wights, ghosts of those who died, and that opening them sets the ghost free."

"Surely you don't believe—"

"Oh, no, of course not, Mr. Holmes," Patchford hastened to reply. His wizened hands smoothed his wild hair back behind his ears. "But I've seen some strange things in the fens and bogs where barrows lie. Swamp gas can only explain so much, sir, so much and no more." His voice grew lower and more confidential. "I removed the stones, one by one, very carefully, from the tumulus and I peered inside with my lantern and what did I see but this very bird staring at me with his great black eyes and I—well, sir, I won't deny it gave me quite a turn."

"I imagine it did indeed," Mycroft replied. His plump hands continued to explore the bird; he ran his fingers over it as if hoping to read some meaning into its shape and heft.

"It was directly in front," Patchford said, "and so I suppose someone must have opened the tomb and placed it there, I mean, that is the only possible explanation, I realize that, but whoever did such a thing covered the tumulus back up with such care, such exactitude, such precision, that I can only assume it was someone as familiar with ancient British burial sites as I myself, and I can tell you, gentlemen, the number of such men in England is infinitesimal. I don't like to boast, gentlemen, but there are accredited professors of archaeology at very prestigious universities who could not have done it. The laying of stone upon stone, sealing the tomb without resort to mortar, and making it appear untouched for centuries—it was a veritable work of art, Mr. Holmes, and it was done with one purpose in mind, of that I am certain."

"To conceal the black bird," Holmes said, almost carelessly, as if confirming a commonplace.

"Just so. But why should anyone conceal such a find, I ask myself?" Patchford settled back in his chair and smiled. "A find like that could make a career. It ought to be in the British Museum or the Ashmolean, not hiding in a barrow."

"If it were stolen," I ventured, and won the little man's smile as a reward for my perception, "that might explain—"

"Exactly, Doctor. If it were stolen, an obscure tomb would be a very good hiding place indeed. It could have lain there another century without anyone disturbing it."

"It might have lain there a half century already," Mycroft observed. "The theft might not be recent at all. Egyptian pyramids have been looted since Roman times and their booty scattered over the entire European continent."

"Enough of this fruitless speculation," Holmes said in a tone that brooked no disagreement. "This first thing to do is find out whether the bird is in fact Egyptian, and if it is, how much it might be worth."

"I know just the man." Mycroft clapped his pudgy hands. "He's a member here, but one sees him rather seldom, since he spends so much time in the Orient. Amateur Egyptologist, quite knowledgeable. We've had several stimulating discussions in this very room after one of his adventures."

"Pray tell me his name," Sherlock Holmes said, leaning forward with the light of curiosity aflame in his grey eyes, "and I shall send for him at once."

"Basil Blakeney," Mycroft replied with an air of great satisfaction. "Knows more about Egypt than men with twice his age and education. Lives near Brighton. He could get up to London in very short order."

MRS. HUDSON ANNOUNCED our visitor, then stepped aside to allow him entry into our sitting room. He was a slender man, with fair hair and large inquisitive blue eyes. He looked rather young for such a renowned expert, and he looked like the last man on earth one would associate with the word "adventure."

"Ah, Mr. Blakeney," Holmes said with a smile. "How good of you to come."

"I am only too glad to be of assistance, Mr. Holmes," the dapper young man replied. He wore a well-cut suit of grey broadcloth and his boots were polished to a high gloss. "I decided to take the opportunity of an unexpected trip to London and spend the evening at the opera."

Blakeney set his hat on a side table, pulled a pair of white cotton sleeve protectors out of his carpetbag, fastened them to his sleeves, and said, "May I see the bird?"

"Certainly," Holmes replied, the ends of his mouth quirking into a near-smile. "I was about to offer you tea, but I admire your single-mindedness."

Holmes had already conducted several chemical tests upon the statue and declared it to be made of basalt, as were many Egyptian funerary statues. He'd scratched the bottom of the figure and found that it was not solid; something inside the bird was made of substances other than the dull black volcanic stone. But without damaging the object, he could do no more, and he dared not damage it without an expert assessment of its value.

The fastidious scholar bent over the bird, which stood on Holmes's old deal chemical table. He reached once more into his capacious carpetbag and pulled out a magnifying glass, a brush, and a small chisel. Holmes quirked a single eyebrow, but I could tell he was impressed.

Holmes ordered tea while Mr. Blakeney's slender fingers poked and prodded, shaved and examined the falcon. After a full ten minutes, he stood up straight, lifted the bird off the table into the air, and dropped it with some force onto the stony hearth.

Pieces of black stone flew into the air. I jumped from my chair and shouted, "What have you done?"

I appealed to Holmes. "My God, he's destroyed it! What will Patchford say? Mr. Blakeney," I cried, running toward the fireplace as if I could somehow reverse the motion of time, turn back the clock to before that appalling act of destruction, "you must be mad!"

Even as I knelt on the hearth picking up pieces, I heard an odd sound behind me. It was Holmes—chuckling.

"Testing your hypothesis, Mr. Blakeney?"

"An untested hypothesis is useless speculation, Mr. Holmes."

"An admirable sentiment," the detective replied with a small bow. "Shall we inspect the results of your little test?"

I was already kneeling on the slate hearthstones, so I turned the broken figure over and gasped, rocking back on my heels.

Inside the basalt covering, partially revealed, was a bird of such magnificence, golden, jewel-encrusted, ruby-eyed, that my eyes blinked at the dazzling display. "Oh, my God," I murmured. "It's—it's wonderful."

"But it is not Egyptian, is it?"

"No," the extraordinary little man replied. He had joined Holmes and me at the fireplace. All three of us huddled over the small figure as if in worship of a pagan idol. "I saw at once that it was fake. I was about to say so, when I caught sight of a thin layer of wax beneath the surface of the basalt, about an inch below the surface. Someone had covered the inside object with wax to protect it, then coated it in a basalt-based plaster to conceal it. The only way to find out what was under the basalt was to break the bird open. And this is the result."

"But what is it?" I turned the figure in my hands, letting the sunlight play upon the sparkling jewels. "And to whom does it belong?"

"Those are pertinent questions, Watson." Holmes shook his head with rueful admiration. "What better way to hide a falcon than inside another falcon? Very clever. Anyone finding it would think, as we did, that it was Egyptian, and when it was discovered to be a fake, it would be dismissed as worthless. Only Mr. Blakeney's daring has permitted us to see the true value of this bird."

Mrs. Hudson brought tea and set it, with a small frown of disapproval, on the old deal table. Holmes poured and offered a cup to our guest, who accepted it without sitting down. Instead he took a single sip, put the cup down, picked up his chisel, and went to work stripping away the remaining basalt from the jeweled bird.

"Faience?" Holmes asked. He stood hovering over the bird like an anxious parent watching a doctor examine a sick child.

"You know it isn't," the Egyptologist replied with some asperity. "But I see the value of eliminating all possibilities before settling upon a conclusion."

"So the gems are real," Holmes murmured, his voice trailing off and his eyes gazing into the distance. "Is it at all Egyptian?"

The fair-haired man shook his head decisively. "No, it is not. If I had to hazard a guess, I'd say it was from the Orient, but of a later period. Persian, perhaps, or Ottoman."

"So my suggestion that it was a Crusader's booty was not so far from the mark," I said with a pardonable air of pride. "Perhaps one of Sir Cadogan's descendants brought it back from the East and placed it in his ancestor's tomb for safekeeping."

"In any case, I have done all that I can," the gentleman said. He took one more sip of tea, unfastened his sleeve-protectors, repacked his carpetbag, and picked up his hat. *"Tosca* awaits. I suggest you contact Gutman at Oxford. Quite the best man for this kind of thing."

GUTMAN OF OXFORD—a man even larger and more rotund than Mycroft Holmes—proved to be a veritable fount of information, so much so that Holmes had a job persuading him to focus upon the essentials. At every turn, he mentioned monographs written in Italian, passages from French histories, obscure biographies of even more obscure Spanish counts, and privately published family histories. My head swam with references to Saracens, Barbarossa, Suleiman the Magnificent, and the Knights Templars.

"But the origin, Professor Gutman," I said at last, "was it in Turkey or Persia? I've lost track, I'm afraid."

"Malta." His dark bushy eyebrows gathered in a frown, as if he disliked dealing with one so dim as to lose the thread of his discourse. "I distinctly said it was undoubtedly—and you should know, sir, that this conclusion will be disputed by those who wish to—well, let us just say that it will be disputed—but I stake my not inconsiderable reputation that this is the authentic article, the *Rara Avis* of song and story, the legendary Maltese Falcon!"

His air of consequence was so enormous that a laugh bubbled up in my throat. "But what exactly does that mean, Professor?"

"It means, for one thing, that this bird is worth a great deal of money," Holmes said, his prosaic manner deliberately chosen to cut through the professor's fustian.

"Priceless, sir, priceless," the professor replied in a soft, silky voice. His gaze had not left the glittering object since he'd entered our rooms. Dark eyes beneath heavy black brows, a full black beard, and fleshy, sensuous lips proclaimed him a man of appetites, and clearly his avariciousness was aroused by the sight of the jeweled avian. But perhaps I wronged him, for he next remarked, "It has been sought by scholars of the Orient for hundreds of years, thought to be lost, then discovered again, then obscured by the mists of time and the smoke of battle. It was once in England, so I should not be surprised to see it here in Baker Street, and yet, I am surprised. Surprised and gratified, shocked and amazed—I had almost begun to think it a chimera, a phantom, a figment of overheated imagination."

"Who made it?" I thought perhaps if my questions were simple to the point of childishness that the answers might become less abstruse.

"The Order of the Hospital of St. John of Jerusalem, later called the Knights of Rhodes, today known as the Knights of Malta," Gutman replied. He folded his hands across his ample stomach and settled back in the leather chair with the air of one about to tell a long story. "Although why they merited the former name is unclear, since Suleiman chased them out of Rhodes in 1523; they settled in Crete and persuaded Emperor Charles V to give them Malta, Gazo, and Tripoli for their own. There was but one condition," he went on, lowering his voice and slowing his speech for dramatic emphasis. "They were to pay the emperor a tribute every year—a tribute of one falcon."

"One falcon like this every year would have left them very poor indeed," Holmes remarked.

The fat man threw his head back and laughed. "Yes, it would have. But this was a special tribute, for the first year only. Bear in mind that the Hospitallers had preyed upon the Saracens for years, looting and gathering spoils of war. They possessed gold and gems, diamonds and rubies, silks and ivories, riches beyond the dreams of avarice. The Holy Wars were to them simply a matter of enriching themselves."

"So they created this bird out of the cream of their booty," Holmes said, "and sent it to the emperor."

"Sent it in a galley commanded by a French knight," Gutman confirmed with a decisive nod. He had the slightest of German accents, overlaid with Oxonian diction.

"Something tells me it never reached Spain," I said. The bird seemed to wink at me, a trick of light, but disconcerting. It had two large rubies for eyes; when the sunlight hit them, they glowed like new-shed blood.

"Something tells you correctly," the professor agreed with a nod of his large head. "Barbarossa, also known as Khair-ed-Din, the Algerian pirate, captured the galley and the bird. There it stayed, in North Africa, for another hundred years until it was carried away by Sir Francis Verney, the famous English adventurer."

"Then it *was* in England," I cried. "Did Verney have a house in the Cotswolds?" All we knew of the barrow's location was that it lay in that most picturesque area of the countryside.

"He did," Gutman replied and I glowed with pride. "But legend has it that the bird left England and made its way to Sicily, then to Spain, and finally to Paris."

"And if that legend was false?" I could not contain myself; the gem-encrusted statue had sparked my imagination. "What if Verney kept the bird and spread a rumor that it was no longer in this country?"

"Or perhaps," Holmes countered, "the bird that left England was a copy and not the true Maltese Falcon. Verney might have concealed the real bird in that barrow."

"Then, Mr. Holmes," Gutman said with an air of great portent, "you have set Arabic scholarship upon its ear and come into possession of the single most valuable artifact of the entire period."

"But to whom does it rightfully belong?" The more I gazed upon the remarkable bird, the more I hated the thought of delivering it into unworthy hands. The thing was a work of art and I began to feel quite strongly that it deserved to be kept in a place where all could see its dazzling glory.

"A case could be made that it ought to be given to the present king of Spain," the professor said. "It was his ancestor, after all, who was its intended recipient."

"Or perhaps," Holmes suggested, "the Knights of Malta should be informed that their gift has been recovered. They undoubtedly paid their falcon rent in less valuable currency and owe the king nothing but one live falcon per annum, as agreed."

"What of the landowner upon whose land the bird was found?" I inquired. "Does the Verney family still own the property, and if so, have they no rights?"

"All very sound legal questions, gentlemen," Professor Gutman observed, "but quite outside my purview. I shall take my leave of you and spend the rest of the day consulting references to the *Rara Avis* in my scholarly books. It is an amazing thing to have seen the bird at last, after so many disappointments." I couldn't help but think he lingered a bit too long beside the jeweled avian; the gleam in his small black eyes seemed to me covetous and grasping.

"I SHOULD LIKE to see the barrow," Holmes said in a patient tone. It seemed a logical request, yet it threw the little professor into a state of stubborn incoherence.

"Oh, but Sir Everard was so very particular about—indeed, he said as much the very first time I made inquiry about opening the site." Professor Patchford's crooked, white fingers twitched in his lap. "He told me no one else was to have access to his land, and he most expressly enjoined me against inviting fellow archeologists. In particular," the little man said, lowering his head and his voice, "he seems to have formed a fixed dislike of General Pitt-Rivers. He made it quite clear that under no circumstances was he to see the burial site, which is quite odd, for, as you are most certainly aware, the general has been appointed as inspector of ancient monuments and is a most meticulous record-keeper."

Holmes steepled his fingers and gazed into the fire blazing in the hearth of the Stranger's Room. "Remarkable," he replied. "The foremost authority on Saxon burial sites not permitted to see a common barrow. Why on earth should Sir Everard Addleton bar a noted expert from his land unless he has something to conceal?"

"What else did you find in the barrow?" I asked.

The little man's face lit up, as if to say that at last someone cared about the truly valuable objects inside the tumulus. "Four marvelous stone jugs, decorated with the geometrical patterns one expects from the Neolithic period, some silver jewelry, an amber necklace, the enamel crowns of the deceased Sir Cadogan—the skeleton was of course quite decayed—five Roman coins—the usual grave goods, but quite informative as to the—"

Holmes cut through the antiquarian's monologue. "Have you informed Sir Everard of your find?"

"I thought it best to wait until I had determined exactly what it was that I found," Professor Patchford said, his watery blue eyes wide with innocence. "I have not been in contact with Sir Everard since he gave me permission to excavate the barrow."

"Have you told anyone else about the black bird?" Holmes asked. He had decided, for reasons of his own, to keep from Professor Patchford the truth about the anomalous object he'd recovered from the burial site. As far as the old man was concerned, he had unearthed an Egyptian funerary statue and nothing more.

"No, indeed not," the antiquarian replied. "I would be very much obliged if you would intercede with Sir Everard on my behalf. I found him rather frightening, I must admit, and I wouldn't like him to think I'd taken liberties."

When Patchford had been ushered out of the Strangers' Room, Holmes said, "Let us send a telegram to Sir Everard and request an audience. Perhaps he can shed some light upon the discovery."

"I wonder why he allowed Patchford to open up his barrow," I remarked as we strode out onto the street in search of a cab, "if he is so adamantly opposed to strangers on his land."

"Ah, Watson, you never fail to stimulate me," my friend replied. As usual, he ignored the first cab in line and made for the second.

My blush of pleasure was hidden, I think, by the thickening dusk.

The news that Professor Hans-Josef Gutman, graduate of Heidelberg University and Fellow of Oxford, had accidentally fallen onto the platform at King's Cross Station and been crushed to death by the 5:14 to Oxford merited but a paragraph in the next morning's *Standard*. Holmes said nothing as he passed me the newspaper, marking with a slender finger the brief notice, but his face was grim as we set forth from Baker Street in search of the truth about the black bird.

SIR EVERARD ADDLETON was an imposing man of about sixty-five years of age, with snow white hair and a large mustache cut in military style. He stood in his library, one gold-headed cane in each hand, leaning heavily upon his sticks.

"So that silly little man thinks he has found the Maltese Falcon in my barrow!" The voice was deep, the tone contemptuous, and the words uttered before any proper greeting had been made.

"You are aware that such a bird exists?" Holmes deliberately kept his voice calm.

"I ought to be," the old man replied. He gestured with one cane toward seats by the fire; I sank gratefully into a leather chair. Sir Everard struggled toward the chair nearest the fire, walking with difficulty. "I was brought up on the story of Sir Francis Verney and the jeweled bird. It was a bedtime tale in my nursery, Mr. Holmes, for my father never ceased boasting about how his ancestor defeated the Barbary pirates at Tripoli and carried off the *Rara Avis*."

"If the bird that sits upon my mantel in Baker Street is not the Maltese Falcon," Holmes said quietly, "then where is the authentic bird?"

"Here, of course," the old man answered, emphasizing his words with a thump of one gold-headed stick. I noticed for the first time that the gold handle was in the form of a falcon's head. "Upstairs in the ballroom. I never ascend stairs, so I have not seen it for several years, but it is there, I assure you."

The situation seemed clear to me: the crippled Sir Everard unable to view his prized object, a venal servant spiriting it away and hiding it in the tomb until his confederate could remove it and sell it to the highest bidder. What a shock it would be for the poor man to realize his bird had flown—and what a welcome surprise it would then be to know it had been recovered.

"May we—" Holmes began, gesturing toward the ceiling.

"Of course," Sir Everard interrupted. "Pray bring it down with you; I should be glad to see it again. It has been many years since I laid eyes upon it." He pulled the bell and a tall butler with a long, cadaverous face appeared. "Barnes, take these gentlemen to the ballroom. They wish to see the Falcon."

"Very good, sir," the servant replied with a bow. He ushered us out of the dimly lit library with a slow, reluctant tread. I fancied I knew the reason for that slowness; undoubtedly, the man was a knave whose thievery was about to be revealed to his indignant master.

Holmes and I followed him up one set of stairs and then another. The ballroom occupied the entire third floor of the house. The huge room was dim, its only light entering through small windows set high on the walls. Unpolished brass sconces gave silent witness to the neglect of the servants; a thick layer of dust overlay the floor and mantel. Muslin coverings squatted over chairs and footstools, tables and ottomans.

The mantel was empty. I was about to remark upon its singular lack of a jeweled avian when the butler, who, despite his large feet, walked as quietly as a cat, stepped over to the largest ottoman and lifted off the muslin cover, raising a cloud of dust that had me coughing. Resting on top of the ottoman's central mound sat a golden bird, the exact same size and dimensions as the one in Baker Street. Even in the dull light of the ballroom, the ruby eyes winked at me.

"Impossible," I gasped. "There cannot be two of them!"

"Why not?" Holmes stepped toward the ottoman and picked up the statue. He turned it in his hands and I saw rainbows glint from its gem-encrusted body. "The creation of one such fowl is an incredible story —how much more fantastic is it to consider that the Knights might have fashioned a second bird? Or that one of these two might be a fake?"

"Come to that," I remarked, entering into the spirit of the thing, "they might both be fakes."

"Indeed, Watson, indeed." He tucked the bird under his arm as if it were a loaf of bread and proceeded, with his long strides, toward the door leading to the stairway. "That is the pleasure and the pitfall of speculation," he continued. "One can consider all possibilities without the necessity of proof. But I am in the proof business, so I shall cease speculating at this point."

Sir Everard radiated a bland calm as Holmes entered the overheated library. In spite of the warmth, the old man had a wool blanket over his knees and his hands were pale from the cold. I mentally diagnosed the slow circulation of an aging man who took little exercise, but I kept my observation to myself.

"I told you it would be there, and there it was. Now," Sir Everard continued, "I would be much obliged if you would tell that fool

Patchford that I will brook no more disturbances on account of that amazingly annoying barrow. I allowed him to open it in return for a promise of complete privacy, and he has broken that promise by bringing you here."

If this ungraciousness bothered Holmes, he managed to conceal the fact. "How long has your family owned this estate, Sir Everard? Was it in your family's possession before Verney fought the Barbary pirates?"

A dry little snigger escaped the thin mouth. "You know better than that, Mr. Holmes. Men who fight pirates do not usually come from landed families. My ancestor purchased the estate with part of his booty from that remunerative battle."

"Then how would he know there was an ancient barrow on his land? He does not sound a scholarly sort of man, and the barrow, like most of its kind, was crafted to resemble a small hillock." We had asked specially to be driven past the gravehill on our way from the railroad station, and it looked to the untrained eye like a slight rise in the countryside, nothing more.

"My ancestor was a man who aspired to better the lot of his children, to send them to fine schools and frank good marriages for them. And if they were able to pass themselves off as landed gentry, so much the better. Landed gentry know every tree and rock on their land, and are only too happy to talk of its history. They preserve old ruins of abbeys and are forever boasting that battles took place on their greenswards and history was made in their great houses. My ancestor wanted that kind of past for his children, and he hired a scholar to research this house. The resulting volume covers Edward the Confessor to Verney himself, and contains maps setting forth all the burial sites and other features of the property."

"Very intelligent of him," Holmes said, and the glint in his grey eyes told me he wanted very much to see this remarkable book. A bit more flattery and the old man gave his consent, ringing the bell once again for Barnes the butler and ordering the book to be brought from his bedchamber to the library.

Sir Everard excused himself, pleading the need for a lie-down before supper. "Not as young as I was," he confessed. Before leaving the library, he took one long last look at the Falcon. "Good to see you again, old friend," he said as he stroked its diamond-studded beak.

Holmes opened the Verney family history, a handsome but well-worn volume, its leather bindings beginning to give and several pages loose inside its covers. I soon tired of watching him peruse the pages, which were written in the old-fashioned script of the eighteenth century. I stood up and prowled the room, gazing at the titles on the shelves.

"Here's a first edition of *Paradise Lost.*" I turned the pages with reverence, then replaced the book next to a cheap copy of *Vanity Fair.* I caught a glimpse of a name that seemed somehow familiar, yet I couldn't recall why.

The book was a slender volume bound in blue cloth. The frontis-piece read ON THE EXCAVATION OF PRIMEVAL SAXON SEPULCHRES: A PRACTICAL MANUAL FOR THE ANTIQUARIAN, BY GENERAL AUGUSTUS PITT-RIVERS.

"Holmes," I cried excitedly, "look at this! A book by the very expert Sir Everard barred from his land."

I turned toward my friend, flushed with excitement, only to see him wave me off. Stung, I took the book to the far corner of the library and perused it on my own. What I saw in its pages doubled my resolution to capture Holmes's attention.

At last, he looked up, his grey eyes glazed with faraway thoughts. "The writing is cryptic, Watson. Hints are given, puns involving birds are used, but nothing solid, nothing I can rely upon. The bird could have flown to Sicily, as the unfortunate Gutman believed, or it could have stood upstairs in that ballroom for one hundred years."

I showed the detective my own find—the pages of Pitt-Rivers's manual demonstrating, stone by stone and layer by layer, how to excavate a Saxon tomb. "Our friend Patchford said few men in England could have restored that barrow. This book, I think, widens that circle considerably. Anyone taking reasonable care could use this as a blueprint for restoring a barrow to a state resembling virginity."

"Watson, you are invaluable. Thanks to you, our time here has been fruitful indeed. Yes," he muttered, "this is suggestive, very suggestive."

By the time Holmes and I rose from the long library table, our legs stiff with sitting, our hands cold, the sun was gone and the evening mists were rising on the river. We thanked our host, refreshed from his nap, and made our way to the nearest public house, where we ate a tolerable dinner and spent the night, planning to return to London the next morning.

Notwithstanding my friend's capricious insistence that two Maltese Falcons were not impossible, the more likely truth emerged upon consultation with experts. The bird Mr. Patchford had unearthed was genuine, insofar as its gems were real and its make of the requisite period. When Holmes informed Sir Everard of this fact, the old soldier commissioned his own test of the bird in his possession and indignantly informed us by telegram that it was a glass-eyed forgery.

Sir Everard, not unnaturally, claimed that he'd been robbed and demanded the return of the authentic jeweled bird. He argued, first, that the statue had been stolen from him and replaced by a fake, and second, that the bird Patchford found belonged to him as the rightful owner of the land on which the barrow lay.

With these points I could find no argument, but Holmes refused to relinquish the falcon until he was satisfied that the actual owner would be the beneficiary of its restoration.

"WATSON HERE IS convinced that someone removed the actual bird from Sir Everard's house and hid it in the barrow," Holmes said as we took our ease yet again in the Strangers' Room at the Diogenes Club.

Mycroft Holmes raised a single eyebrow. "It is the most likely explanation," he remarked as he lifted a heavily laden scone to his thick lips.

"But it is not the only one," my friend replied, contenting himself with a cup of sugarless tea. "I can think of a dozen explanations for the bird's presence in the tomb, and I daresay you, brother, can think of a dozen more."

"I thought you were in the business of proof and not speculation," I remarked with an air of innocence. "Where can proof be obtained that will settle this matter once and for all?"

Another thought struck me as I reached for a scone. "You once said you suspected why Sir Everard granted Patchford permission to excavate the barrow. Did you mean to imply that he knew the falcon was there and wanted it found?"

"I did. I always suspect people who behave differently from their usual patterns, and Sir Everard is known as a man who guards his privacy. Why would such a man, who had never expressed the slightest interest in the ancient burial sites on his land, suddenly allow an untrained amateur to go pot hunting? And why did he expressly refuse access to a noted expert like General Pitt-Rivers unless he feared that the general would realize the tomb had already been opened?"

"But why would he steal his own bird?"

"If it was his own bird," Mycroft Holmes replied, "then I can think of several reasons why he might have had it stolen. Perhaps he wished to have someone blamed for the theft."

"But as far as we know, he has taken no action in that regard," I pointed out. "He has blamed no one, fired no servants, cut no one out of his will."

"These are deep waters," Sherlock Holmes said. "I am on my second pipe, and I see no glimmer as yet. I am convinced utterly that Sir Everard deliberately permitted Patchford to open the barrow so as to find the falcon, and I see no reason for him to have behaved in that fashion if the falcon was his legitimately. Therefore, he set upon a course of action designed to bring the falcon to him, to cement his rightful ownership of it, but—where did the falcon come from? Where was it before it was placed in the barrow?"

"When was it placed there, and by whom?" Mycroft Holmes spread jam on his cream-laden scone and took a bite.

"If it was stolen from someone else," I pointed out, "then why hasn't there been a hue and cry?"

"Who made the fake, and when?" Mycroft said, ignoring my observation. "How long has Sir Everard really known his bird was not genuine?"

Holmes turned toward his brother. "I have taken a great liberty," he said. "I know how much you dislike bestirring yourself, so I invited someone to join us, someone who may shed some light upon this dark matter."

"Of course, Sherlock," the large man replied. He settled himself into the capacious leather chair. "I have already instructed the door-keeper to admit him, although he is not the sort of person the Club usually cares to see within its doors."

"Then you anticipated me," Holmes replied with a smile. "I should have expected as much."

"How does one learn about a theft?" Mycroft spread his plump hands. "One asks a thief—or if not a thief, then a receiver."

"In this case, the King of Receivers," Holmes answered, gesturing toward the man making his way toward us across the Strangers' Room, led by a very disapproving waiter.

"Ah, Magpie, sit down and take some tea with us," he invited. The little ferret of a man who followed the waiter nodded at us and took his ease in a straight-backed chair.

His trousers were loudly checked, his jacket plaid, his shirt a violent puce, and his neck cloth bright yellow. Pointed boots of an unfortunate color emerged from the pegged trousers, and the cap in his hand was forest green.

"Don't mind if I do," was his gracious reply. He poured himself a cup, drank it down in one gulp, proclaimed himself famished, and asked if the Club could provide fairy-cakes.

I was relieved to discover that it could not. Scones with extra jam were ordered, along with a second pot of tea, China this time.

Upon being formally introduced, the little man extended a brown hand and said affably, "I'm Magpie by name and Magpie by nature. See anything shinylike and I've got to 'ave it. Mebbe not to keep, it's my business to turn things over to others for a profit, but if it's of value and if it's in the marketplace, so to speak, then I know about it or I'll know the reason why."

"Do you know anything about a singular bird?" Holmes asked.

"Shall we speak of the black bird, then?" Magpie slathered jam on his scone and licked the knife before popping the entire pastry into his mouth.

Holmes's voice was a near-whisper. "Was it black when you saw it?"

A broad smile, revealing several broken and brown teeth, as well as a good deal of Devonshire cream, graced the weasel face. "You're a downy one, Mr. 'Olmes, and no mistake. 'Was it black when you saw it?' I'd never 'ave credited it, Mr. 'Olmes—why you know as much as anyone in the game. You could make a fair livin', you could, if you was to take to my profession, and, sir, it'd be an honor to 'ave you, really it would."

"I shall bear it in mind," Holmes replied graciously, while Mycroft stifled a laugh with his napkin.

"Let's just say I've seen it black and I've seen it not so black," Magpie said, lifting a finger to the side of his nose. "Less said the better, right, Mr. 'Olmes?"

Holmes nodded. "Less said the better, Magpie, but are you certain that the bird you saw was the genuine article and not a fake?"

"Mr. 'Olmes!" The little man was aghast. "I'm wounded, really I am. You think so little of me as that? You think I could be taken in by a rum sparkler? Me what learned me gems at the knee of me old granddad and 'im the greatest receiver what ever lived?" He drew himself up to his full five-foot height and said with exaggerated dignity, "That bird was crusted with 'em. Fairly crusted, like a ham dotted with cloves." Having seen the bird in question, I nodded at his description, which was so apt as to verge upon poetry. "And they was real, I'll stake me reputation on it. Real as the Crown Jewels themselves."

"Where did you see it?" I asked. "Who brought it to you?"

The little man narrowed his birdlike black eyes. "It wouldn't be good for business, would it, if I was to tell the names of all the gentlemen I dealt with?"

"Come, Magpie," Holmes said with a knowing smile, "none of your associates can be described as 'gentlemen,' now, can they? Who was your principal? I assure you I have no intention of going to the police."

The little man shook his head. "I've 'eard what I've 'eard and not a bit more," he said. "The bird was said to be the property of a man named Cairo, a Greek. Then it went missing, and 'is cries of anguish could be 'eard round the world."

"That would be Aristophanes Cairo, I believe," Mycroft said with a complacent smile. "Shady chap. Mentioned in the newspapers every so often in connection with art and antiques of dubious provenance."

"All I know is a large reward was offered, no questions asked. So when I seen the—well, when I seen what I seen, I thought I'd better get on to Cairo, 'e's a nasty man when crossed."

"Have you told Cairo everything you told me?"

"'Course I did. No desire to wake up with me throat slit, 'ave I?"

"Including the name of the person who brought you the bird?"

"I never knew the name," the little man protested. "I took it from one bloke I didn't know and gave it to another, no names mentioned. That's 'ow it is in my business."

Descriptions were elicited, and when the receiver was finished, I looked at Holmes with surprise written on my face. The man Magpie gave the bird to sounded very much like Sir Everard's tall, lugubrious butler, Barnes.

"But why?" I murmured. We had moved from tea to whisky and soda; the sun lowered itself behind the grey buildings of London and yet we sat in our leather chairs, our brains cogitating over this intractable puzzle. "Why would Sir Everard steal his own falcon?"

"He didn't," both Holmes brothers replied at once. They looked at one another and smiled. The fraternal resemblance I had never before noticed was readily apparent in that smile; in spite of Mycroft's bulk and Sherlock's lean intensity, they shared the same quirk of the upper lip when registering amusement. Sherlock Holmes continued, "He stole the original after he learned that the one he'd grown up with was a fake. Someone informed him that the gems in his falcon weren't real, and he set out to obtain the genuine bird at all costs."

Mycroft took up the tale. "He tracked the bird to Cairo, heaven knows how, and arranged to have it stolen from Cairo's shop in Constantinople."

"But why hide it in the barrow?" I cried, thoroughly frustrated by my inability to understand. "Why not just take it home and substitute it for the one in his ballroom?"

"Because someone else knew that bird was a fake," Holmes pointed out. "How could he explain that a bird covered in glass gems suddenly became a bird bedecked in diamonds, rubies, and emeralds?"

"He could have said the person who told him it was fake was mistaken," I objected.

Mycroft Holmes shook his large head. "No, he could not," he said, "for the person who told him was a great expert, whose word would certainly carry a great deal of weight."

"And that person was?" I spread my hands in supplication.

"Herr Professor Gutman of Magdalen College, Oxford," Holmes said, emphasizing the Germanic consonants of the man's name. "He told us he was pleased to see the genuine bird 'after so many disappointments.' Those words can only mean that he'd seen fake birds in the past."

"And now he is dead," I said, a chill running through me.

Within a week, the newspapers carried the news that Sir Everard Addleton was the victim of a particularly vicious burglary on his country estate. He was killed with a poker, his head struck from behind. The local police were said to be baffled, since several small and very valuable objects remained in place, though surely any competent burglar would have known their value.

"He was a fool," Holmes said in a harsh tone. "He stole the bird from a man he knew to be ruthless and determined, and he paid the consequences of his folly."

The newspapers trumpeted shrill calls for increased police protection. What, they asked, was the world coming to if a man couldn't live in peace in the peaceful English countryside without being killed in his own study by marauders?

The bird went unmentioned. For all readers of the *Mirror* knew, the burglars escaped with little, having murdered a war hero for a pittance. The lugubrious butler had fled; the police wished him to assist them with their inquiries, which meant they suspected him of working hand in hand with the thieves.

"Cairo's reach is long," I remarked.

"His reach *is* long," Holmes replied with a grim smile, "but he will find a rat trap of my making at the end of it when he tries again."

I looked up, startled. "You mean you think he might come—" I broke off uneasily and looked at the mantel, where the falcon winked at me as if amused by my stupidity. I cleared my throat. "You expect an attempt to steal the falcon from this room?"

"He will soon realize he has a fake," Holmes said, and, noting my inadvertent glance at our front door, hastened to add, "I have taken precautions, my dear Watson. You need not fear on Mrs. Hudson's account."

"Do you have any notion as to when this event might occur? Are we to lurk in the shadows, pistols drawn, indefinitely?"

"Turn to page six," my friend replied, waving a languid hand at the newspaper on my lap.

Page six—the agony column, one of Holmes' favorite parts of any newspaper—contained the following notice: ANY PERSON HAVING KNOWLEDGE OF A PARTICULARLY SPECTACULAR BIRD OF FOREIGN ORIGIN WILL BE AMPLY REWARDED BY APPLYING TO MR. SHERLOCK HOLMES, 221B BAKER STREET, LONDON, AT THE EARLIEST OPPORTUNITY.

"Inviting the cat among the pigeons," I remarked. "I had better clean and oil my revolver." I spoke as if anticipating the arrival of a notoriously ruthless criminal were not only an everyday but also a much desired occurrence, but my heart beat a little faster and a mild sweat broke out on my forehead. I could not help recalling the doomed Professor Gutman and the tragedy of Addleton's murder.

That evening after supper we whiled away the time with a round of whist. My cards were good and I settled into a pleasant frame of mind, resolutely pushing away thoughts of what was to come.

When Mrs. Hudson came upstairs, Inspector Lestrade in tow, I jumped from my seat, all pretense of normality gone. "Inspector, are you prepared for tonight's vigil?"

The inspector rubbed his hands together and made for the fire. "Indeed, I am," he said with a jaunty air. "I might have wished Mr. Holmes had told me about this fabulous bird a bit earlier, but better late than never, doctor, better late than never."

"How many men have you deployed?" Holmes stood at the door, coat in one hand, muffler in the other. "Are all the doorways and windows watched?"

"There are six in all," Lestrade replied. "Two in front, two in back, and two on the roof." His gaze moved from the fire to the mantel above it. His right hand, as if moved by a will of its own, reached for the golden bird.

"My God," he said in a reverent tone. "I've seen some wonderful jewels in my day, Mr. Holmes. Emerald necklaces and diamond tiaras, one of those Russian eggs all covered with rubies, but I've never seen anything like this."

"Few people have," Holmes replied.

"I see why someone would kill to get it back." He shook his head and replaced the statue. "I still think you should have listened to me and sent the thing to the British Museum. Let them guard it."

"They cannot keep it safe from Cairo," Holmes replied. "Indeed, I'm not sure anyone can in the long run. All I can do is make certain Cairo's representatives now in England can't get the bird. He will send more eventually, but we'll deal with them in due time. For tonight," he said, flinging his scarf around his neck and uttering the words that never failed to thrill my blood, "The game's afoot!"

IT WAS A sharp night. Damp and cold seeped into my very bones as I stood motionless, watching the shadows dance in the flickering light from the street lamps. We'd stood our post for three hours and my legs were growing numb. My feet, even in stout boots, felt like concrete blocks, and my fingers tingled in their leather gloves.

The sounds of Baker Street filled my ears. Even at this late—or was it early?—hour, the street clattered with hoofs and carriage wheels. Deliverymen and dray horses made their way through the narrow street, boxes and barrels jounced atop flat carts, workmen called to one another, and horses whinnied and stamped their hooves against the cold, filling the air with clouds of warm breath.

I marveled at the great city's liveliness at this unearthly hour, when most were asleep in comfortable beds. Men in cloth caps and thin jackets hefted goods from carts into shops, and shopkeepers in white aprons received their deliveries with sleepy smiles. Cats prowled and meowed, showing particular interest in the dairyman's cart, as if they gathered there every night to engage in high-pitched demands, or hopes that a few drops might spill on the sidewalk for pink tongues to lap up.

A quick movement, a trick of the shadow, caught my attention. I glanced at the rooftop of 221B Baker Street and saw what looked like a boy opening the trap door that led to the back staircase. I pointed; Holmes nodded and made a signal to Lestrade. Police officers moved stealthily forward, ready to surround and capture the burglar when he emerged with the falcon.

Excitement flooded my veins with the same intensity that, I imagined, cocaine swept through my friend's bloodstream. I put my hand on the butt of my gun and waited in unnatural stillness as booted feet approached. Our trap was ready for the springing, and a nice fat mouse had grasped at the cheese.

Five minutes later, a loud, triumphant cry went up. "Got him!"

On the rooftop stood two uniformed policemen, one on either side of the small burglar. He struggled in their grasp, but could not get loose. A large cloth sack hung from his shoulder, and I envisioned the jeweled bird inside.

Holmes and I raced from our hiding place across the street toward the building. I didn't see what happened next, but I heard shouts from below and looked up to see the small man running away, the two large policemen chasing him, curses on their lips.

"'E's gone, 'e's scarpered," came a high-pitched shout. "After him, boys."

The quiet night erupted in sounds of feet running, men calling to one another, and, in the distance, a horse neighing. The little man jumped from one rooftop to another like a circus aerialist; the heavier, taller policemen dared not follow.

"We'll get 'im down 'ere," someone ahead of me cried, as several officers made for the alleyway. "'E can't stay up there forever!"

I stopped running, bending over to catch my breath. The pain in my leg was excruciating, and I realized I wasn't really necessary to the chase. I waited for the police to surround and capture the burglar. Several minutes later, Lestrade stepped towards me, rubbing his hands with satisfaction. "We've got our man," he said, pardonable pride in his voice.

I looked up the street to see a phalanx of police officers leading a small, ferretlike man, his hands in iron cuffs, toward us. As they came closer, I recognized the sharp little face, the sparrow eyes.

"Magpie."

"The same, guvnor, and 'ow are you this fine morning, doctor?" The little man had the effrontery to make a little bow, quite as if we'd met strolling along Pall Mall.

The complacency of his smile and the insouciance of his manner should have told me what we learned after a thorough search of the receiver's person. He didn't have the bird, and the capacious sack he carried over his shoulder contained nothing more than old clothes wrapped in bundles.

"Where did you hide it?" Lestrade demanded, seizing Magpie's lapels and giving him a shake. "Dropped it down a drainpipe, did you?"

Holmes murmured, "How many officers did you say were with you, Inspector?"

"Six," Lestrade replied with a touch of impatience, "but that hardly matters now, does it?"

"How many are here right now?"

"Six," Lestrade answered, then realized where Holmes was headed. He addressed his men. "Which of you were on the rooftop?"

No one replied. They looked at one another, shrugged, shuffled their feet, but none admitted to being the officers who'd captured Magpie and then lost him.

I turned toward Holmes, enlightenment dawning. "They weren't police, were they?"

He shook his head. "Cairo's men. They sent Magpie here to effect entry into our rooms and steal the bird. Then they pretended to arrest him, took the bird from him, and let him pretend to escape. We watched without interference thinking the police had the burglar, when all the time, he was simply delivering the booty into the hands of those who'd hired him in the first place."

Holmes fixed Magpie with stern grey eyes. "Tell the truth now, Magpie. You were the decoy in this little scheme, weren't you? You let yourself be caught by those two 'policemen' so that they could take the bird from you without our interfering."

"Can't convict a man for burglary what 'asn't got the loot, guv," Magpie said jauntily. "I expect I'll get sent up for breaking and entering, but that's not a long sentence, not compared to some I done."

"And I'm sure you were handsomely compensated for your trouble," Holmes agreed.

"As to that, guv, I always 'ad a fancy for pretty sparklers. And though it ain't worth much, it's still going to look mighty 'andsome on the mantelpiece in my flat in Soho."

I gazed at Holmes in sudden enlightenment. "You can't mean—"

A chuckle of genuine amusement escaped my friend. Lestrade said, "What is he talking about, and what can you find to laugh about, Mr. Holmes?"

"He's got the fake," I explained. "That was his payment. Cairo's men said he could have the fake bird in exchange for stealing the genuine falcon for them."

"That bird belonged to the late Sir Everard Addleton," Lestrade protested. "It's stolen property."

"I doubt that Sir Everard has much use for it now," Holmes said. "Let us admit it, Lestrade. We've been well and truly hoodwinked and our friend here has earned his fee. He pays for it with several years in

Wormwood Scrubs for breaking and entering, so you don't go back to the Yard completely empty-handed."

The bird had flown.

"If you were ever," Holmes suggested, "to recount the adventure of the *Rara Avis,* you might call it the Addleton tragedy, for his was surely the most precipitous fall. A man of honor reduced to a petty grasper, a liar, and a murderer—now there is a tale to freeze the blood of honest men."

"And it all began with the singular contents of an ancient British barrow," I remarked. "But I will think long and hard before recounting the tale, for the world is not prepared to learn about so valuable an object. Talking about the Black Bird will only lead to more deception, theft, betrayal, and murder. I think its secret is best kept within our small circle."

Holmes shook his head. "I have no doubt," he said, "that you are right, but I also have no doubt that the world has not heard the last of the Maltese Falcon."

THE ADVENTURE
OF THE AGITATED ACTRESS

Daniel Stashower

"WE'VE ALL HEARD stories of your wonderful methods, Mr.
Holmes," said James Larrabee, drawing a cigarette from a
silver box on the table. "There have been countless tales of your marvellous insight, your ingenuity in picking up and following clues, and
the astonishing manner in which you gain information from the most
trifling details. You and I have never met before today, but I dare say
that in this brief moment or two you've discovered any number of
things about me."

Sherlock Holmes set down the newspaper he had been reading and
gazed languidly at the ceiling. "Nothing of consequence, Mr.
Larrabee," he said. "I have scarcely more than asked myself why you
rushed off and sent a telegram in such a frightened hurry, what possible excuse you could have had for gulping down a tumbler of raw
brandy at the 'Lion's Head' on the way back, why your friend with the
auburn hair left so suddenly by the terrace window, and what there
can possibly be about the safe in the lower part of that desk to cause
you such painful anxiety." The detective took up the newspaper and
idly turned the pages. "Beyond that," he said, "I know nothing."

"Holmes!" I cried. "This is uncanny! How could you have possibly
deduced all of that? We arrived in this room not more than five minutes ago!"

My companion glanced at me with an air of strained abstraction, as though he had never seen me before. For a moment he seemed to hesitate, apparently wavering between competing impulses. Then he rose from his chair and crossed down to a row of blazing footlights. "I'm sorry, Frohman," he called. "This isn't working out as I'd hoped. We really don't need Watson in this scene after all."

"Gillette!" came a shout from the darkened space across the bright line of lights. "I do wish you'd make up your mind! Need I remind you that we open tomorrow night?" We heard a brief clatter of footsteps as Charles Frohman—a short, solidly built gentleman in the casual attire of a country squire—came scrambling up the side access stairs. As he crossed the forward lip of the stage, Frohman brandished a printed handbill. It read: "William Gillette in his Smash Play! Sherlock Holmes! Fresh from a Triumphant New York Run!"

"He throws off the balance of the scene," Gillette was saying. "The situation doesn't call for an admiring Watson." He turned to me. "No offense, my dear Lyndal. You have clearly immersed yourself in the role. That gesture of yours—with your arm at the side—it suggests a man favoring an old wound. Splendid!"

I pressed my lips together and let my hand fall to my side. "Actually, Gillette," I said, "I am endeavoring to keep my trousers from falling down."

"Pardon?"

I opened my jacket and gathered up a fold of loose fabric around my waist. "There hasn't been time for my final costume fitting," I explained.

"I'm afraid I'm having the same difficulty," said Arthur Creeson, who had been engaged to play the villainous James Larrabee. "If I'm not careful, I'll find my trousers down at my ankles."

Gillette gave a heavy sigh. "Quinn!" he called.

Young Henry Quinn, the boy playing the role of Billy, the Baker Street page, appeared from the wings. "Yes, Mr. Gillette?"

"Would you be so good as to fetch the wardrobe mistress? Or at least bring us some extra straight pins?" The boy nodded and darted backstage.

Charles Frohman, whose harried expression and lined forehead told of the rigors of his role as Gillette's producer, folded the handbill and replaced it in his pocket. "I don't see why you feel the need to tinker with the script at this late stage," he insisted. "The play was an enormous success in New York. As far as America is concerned, you *are* Sherlock Holmes. Surely the London audiences will look on the play with equal favor?"

Gillette threw himself down in a chair and reached for his prompt book. "The London audience bears little relation to its American counterpart," he said, flipping rapidly through the pages. "British tastes have been refined over centuries of Shakespeare and Marlowe. America has only lately weaned itself off of *Uncle Tom's Cabin.*"

"Gillette," said Frohman heavily, "you are being ridiculous."

The actor reached for a pen and began scrawling over a page of script. "I am an American actor essaying an English part. I must take every precaution, and make every possible refinement before submitting myself to the fine raking fire of the London critics. They will seize on a single false note as an excuse to send us packing." He turned back to Arthur Creeson. "Now, then. Let us continue from the point at which Larrabee is endeavoring to cover his deception. Instead of Watson's expression of incredulity, we shall restore Larrabee's evasions. Do you recall the speech, Creeson?

The actor nodded.

"Excellent. Let us resume."

I withdrew to the wings as Gillette and Creeson took their places. A mask of impassive self-possession slipped over Gillette's features as he stepped back into the character of Sherlock Holmes. "Why your friend with the auburn hair left so suddenly by the terrace window," he said, picking up the dialogue in midsentence, "and what there can possibly be about the safe in the lower part of that desk to cause you such painful anxiety."

"Ha! Very good!" cried Creeson, taking up his role as the devious James Larrabee. "Very good indeed! If those things were only true, I'd be wonderfully impressed. It would be absolutely marvellous!"

Gillette regarded him with an expression of weary impatience. "It won't do, sir," said he. "I have come to see Miss Alice Faulkner and will not leave until I have done so. I have reason to believe that the young lady is being held against her will. You shall have to give way, sir, or face the consequences."

Creeson's hands flew to his chest. "Against her will? This is outrageous! I will not tolerate—"

A high, trilling scream from backstage interrupted the line. Creeson held his expression and attempted to continue. "I will not tolerate such an accusation in my own—"

A second scream issued from backstage. Gillette gave a heavy sigh and rose from his chair as he reached for the prompt book. "Will that woman never learn her cue?" Shielding his eyes against the glare of the footlights, he stepped again to the lip of the stage and sought out Frohman. "This is what comes of engaging the company locally," he said in an exasperated tone. "We have a mob of players in ill-fitting costumes who don't know their scripts. We should have brought the New York company across, hang the expense." He turned to the wings. "Quinn!"

The young actor stepped forward. "Yes, sir?"

"Will you kindly inform—"

Gillette's instructions were cut short by the sudden appearance of Miss Maude Fenton, the actress playing the role of Alice Faulkner, who rushed from the wings in a state of obvious agitation. Her chestnut hair fell loosely about her shoulders and her velvet shirtwaist was imperfectly buttoned. "Gone!" she cried. "Missing! Taken from me!"

Gillette drummed his fingers across the prompt book. "My dear Miss Fenton," he said, "you have dropped approximately seventeen pages from the script."

"Hang the script!" she wailed. "I'm not playing a role! My brooch is missing! My beautiful, beautiful brooch! Oh, for heaven's sake, Mr. Gillette, someone must have stolen it!"

Selma Kendall, the kindly, auburn-haired actress who had been engaged to play Madge Larrabee, hurried to Miss Fenton's side. "It can't be!" she cried. "He only just gave it—that is to say, you've only just acquired it! Are you certain you haven't simply mislaid it?"

Miss Fenton accepted the linen pocket square I offered and dabbed at her streaming eyes. "I couldn't possibly have mislaid it," she said between sobs. "One doesn't mislay something of that sort! How could such a thing have happened?"

Gillette, who had cast an impatient glance at his pocket watch during this exchange, now stepped forward to take command of the situation. "There, there, Miss Fenton," he said, in the cautious, fal-tering tone of a man not used to dealing with female emotions. "I'm sure this is all very distressing. As soon as we have completed our run-through, we will conduct a most thorough search of the dressing areas. I'm sure your missing bauble will be discovered presently."

"Gillette!" I cried. "You don't mean to continue with the rehearsal? Can't you see that Miss Fenton is too distraught to carry on?"

"But she must," the actor declared. "As Mr. Frohman has been at pains to remind us, our little play has its London opening tomorrow evening. We shall complete the rehearsal, and then—after I have given a few notes—we shall locate the missing brooch. Miss Fenton is a fine actress, and I have every confidence in her ability to conceal her dis-tress in the interim." He patted the weeping actress on the back of her hand. "Will that do, my dear?"

At this, Miss Fenton's distress appeared to gather momentum by steady degrees. First her lips began to tremble, then her shoulders commenced heaving, and lastly a strange caterwauling sound emerged from behind the handkerchief. After a moment or two of this, she threw herself into Gillette's arms and began sobbing lustily upon his shoulder.

"Gillette," called Frohman, straining to make himself heard above the lamentations, "perhaps it would be best to take a short pause."

Gillette, seemingly unnerved by the wailing figure in his arms, gave a strained assent. "Very well. We shall repair to the dressing area. No doubt the missing object has simply slipped between the cushions of a settee."

With Mr. Frohman in the lead, our small party made its way through the wings and along the backstage corridors to the ladies' dressing area. As we wound past the scenery flats and crated property trunks, I found myself reflecting on how little I knew of the other members of our troupe. Although Gillette's play had been a great success in America, only a handful of actors and crewmen had transferred to the London production. A great many members of the cast and techni-cal staff, myself included, had been engaged locally after a brief open call. Up to this point, the rehearsals and staging had been a rushed affair, allowing for little of the easy camaraderie that usually develops among actors during the rehearsal period.

As a result, I knew little about my fellow players apart from the usual backstage gossip. Miss Fenton, in the role of the young heroine Alice Faulkner, was considered to be a promising ingenue. Reviewers frequently commented on her striking beauty, if not her talent. Selma Kendall, in the role of the conniving Madge Larrabee, had established herself in the provinces as a dependable support player, and was regarded as something of a mother hen by the younger actresses. Arthur Creeson, as the wicked James Larrabee, had been a promising romantic lead in his day, but excessive drink and gambling had marred his looks and scotched his reputation. William Allerford, whose high, domed forehead and startling white hair helped to make him so effective as the nefarious Professor Moriarty, was in fact the most gentle of men, with a great passion for tending the rose bushes at his cottage in Hove. As for myself, I had set out to become an opera singer in my younger days, but my talent had not matched my ambition, and over time I had evolved into a reliable, if unremarkable second lead.

"Here we are," Frohman was saying as we arrived at the end of a long corridor. "We shall make a thorough search." After knocking on the unmarked door, he led us inside.

As was the custom of the day, the female members of the cast shared a communal dressing area in a narrow, sparsely appointed chamber illuminated by a long row of electrical lights. Along one wall was a long mirror with a row of wooden makeup tables before it. A random cluster of coat racks, reclining sofas, and well-worn armchairs were arrayed along the wall opposite. Needless to say, I had never been in a ladies' dressing room before, and I admit that I felt my cheeks redden at the sight of so many underthings and delicates thrown carelessly over the furniture. I turned to avert my eyes from a cambric corset cover thrown across a ladderback chair, only to find myself gazing upon a startling assortment of hosiery and lace-trimmed drawers laid out upon a nearby ottoman.

"Gracious, Mr. Lyndal," said Miss Kendall, taking a certain delight in my discomfiture. "One would almost think you'd never seen linens before."

"Well, I—perhaps not so many at once," I admitted, gathering my composure. "Dr. Watson is said to have an experience of women which extends over many nations and three separate continents. My own experience, I regret to say, extends no further than Hatton Cross."

Gillette, it appeared, did not share my sense of consternation. No sooner had we entered the dressing area than he began making an energetic and somewhat indiscriminate examination of the premises, darting from one side of the room to the other, opening drawers and tossing aside cushions and pillows with careless abandon.

"Well," he announced, after five minutes' effort, "I cannot find your brooch. However, in the interests of returning to our rehearsals as quickly as possible, I am prepared to buy you a new one."

Miss Fenton stared at the actor with an expression of disbelief. "I'm afraid you don't understand, Mr. Gillette. This was not a common piece of rolled plate and crystalline. It was a large, flawless sapphire in a rose gold setting, with a circle of diamond accents."

Gillette's eyes widened. "Was it, indeed? May I know how you came by such an item?"

A flush spread across Miss Fenton's cheek. "It was—it was a gift from an admirer," she said, glancing away. "I would prefer to say no more."

"Be that as it may," I said, "this is no small matter. We must notify the police at once!"

Gillette pressed his fingers together. "I'm afraid I must agree. This is most inconvenient."

A look of panic flashed across Miss Fenton's eyes. "Please, Mr. Gillette! You must not involve the police! That wouldn't do at all!"

"But your sapphire—?"

She tugged at the lace trimming of her sleeve. "The gentleman in question—the man who presented me with the brooch—he is of a certain social standing, Mr. Gillette. He—that is to say, I—would prefer to keep the matter private. It would be most embarrassing for him if his—if his attentions to me should become generally known."

Frohman gave a sudden cough. "It is not unknown for young actresses to form attachments with certain of their gentlemen admirers," he said carefully. "Occasionally, however, when these matters become public knowledge, they are attended by a certain whiff of scandal. Especially if the gentleman concerned happens to be married." He glanced at Miss Fenton, who held his gaze for a moment and then looked away. "Indeed," said Frohman. "Well, we can't have those whispers about the production, Gillette. Not before we've even opened."

"Quite so," I ventured, "and there is Miss Fenton's reputation to consider. We must discover what happened to the brooch without involving the authorities. We shall have to mount a private investigation."

All eyes turned to Gillette as a mood of keen expectation fell across the room. The actor did not appear to notice. Having caught sight of himself in the long mirror behind the dressing tables, he was making a meticulous adjustment to his waistcoat. At length, he became aware that the rest of us were staring intently at him.

"What?" he said, turning away from the mirror. "Why is everyone looking at me?"

"I AM NOT Sherlock Holmes," Gillette said several moments later, as we settled ourselves in a pair of armchairs. "I am an actor *playing* Sherlock Holmes. There is a very considerable difference. If I did a turn as a pantomime horse, Lyndal, I trust you would not expect me to pull a dray wagon and dine on straw?"

"But you've studied Sherlock Holmes," I insisted. "You're examined his methods and turned them to your own purposes. Surely you might be able to do the same in this instance? Surely the author of such a fine detective play is not totally lacking in the powers of perception?"

Gillette gave me an appraising look. "Appealing to my vanity, Lyndal? Very shrewd."

We had been arguing back and forth in this vein for some moments, though by this time—detective or no—Gillette had reluctantly agreed to give his attention to the matter of the missing brooch. Frohman had made him see that an extended disruption would place their financial interests in the hazard, and that Gillette, as head of the company, was the logical choice to take command of the situation. Toward that end, it was arranged that Gillette would question each member of the company individually, beginning with myself.

Gillette's stage manager, catching wind of the situation, thought it would be a jolly lark to replace the standing set of James Larrabee's drawing room with the lodgings of Sherlock Holmes at Baker Street, so that Gillette might have an appropriate setting in which to carry out his investigation. If Gillette noticed, he gave no sign. Stretching his arm toward a side table, he took up an outsize calabash pipe and began filling the meerschaum bowl.

"Why do you insist on smoking that ungainly thing?" I asked. "There's no record whatsoever of Sherlock Holmes having ever touched a calabash. Dr. Watson tells us that he favors an oily black clay pipe as the companion of his deepest meditations, but is wont to replace it with his cherrywood when in a disputatious frame of mind."

Gillette shook his head sadly. "I am *not* Sherlock Holmes," he said again. "I am an actor *playing* Sherlock Holmes."

"Still," I insisted, "it does no harm to be as faithful to the original as possible."

Gillette touched a flame to the tobacco and took several long draws to be certain the bowl was properly ignited. For a moment, his eyes were unfocused and dreamy, and I could not be certain that he had heard me. His eyes were fixed upon the fly curtains when he spoke again. "Lyndal," he said, "turn and face down stage."

"What?"

"Humor me. Face down stage."

I rose and looked out across the forward edge of the stage.

"What do you see?" Gillette asked.

"Empty seats," I said.

"Precisely. It is my ambition to fill those seats. Now, cast your eyes to the rear of the house. I want you to look at the left-hand aisle seat in the very last row."

I stepped forward and narrowed my eyes. "Yes," I said. "What of it?"

"Can you read the number plate upon that seat?"

"No," I said. "Of course not."

"Nor can I. By the same token, the man or woman seated there will not be able to appreciate the difference between a cherrywood pipe and an oily black clay. This is theater, Lyndal. A real detective does not do his work before an audience. I do. Therefore I am obliged to make my movements, speech, and stage properties readily discernible." He held the calabash aloft. "This pipe will be visible from the back row, my friend. An actor must consider even the smallest object from every possible angle. That is the essence of theater."

I considered the point. "I merely thought, inasmuch as you are attempting to inhabit the role of Sherlock Holmes, that you should wish to strive for authenticity."

Gillette seemed to consider the point. "Well," he said, "let us see how far that takes us. Tell me, Lyndal. Where were you when the robbery occurred?"

"Me? But surely you don't think that I—"

"You are not the estimable Dr. Watson, my friend. You are merely an actor, like myself. Since Miss Fenton had her brooch with her when she arrived at the theater this morning, we must assume that the theft occurred shortly after first call. Can you account for your movements in that time?"

"Of course I can. You know perfectly well where I was. I was standing stage right, beside you, running through the first act."

"So you were. Strange, my revision of the play has given you a perfect alibi. Had the theft occurred this afternoon, after I had restored the original text of the play, you should have been high on the list of suspects. A narrow escape, my friend." He smiled and sent up a cloud of pipe smoke. "Since we have established your innocence, however, I wonder if I might trouble you to remain through the rest of the interviews?"

"Whatever for?"

"Perhaps I am striving for authenticity." He turned and spotted young Henry Quinn hovering in his accustomed spot in the wings near the scenery cleats. "Quinn!" he called.

The boy stepped forward. "Yes, sir?"

"Would you ask Miss Fenton if she would be so good as to join us?"

"Right away, sir."

I watched as the boy disappeared down the long corridor. "Gillette," I said, lowering my voice, "this Baker Street set is quite comfortable in its way, but do you not think a bit of privacy might be indicated? Holmes is accustomed to conducting his interviews in confidence. Anyone might hear what passes between us here at the center of the stage."

Gillette smiled. "I am *not* Sherlock Holmes," he repeated.

After a moment or two Quinn stepped from the wings with Miss Fenton trailing behind him. Miss Fenton's eyes and nose were red with weeping, and she was attended by Miss Kendall, who hovered protectively by her side. "May I remain, Mr. Gillette?" asked the older actress. "Miss Fenton is terribly upset by all of this."

"Of course," said Gillette in a soothing manner. "I shall try to dispense with the questioning as quickly as possible. Please be seated." He folded his hands and leaned forward in his chair. "Tell me, Miss Fenton, are you quite certain that the brooch was in your possession when you arrived at the theater this morning?"

"Of course," the actress replied. "I had no intention of letting it out of my sight. I placed the pin in my jewelry case as I changed into costume."

"And the jewelry case was on top of your dressing table?"

"Yes."

"In plain sight?"

"Yes, but I saw no harm in that. I was alone at the time. Besides, Miss Kendall is the only other woman in the company, and I trust her as I would my own sister." She reached across and took the older woman's hand.

"No doubt," said Gillette, "but do you mean to say that you intended to leave the gem in the dressing room during the rehearsal? Forgive me, but that seems a bit careless."

"That was not my intention at all, Mr. Gillette. Once in costume, I planned to pin the brooch to my stockings. I should like to have worn it in plain view, but James—that is to say, the gentleman who gave it to me—would not have approved. He does not want anyone—he does not approve of ostentation."

"In any case," I said, "Alice Faulkner would hardly be likely to own such a splendid jewel."

"Yes," said Miss Fenton. "Just so."

Gillette steepled his fingers. "How exactly did the jewel come to be stolen? It appears that it never left your sight."

"It was unforgivable of me," said Miss Fenton. "I arrived late to the theater this morning. In my haste, I overturned an entire pot of facial powder. I favor a particular type, Gervaise Graham's Satinette, and I wished to see if I could persuade someone to step out and purchase a fresh supply for me. I can only have been gone for a moment. I stepped into the hallway looking for one of the stagehands, but of course they were all in their places in anticipation of the scene three

set change. When I found no one close by, I realized that I had better finish getting ready as best I could without the powder."

"So you returned to the dressing area?"

"Yes."

"How long would you say that you were out of the room?"

"Two or three minutes. No more."

"And when you returned the brooch was gone?"

She nodded. "That was when I screamed."

"Indeed." Gillette stood and clasped his hands behind his back.
"Extraordinary," he said, pacing a short line before a scenery flat decorated to resemble a bookcase. "Miss Kendall?"

"Yes?"

"Has anything been stolen from you?" he asked.

"No," she answered. "Well, not this time."

Gillette raised an eyebrow. "Not this time?"

The actress hesitated. "I'm sure it's nothing," she said. "From
time to time I have noticed that one or two small things have gone
astray. Nothing of any value. A small mirror, perhaps, or a copper
or two."

Miss Fenton nodded. "I've noticed that as well. I assumed that I'd
simply misplaced the items. It was never anything to trouble over."

Gillette frowned. "Miss Fenton, a moment ago, when the theft
became known, it was clear that Miss Kendall was already aware that
you had the brooch in your possession. May I ask who else among the
company knew of the sapphire?"

"No one," the actress said. "I only received the gift yesterday, but I
would have been unlikely to flash it about, in any case. I couldn't resist
showing it to Selma, however."

"No one else knew of it?"

"No one."

Gillette turned to Miss Kendall. "Did you mention it to anyone?"

"Certainly not, Mr. Gillette."

The actor resumed his pacing. "You're quite certain? It may have
been a perfectly innocent remark."

"Maude asked me not to say anything to anyone," said Miss Kendall.
"We women are rather good with secrets."

Gillette's mouth pulled up slightly at the corners. "So I gather, Miss Kendall. So I gather." He turned and studied the false book spines on the painted scenery flat. "Thank you for your time, ladies."

I watched as the two actresses departed. "Gillette," I said after a moment, "if Miss Kendall did not mention the sapphire to anyone, who else could have known that it existed?"

"No one," he answered.

"Are you suggesting—" I leaned forward and lowered my voice. "Are you suggesting that Miss Kendall is the thief? After all, if she was the only one who knew—

"No, Lyndal. I do not believe Miss Kendall is the thief."

"Still," I said, "there is little reason to suppose that she kept her own counsel. A theatrical company is a hotbed of gossip and petty jealousies." I paused as a new thought struck me. "Miss Fenton seems most concerned with protecting the identify of her gentleman admirer, although this will not be possible if the police have to be summoned. Perhaps the theft was orchestrated to expose him." I considered the possibility for a moment. "Yes, perhaps the intended victim is really this unknown patron, whomever he might be. He is undoubtedly a man of great wealth and position. Who knows? Perhaps this sinister plot extends all the way to the—"

"I think not," said Gillette.

"No?"

"If the intention was nothing more than to expose a dalliance between a young actress and a man of position, one need not have resorted to theft. A word in the ear of certain society matrons would have the same effect, and far more swiftly." He threw himself back down in his chair. "No, I believe that this was a crime of opportunity, rather than design. Miss Kendall and Miss Fenton both reported having noticed one or two small things missing from their dressing area on previous occasions. It seems that we have a petty thief in our midst, and that this person happened across the sapphire during those few moments when it was left unattended in the dressing room."

"But who could it be? Most of us were either on stage or working behind the scenes, in plain view of at least one other person at all times."

"So it would seem, but I'm not entirely convinced that someone couldn't have slipped away for a moment or two without being noticed. The crew members are forever darting in and out. It would not have drawn any particular notice if one of them had slipped away for a moment or two."

"Then we shall have to question the suspects," I said. "We must expose this nefarious blackguard at once."

Gillette regarded me over the bowl of his pipe. "Boucicault?" he asked.

"Pardon?"

"That line you just quoted. I thought I recognized it from one of Mr. Boucicault's melodramas."

I flushed. "No," I said. "It was my own."

"Was it? How remarkably vivid." He turned to young Henry Quinn, who was awaiting his instructions in the wings. "Quinn," he called, "might I trouble you to run and fetch Mr. Allerford? I have a question or two I would like to put to him."

"Allerford," I said, as the boy disappeared into the wings. "So your suspicions have fallen upon the infamous Professor Moriarty, have they? There's a bit of Holmes in you, after all."

"Scarcely," said Gillette with a weary sigh. "I am proceeding in alphabetical order."

"Ah."

Young Quinn returned a moment later to conduct Allerford into our presence. The actor wore a long black frock coat for his impersonation of the evil professor, and his white hair was pomaded into a billowing cloud, exaggerating the size of his head and suggesting the heat of the character's mental processes.

"Do sit down, Allerford," Gillette said as the actor stepped onto the stage, "and allow me to apologize for subjecting you to this interview. It pains me to suggest that you may in any way have—"

The actor held up his hands to break off the apologies. "No need, Gillette. I would do the same in your position. I presume you will wish to know where I was while the rest of you were running through the first act?"

Gillette nodded. "If you would be so kind."

"I'm afraid the answer is far from satisfactory. I was in the gentlemen's dressing area."

"Alone?"

"I'm afraid so. All the others were on stage or in the costume shop for their fittings." He gathered up a handful of loose fabric from his waistcoat. "My fitting was delayed until this afternoon. So I imagine I would have to be counted as the principal suspect, Gillette." He allowed his features to shift and harden as he assumed the character of Professor Moriarty. "You'll never hang this on me, Mr. Sherlock Holmes," he hissed, as his head oscillated in a reptilian fashion. "I have an ironclad alibi! I was alone in my dressing room reading a magazine!" The actor broke character and held up his palms in a gesture of futility. "I'm afraid I can't offer you anything better, Gillette."

"I'm sure nothing more will be required, Allerford. Again, let me apologize for this intrusion."

"Not at all."

"One more thing," Gillette said as Allerford rose to take his leave.

"Yes?"

"The magazine you were reading. It wasn't *The Strand,* by any chance?"

"Why, yes. There was a copy lying about on the table."

"A Sherlock Holmes adventure, was it?"

Allerford's expression turned sheepish. "My tastes don't run in that direction, I'm afraid. There was an article on the sugar planters of the Yucatan. Quite intriguing, if I may say."

"I see." Gillette began refilling the bowl of his pipe. "Much obliged, Allerford."

"Gillette!" I said in an urgent whisper, as Allerford retreated into the wings. "What was that all about? Were you trying to catch him out?"

"What? No, I was just curious." The actor's expression grew unfocused as he touched a match to the tobacco. "Very curious." He sat quietly for some moments, sending clouds of smoke up into the fly curtains.

"Gillette," I said after a few moments, "shouldn't we continue? I believe Mr. Creeson is next."

"Creeson?"

"Yes. If we are to proceed alphabetically."

"Very good. Creeson. By all means. Quinn! Ask Mr. Creeson to join us, if you would."

With that, Gillette sank into his chair and remained there, scarcely moving, for the better part of two hours as a parade of actors, actresses, and stagehands passed before him. His questions and attitude were much the same as they had been with Allerford, but clearly his attention had wandered to some distant and inaccessible plateau. At times he appeared so preoccupied that I had to prod him to continue with the interviews. At one stage he drew his legs up to his chest and encircled them with his arms, looking for all the world like Sidney Paget's illustration of Sherlock Holmes in the grip of one of his three-pipe problems. Unlike the great detective, however, Gillette soon gave way to meditations of a different sort. By the time the last of our interviews was completed, a contented snoring could be heard from the actor's armchair.

"Gillette," I said, shaking him by the shoulder. "I believe we've spoken to everyone now."

"Have we? Very good." He rose from the chair and stretched his long limbs. "Is Mr. Frohman anywhere about?"

"Right here, Gillette," the producer called from the first row of seats. "I must say this appears to have been a colossal waste of time. I don't see how we can avoid going to the police now."

"I'm afraid I have to agree," I said. "We are no closer to resolving the matter than we were this morning." I glanced at Gillette, who was staring blankly into the footlights. "Gillette? Are you listening?"

"I think we may be able to keep the authorities out of the matter," he answered. "Frohman? Might I trouble you to assemble the company?"

"Whatever for?" I asked. "You've already spoken to—say! You don't mean to say that you know who stole Miss Fenton's brooch?"

"I didn't say that."

"But then why should you—?"

He turned and held a finger to his lips. "I'm afraid you'll have to wait for the final act."

The actor would say nothing more as the members of the cast and crew appeared from their various places and arrayed themselves in the first two rows of seats. Gillette, standing at the lip of the stage, looked over them with an expression of keen interest. "My friends," he said after a moment, "you have all been very patient during this unpleasantness. I appreciate your indulgence. I'm sure that Sherlock Holmes would have gotten to the bottom of the matter in just a few moments, but as I am not Sherlock Holmes, it has taken me rather longer."

"Mr. Gillette!" cried Miss Fenton. "Do you mean to say you've found my brooch?"

"No, dear lady," he said, "I haven't. But I trust that it will be back in your possession shortly."

"Gillette," said Frohman, "this is all very irregular. Where is the stone? Who is the thief?"

"The identity of the thief has been apparent from the beginning," Gillette said placidly. "What I did not understand was the motivation."

"But that's nonsense!" cried Arthur Creeson. "The sapphire is extraordinarily valuable! What other motivation could there be?"

"I can think of several," Gillette answered, "and our 'nefarious blackguard,' to borrow a colorful phrase, might have succumbed to any one of them."

"You're talking in circles, Gillette," said Frohman. "If you've known the identity of the thief from the first, why didn't you just say so?"

"I was anxious to resolve the matter quietly," the actor answered. "Now, sadly, that is no longer possible." Gillette stretched his long arms. Moving upstage, he took up his pipe and slowly filled the bowl with tobacco from a ragged Persian slipper. "It was my hope," he said, "that the villain would come to regret these actions—the rash decision of an instant—and make amends. If the sapphire had simply been replaced on Miss Fenton's dressing table, I should have put the incident behind and carried on as though I had never discerned the guilty party's identity. Now, distasteful as it may be, the villain must be unmasked, and I must lose a member of my company on the eve of our London opening. Regrettable, but it can't be helped."

The members of the company shifted uneasily in their seats. "It's one of us, then?" asked Mr. Allerford.

"Of course. That much should have been obvious to all of you." He struck a match and ran it over the bowl of his pipe, lingering rather longer than necessary over the process. "The tragedy of the matter is that none of this would have happened if Miss Fenton had not stepped from her dressing room and left the stone unattended."

The actress' hands flew to her throat. "But I told you, I had spilled a pot of facial powder."

"Precisely so. Gervaise Graham's Satinette. A very distinctive shade. And so the catalyst of the crime now becomes the instrument of its solution."

"How do you mean, Gillette?" I asked.

Gillette moved off to stand before the fireplace—or rather the canvas-and-wood strutting that had been arranged to resemble a fireplace. The actor spent a moment contemplating the plaster coals that rested upon a balsa grating. "Detective work," he intoned, "is founded upon the observation of trifles. When Miss Fenton overturned that facial powder she set in motion a chain of events that yielded a clue—a clue as transparent as that of a weaver's tooth or a compositor's thumb—and one that made it patently obvious who took the missing stone."

"Gillette!" cried Mr. Frohman. "No more theatrics! Who took Miss Fenton's sapphire?"

"The thief is here among us," he declared, his voice rising to a vibrant timbre. "And the traces of Satinette facial powder are clearly visible upon—wait! Stop him!"

All at once, the theater erupted into pandemonium as young Henry Quinn, who had been watching from his accustomed place in the wings, suddenly darted forward and raced towards the rear exit.

"Stop him!" Gillette called to a pair of burly stagehands. "Hendricks! O'Donnell! Don't let him pass!"

The fleeing boy veered away from the stagehands, upsetting a flimsy side table in his flight, and made headlong for the forward edge of the stage. Gathering speed, he attempted to vault over the orchestra pit, and would very likely have cleared the chasm, but for the fact that his ill-fitting trousers suddenly slipped to his ankles, entangling his legs and causing him to land in an awkward heap at the base of the pit.

"He's out cold, Mr. Gillette," came a voice from the pit. "Nasty bruise on his head."

"Very good, Hendricks. If you would be so good as to carry him into the lobby, we shall decide what to do with him later."

Miss Fenton pressed a linen handkerchief to her face as the unconscious figure was carried past. "I don't understand, Mr. Gillette. Henry took my sapphire? He's just a boy! I can't believe he would do such a thing!"

"Strange to say, I believe Quinn's intentions were relatively benign," said Gillette. "He presumed, when he came across the stone on your dressing table, that it was nothing more than a piece of costume jewelry. It was only later, after the alarm had been raised, that he realized its value. At that point, he became frightened and could not think of a means to return it without confessing his guilt."

"But what would a boy do with such a valuable stone?" Frohman asked.

"I have no idea," said Gillette. "Indeed, I do not believe that he had any interest whatsoever in the sapphire."

"No interest?" I said. "What other reason could he have had for taking it?"

"For the pin."

"What?"

Gillette gave a rueful smile. "You are all wearing costumes that are several sizes too large. Our rehearsals have been slowed for want of sewing pins to hold up the men's trousers and pin back the ladies' frocks. I myself dispatched Quinn to find a fastener for Mr. Lyndal."

"The essence of theater," I said, shaking my head with wonder.

"Pardon me, Lyndal?"

"As you were saying earlier. An actor must consider even the smallest object from every possible angle. We all assumed that the brooch had been taken for its valuable stone. Only you would have thought to consider it from the back as well as the front." I paused. "Well done, Gillette."

The actor gave a slight bow as the company burst into spontaneous applause. "That is most kind," he said, "but now, ladies and gentlemen, if there are no further distractions, I should like to continue with our rehearsal. Act one, scene four, I believe. . . ."

IT WAS SEVERAL hours later when I knocked at the door to Gillette's dressing room. He bade me enter and made me welcome with a glass of excellent port. We settled ourselves on a pair of makeup stools and sat for a few moments in a companionable silence.

"I understand that Miss Fenton has elected not to pursue the matter of Quinn's theft with the authorities," I said, after a time.

"I thought not," Gillette said. "I doubt if her gentleman friend would appreciate seeing the matter aired in the press. However, we will not be able to keep young Quinn with the company. He has been dismissed. Frohman has been in touch with another young man I once considered for the role. Charles Chapman."

"Chaplin, I believe."

"That's it. I'm sure he'll pick it up soon enough."

"No doubt."

I took a sip of port. "Gillette," I said, "there is something about the affair that troubles me."

He smiled and reached for a pipe. "I thought there might be," he said.

"You claimed to have spotted Quinn's guilt by the traces of face powder on his costume."

"Indeed."

I lifted my arm. "There are traces of Miss Fenton's powder here on my sleeve as well. No doubt I acquired them when I was searching for the missing stone in the dressing area—after the theft had been discovered."

"No doubt," said Gillette.

"The others undoubtedly picked up traces of powder as well."

"That is likely."

"So Quinn himself might well have acquired his telltale dusting of powder *after* the theft had occurred, in which case it would not have been incriminating at all."

Gillette regarded me with keen amusement. "Perhaps I noticed the powder on Quinn's sleeve before we searched the dressing area," he offered.

"Did you?"

He sighed. "No."

"Then you were bluffing? That fine speech about the observation of trifles was nothing more than vain posturing?"

"It lured a confession out of Quinn, my friend, so it was not entirely in vain."

"But you had no idea who the guilty party was! Not until the moment he lost his nerve and ran!"

Gillette leaned back and sent a series of billowy smoke rings toward the ceiling. "That is so," he admitted, "but then, as I have been at some pains to remind you, I am *not* Sherlock Holmes."

THE CASE OF THE HIGHLAND HOAX

Anne Perry and Malachi Saxon

I WALKED BRISKLY down Baker Street towards the residence of my good friend Sherlock Holmes, as I was in a hurry to share my news with him. I knew he would be disappointed, but the offer I had received was one that I was not in a position to turn down. I was certain that he would understand. It did, however, mean that I would not be able to go with him on his holiday to Switzerland. He had been most enthusiastic that we should visit the Reichenbach Falls together.

Mrs. Hudson greeted me at the door. "Good morning, Dr. Watson," she said, "Do come in. Mr. Holmes was rather expecting you. Please go on—you know the way."

"Come in, come in, my dear Watson!" Holmes invited. "Come over and stand by the window so that I can see you in the light. Let me admire your new outfit."

I dutifully walked over towards the window under the watchful gaze of Holmes. He reached towards his desk and picked up a large magnifying glass, then with exaggerated attention proceeded to examine me closely up and down.

"What are you up to, Holmes?" I exclaimed. "All I have done is buy a new set of clothes for my holiday."

"And very smart, too, if I may say so," he agreed. "The jacket is excellent—a good quality Harris Tweed, with nice big pockets. I definitely like the deerstalker—I wonder where you got the inspiration for that! Plus-fours and a stout pair of walking shoes." He put the magnifying glass back onto the table, picked up his pipe and solemnly lit it. He puffed away intently as he walked over to his favorite armchair and sat down. Curls of thick blue smoke climbed slowly into the air around his head. I was intrigued and puzzled.

Holmes took the pipe out of his mouth, pointed the stem at me, and said, "Watson, I believe you have presented me with enough evidence to deduce the news that you were about to tell me!"

"Well, Holmes, I await the conclusions of your cerebrations," I said with a deliberate air of pomposity.

He regarded me with complete solemnity. "You will not be able to come with me to Switzerland, because tomorrow evening you will be taking the night train from King's Cross here in London to Aberdeen, then changing to the Great North of Scotland Deeside branch to Ballater, to holiday in the Scottish Highlands, somewhere near, I would say, Dunkeld. You plan to stay about three weeks, catch up on your much-neglected pastime of fly fishing, before returning to London." He leaned back in his chair, took a puff on his pipe, and raised his eyebrows slightly. "Am I right, Watson?"

I was astounded. "Holmes," I said, "I have the highest admiration for your powers of deduction, but this time you have excelled even yourself. Did you work that out from the jacket?"

"No."

"Was it the deerstalker?"

"No, much as I admire it!"

"The walking shoes?"

"No, my dear friend," Holmes said as he leaned forwards, "I have a confession to make. This has been my humble attempt at a spot of humor. I am afraid I have played a practical joke on you. Let me explain." He gestured me to take a seat. "With the mail that arrived this morning," he continued, "there was a letter which had been delivered by private messenger. It was addressed to me, so naturally I opened it. Out fell a first-class return ticket to Ballater, for the night train, tomorrow evening. This struck me as most curious. I checked further in the envelope, and found a note that stated, 'For the attention of Dr. John Watson.' That was how I came to be in possession of this knowledge.

Naturally, if I had known that it was for you, I would never have dreamed of opening it. I apologize, but it leaves me a bit puzzled, Watson."

"Let me explain from the beginning," I said. "My sister, Harriet, is married to the Reverend Talbot Ridley. He had just turned sixty-five, and had announced his intention to retire, when out of the blue, he received from a parishioner—who wished to remain anonymous—the offer of a holiday in the Scottish Highlands, all expenses paid. A most generous offer, you must admit, and it was for a party of up to six people. The accommodation would be in a small castle whose owner was away in the United States for a few months, and all the domestic staff would still be there. Included are the hunting and fishing rights in the nearby countryside. Well, Harriet and Talbot insisted that I accompany them, which I could not refuse, and of course extended the invitation to you, Holmes. I was on my way round here to tell you, in the hope that you might change your mind about going to Switzerland, and come with us, instead."

Holmes looked at me candidly, and said, "It is indeed a most generous offer, and you were quite right to accept it, Watson. However, I feel I cannot intrude on you, and will continue with my journey to the Continent, and trust that you all will have a wonderful reunion. How do you intend to spend your time, granted that you have some reasonable weather?"

"I expect that Talbot will take his box of watercolor paints and endeavor to capture the beauty of the landscape," I replied. "I will turn my hand to some fishing and I expect that we will do a lot of walking and talking. Harriet and I will have much to catch up on." Just thinking about it had made me feel quite excited. "Are you sure, Holmes, that you cannot join us?" I urged.

"Quite sure, my dear friend. In a week's time I will be in Switzerland, looking at the grandeur of those rocks and swirling water," Holmes answered. "When we both return from our respective holidays, we will have much to tell each other!"

"If you change your mind . . . " I ventured.

"Of course. But may I ask you a question?"

"Indeed, Holmes. What about?"

"At the travel agency where you booked your tickets, was there anybody who smoked a pipe?"

"Not that I recall. Why do you ask?"

"The envelope that contained your documents had been freshly sealed. I thought that I could detect the smell of tobacco in the saliva that had been applied. I would say that the person smoked a rather unusual mixture of Virginia, Latakia—to give it strength—and some Turkish blend, to produce a rather individual aromatic texture. Not unpleasing, mind you."

"You are ever the detective, Holmes," I quipped. "It will be a sad day when smoking a pipe becomes a criminal offence!"

"Your turn to jest, Watson! I was just using my powers of observation! Let me ask Mrs. Hudson to prepare us tea and scones, and then you can tell me all your other news."

We chatted for a while, and then I bade Holmes farewell, as I had to return to my rooms and complete preparations for my departure next evening.

I ARRIVED EARLY at King's Cross Station. A porter presented himself and asked if he could take my luggage and which train I was catching. Deftly he stacked my suitcases on his trolley, and I followed him as he navigated his way through the crowd towards the platform where my train would be waiting. I pondered how Harriet and Talbot would have changed in the years since we last met. Like all of us, probably put on a little weight! I remembered Talbot as a man of quiet energy who seemed to get a great deal accomplished with the minimum of fuss. He was not an imposing man, about average height, pleasant features but by no means handsome, and with a gentle and ready sense of humor which was never at anyone's expense, except perhaps his own! He and Harriet seemed made for each other.

Talbot was a clergyman who believed that the best sermon he could give was not from the pulpit, but by the example of his own life. After many busy and exciting years in the Colonies, with Harriet as his devoted and capable companion, he had settled down in the rural parish of St. Luke's in West Dorset. Their one son, Martin, was now an established lawyer in Watford.

They were already at the railway carriage, organizing their luggage being loaded onto the train when I reached it. I waved and shouted hello, and they turned and waved excitedly back at me. Within no time, we had greeted each other and asked all the usual questions that one does—never listening to the answers! How are you? You do look well. How have you been keeping? You haven't changed a bit!

Having settled down in our seats, and the initial rush of excitement gone, we got down to more levelheaded conversation. Harriet asked how my medical practice was going, and how on earth did I find the time to assist my good friend Sherlock Holmes, and expressed the hope that he, too, was in excellent health. I assured her that he was in fine fettle and would be taking his holiday in Switzerland, and how he much regretted not being able to join us. She knew adventures with Holmes were an integral part of my existence, and that things were busy, even chaotic at times, but I treasured every moment of it! However, a holiday was just what I needed right now, and I hoped that Holmes would have a similarly relaxing time. He needed a break from pitting his wits against the criminal mind, and the police would have to solve their own problems. Perhaps the criminals might take a holiday as well, just as long as they did not go to Switzerland for it!

I remarked that I thought it a marvelous gesture on the part of the well-wisher in St.Luke's parish to provide this holiday for us all. Harriet acknowledged that it was most generous, but nothing less than Talbot deserved after all the devoted service he had given. Talbot, modest as ever, asserted that he had done no more than his duty. He confessed, however, that he welcomed the break from his pastoral commitments and looked forward to getting out his much-neglected box of watercolor paints. Then with a touch of mock solemnity, he asked us all if we would petition the Almighty to grant us some clement weather!

The time passed quickly in happy conversation. We took a light supper in the dining car, and then retired to our sleeping compartments. The morning found us in Aberdeen, and as we stepped out of the carriage, we could feel that the air was a few degrees cooler that in London, but so much fresher and more invigorating. A porter took our luggage and escorted us to the platform where we would board the Great North of Scotland train to Ballater. This journey was different. In the bright morning sunshine we watched the local people get on and off at each small station. The countryside was alive with laborers busy about their work.

Before long we had pulled in at the long curved platform of Ballater Station. It had been especially extended to cope with the Royal Train in which Her Majesty Queen Victoria and her entourage would travel. She loved to sneak away to her beloved Balmoral castle, much to the consternation and discomfort of her government, because they had to follow after her, and commute backwards and forwards from London with all sorts of documents of state which needed her attention.

We alighted and were soon approached by a man who seemed to be expecting us.

He was of middle age, had a handsome red beard just beginning to get some touches of gray. He wore a kilt and sporran, and a stout tweed jacket.

He addressed Talbot, "Excuse me, sir, but would you be the Reverend Mr. Ridley?"

"I am that," Talbot replied, "This is my wife, and my brother-in-law, Dr. Watson."

"My name is Taggart, sir, head ghillie to the laird MacLeod, at whose castle you will be staying. The trap is waiting. I'll get Angus to bring your luggage."

We followed him out to the horse and buggy that was standing obediently at the kerb, and I assisted Harriet up.

"John," she whispered quietly to me, "Do you think Taggart is his Christian name or his surname? A bit dour, isn't he? Very economical with words. Perhaps he thinks they cost money!"

"You always did have a mischievous sense of humor, Harriet. I am sure it will get us all into trouble some day," I said trying to look just a bit schoolmasterish.

She smiled back at me, ignoring my expression entirely, as she always had. She continued, "I am certain the weather will be kind to us. We have so much to do, before it is too late, and it seems God has granted us the time, the opportunity, and the good health with which to do it."

I realized how deeply I loved my sister and how much I had missed her company recently, and that of her husband as well.

Taggart had the reins, and skillfully he maneuvered our way out of Station Square, and off down the country lanes towards our castle. Perhaps castle was too grand a title for it, but it was certainly an imposing structure. It was three stories high, built of solid granite to keep out the winter cold, and was set in rolling parkland. To experience the beauty of the Highlands on a sunlit summer morning is to have the senses filled with a simple but profound pleasure. We looked at each other, and felt how blessed we were to be sharing this splendor.

Mrs. MacPhail, the housekeeper and cook, had assembled the staff at the front entrance to greet us. We were introduced to Shona and Morag, the two maids, James, the head gardener, and Ian his assistant, and to Wee Jamie and Callum, the stable boys. Taggart and Angus brought our luggage in, and Mrs. MacPhail showed us around the house. The drawing room was spacious, with oak paneling, and comfortable armchairs situated close to the fire. Scenic paintings and photographs in abundance were all round the room, giving it a sense of coziness. The corridors were lined with oil paintings of ancestors, the men looking most impressive in full Highland costume, and the women very demure. There were also claymores, leather shields, and trophies of deer's antlers and the occasional stuffed pheasant. It was another world from Baker Street.

"I do believe we are on the doorstep of Heaven!" Harriet remarked.

After we had been shown to our rooms and unpacked our bags, we assembled in the dining room for a light lunch and discussed our plans for the rest of the day. We decided to ask Taggart to take us for a drive around the local countryside, so that Talbot could choose a suitable place for his painting, and I could perhaps find a stretch of the river where I could turn my hand at landing some trout.

For supper, Mrs. MacPhail had prepared a traditional Scottish haggis, and Taggart "piped it in" with a rousing tune, to make us all feel welcome, and, no doubt, to impress upon us that we were a long way from England!

We discussed our plans for the morrow. I would try fishing again, Talbot would embark on his painting, and Harriet would stay here and just walk around the estate. We all retired to bed early, as it had been a long day, and we wished to be up with the lark and suitably refreshed for an energetic day of pleasure.

I awoke to find the sunshine streaming into my room, and the house bustling with activity. We English do not realize how far north the Highlands are, and therefore how early the sun rises in midsummer, and also how late it sets! After a breakfast of oats porridge, taken the proper way, with salt (and a sprinkling of sugar, when Mrs. MacPhail was not looking), Talbot and I were on our way in the carriage. We each had a small hamper containing some refreshment, and Taggart said he would pick us up at about four o'clock.

It was a long time since I had done any fly fishing, and I tried to remember all the rules I had once learned, especially not to let my shadow fall across the water where I was going to cast my line. There were no serious mishaps, I did not get my line caught up in the bushes, and eventually my patience and diligence were rewarded with a catch of three rainbow trout. I would return home in good time for Mrs. MacPhail to prepare these for our supper—one each. Already I was feeling that London with all its bustle and smell was a thousand miles away!

Talbot was delighted to be back painting again, and when I rejoined him to return home, he flatly refused to let me see his work until it was finished. Then, he said good-naturedly, he would hold a "grand exhibition of his summer collection" in the drawing room to which we would all be invited!

"I'm afraid I do not like people to see my paintings until I have finished them," he apologized. "I feel myself getting a little short-tempered when people insist on looking over my shoulder when I paint, and it is even worse when they start asking me silly questions!"

"I promise not to do any of that, Talbot," I reassured him.

"I felt certain you would not!" he smiled. "I had one passerby this morning who did get me a bit angry, but as he was a fellow clergyman, I was loath to shoo him away. We chatted and found that we got on really rather well. Reverend Edwin Murray was his name. A bit younger than I am, I would say. His brother is in the chemical industry and has made a lot of money, and is persuading Edwin to retire, or at least take a good break away from it all to think about it. Consequently, he has come up to the Highlands, hoping that some fresh air and good stiff exercise will help him sort out his thoughts. I had more than enough lunch in my hamper, so I shared it with him. After that, he thanked me most generously, and apologized for any intrusion, and was off on his way."

"When I go on holiday, Talbot, the last thing I want to do is meet another doctor, and find myself talking shop!" I retorted.

"Quite right, John," he nodded in agreement. "We did not talk theology at all, nor did we compare notes about our parishes or parishioners. I don't suppose that we will meet again."

But they did. That evening we each recounted what we had done during the day, and how exhilarating it was to be breathing a different air and gazing upon different scenery. I decided that tomorrow I would revisit the place where I had caught my three trout, and Harriet would accompany Talbot while he put the finishing touches to his painting. Close to lunchtime, I decided to take my luncheon over to join them, and had just sat down on the grass, when the Reverend Edwin Murray reappeared, this time carrying a hamper of food and insisting that we join him.

"Trout again tonight, John?" Harriet asked me.

I assured her that that was on the menu, if she so wished.

"Yes, please," she replied enthusiastically. "I am very partial to fish, and I don't think I am quite ready for more haggis—no offence to Mrs. MacPhail!" She turned to Murray, "And we would be delighted if you would come and join us for supper tomorrow."

"An excellent idea," he agreed enthusiastically. "And in perfect time, as I plan to leave for the Isle of Skye the day after. I would enjoy that very much—even with haggis!"

"I don't think you need to stretch it so far," Talbot said, with a wide smile. "I am sure if John turns his attention to it, he will be able to catch us something more to our taste." He looked across at me encouragingly.

"I am sure I can!" I assured them. "Perhaps even a salmon."

THE NEXT DAY was perfect. Harriet and Talbot spent it together, and I landed a very fine salmon that would do splendidly for our evening meal, guest included. Just after seven o'clock, Edwin arrived in his carriage, and we enjoyed a sherry before going to the dining room. Conversation flowed easily. It transpired that Edwin had been to many parts of the world where Talbot and Harriet had worked.

"It is unfortunate that we had never met while abroad," Talbot remarked.

"With you there, I am sure they had no need of my humble services!" Edwin replied, to much laughter.

"Come, come, Edwin, I can assure you that there were more than enough sinners for both of us to cope with!" Talbot retorted.

Edwin asked how it was that we came to be holidaying in the High-lands and Harriet explained the story of the generous parishioner who had donated this to us. She also pointed out that it was hoped that there would be another member to our party, Mr. Sherlock Holmes, the detective.

At this, Edwin became most excited.

"*The* Sherlock Holmes? You mean you are acquainted with him?" he asked.

"Well, it is my brother, here, who is his great friend," Harriet explained, looking at me.

"Then you must be *The* Dr. Watson!" Edwin exclaimed with delight. "I am indeed honored to meet you, sir. There is scarcely a mention of Mr. Holmes but that your name is not alongside his."

I blushed. "You do me undue honor, sir," I replied.

Edwin continued, "I follow his exploits with great enthusiasm. Such a gifted mind, so logical, such powers of reasoning! It is such a pity he could not be with us, but I fear I would make a dreadful bore of myself, pestering him with questions, if he were here."

"I did try to persuade him to come," I answered, "but he had prior arrangements to go to Switzerland, to view the Reichenbach Falls. In fact, he should be setting off on his journey in two days' time."

"What a coincidence!" Edwin exclaimed. "I and my brother James plan to be there soon, as well. I would like to take the liberty of intro-ducing myself should I meet him, if for no other reason than to say what excellent hosts you have been to me, and how much you appear to be enjoying your holiday."

"Our holiday could not be better, could it, my dear," Talbot said as he turned to Harriet. "Would you not agree, John?"

"Wholeheartedly. Perhaps you can make him jealous that he did not come with us." I responded.

By the end of the meal, we felt we had been in the company of an old friend, not a new acquaintance. We returned to the drawing room and in a leisurely manner sipped our coffee, and the gentlemen smoked their pipes. Harriet decided to retire, while we continued to talk and enjoy some vintage tawny port. Edwin said that he had brought a contribution for this evening, a half bottle of the most excellent port he had ever tasted. Talbot declined courteously, saying that as host, he insisted on providing. Edwin seemed genuinely upset that his offer had been rejected, even though most politely. However it was amicably agreed that Talbot would accept the bottle and of course would be sure to sample it later.

I had had a strenuous but rewarding day, so at about half past eleven, I decided to retire. Edwin felt that it was time for him also to bid us good night, and thanked us for one of the most delightful evenings he had ever spent. I left Talbot seated comfortably in an armchair in the drawing room, taking his first sips from the bottle that Edwin had left.

"Good night, John," he said dreamily. "Hmm, this port is truly exceptional. If Heaven is half as good as life is at this moment, I sincerely hope that the Almighty will number me amongst His chosen— but I ask Him not to call me just yet! See you in the morning."

"Good night, Talbot," I said, and turned to climb up the stairs.

IT WAS MOST undignified for me, as a respected member of the medical profession, to find myself astride one of these beasts! The Highland cattle, with their long shaggy red hair and their huge curved horns that point forwards so menacingly, look like relics from the Ice Age. And this brute had a temper to go with it; no wonder he was trying to throw me off! Me, a doctor, doctor, doctor . . .

I awoke from this silly dream to find Morag shaking me rigorously and calling, "Doctor, doctor!"

I gathered my wits about me as quickly as I could, and I saw that she was in great distress.

"Calm yourself down, girl, and tell me what all the fuss is about." I said, sitting up and reaching for my dressing robe.

"It's the Reverend, sir," she gasped. "Something dreadful, oh please come and look, sir!"

It was only half past five in the morning, but the sun was streaming in through the window. I got out of bed in great haste, and pulled on my robe.

"Lead the way," I instructed, and followed as she went down the stairs to the drawing room. She stopped at the door, and beckoned that I should go in. I entered, and by the light that was shining through where one curtain had been pulled back, I could see Talbot slouched in the armchair, his glass spilled on the floor, his head lolled to one side, and his eyes half closed, his lower jaw sagging. I knew that he was dead. I walked over and felt for the radial pulse, knowing that it would be absent. Then I felt for the carotid, but I knew the answer before I tried. It was just an instinctive thing for me to do as a doctor, while I braced myself.

A wave of sadness came over me, and there was a sinking sensation in the pit of my stomach. I would have to break the news to Harriet, and I have always found that to be the most wretched and unwelcome task that befalls a doctor. There is no easy way to tell a relative that a loved one has died. One must be firm but polite, and yet put it across in words that cannot be misunderstood. And now I must tell my dear sister.

I walked out of the room, and closed the door. Morag was sitting at the foot of the stairs, sobbing and choking the tears back, as Shona sat beside her trying to comfort her. Just at that moment, Mrs. MacPhail came in through the front door with Taggart.

"It seems that the Reverend died in his sleep last night," I said solemnly. "It must have been a stroke or a heart attack. I will go and inform Mrs. Ridley. Mrs. MacPhail, please could you put the kettle on. I think a pot of tea will be helpful. Taggart, if you would be so kind as to contact the local doctor, and an undertaker, and I suppose you had better call the local police, as well. Come, we all have things to do."

I took a deep breath and with feet like lead, I trudged up the stairs, and paused briefly at the landing. The sun was streaming in through the open curtain and outside was that magnificent land in all its splendor.

"Here we are," I thought to myself, "next to Heaven itself, and I must wake my dear sister to plunge her into a hellish agony. Why should such a cruel twist of fate strike us down now!"

With an air of numbed resignation, I opened the door to Harriet's bedroom, pulled back a curtain, and went over to the double bed. She awoke gradually, and turned to give me a sleepy smile.

"Good morning, John. What a glorious day!" She said. She looked at me and began to register my distress. She reached her arm to the other side of the bed. "Where's Talbot?" she asked, with a sudden anxiety in her voice.

The words that I knew I had to say stuck in my throat, but Harriet understood the dreadful tidings that I had to bring. I saw the pain cut deep into her, and I tried to comfort her the best I could.

THUS BEGAN THE most wretched morning of my life. I remember going about my duties in a state of shock and numbness. The local doctor came and agreed with my findings. The constable from the nearby police station arrived soon after. They conferred together, and came to the conclusion that there was nothing suspicious about Talbot's death, and that a certificate stating it to be from natural causes was in order. The undertakers arrived and took away the body. It was agreed that we would all return to London tomorrow during the day, taking the body with us, and that after the funeral, Talbot would be buried in the graveyard of his own parish.

I did not feel like lunch, so Taggart took me into Ballater, to the Post Office, and I sent a telegram to Martin Ridley, to inform him of the sad news. It occurred to me that I had better tell Holmes as well.

An hour after I arrived back, two telegrams were delivered. The first, from Martin, said that he would be on the overnight train, and requested that someone pick him up at Ballater Station, and the second one was from Holmes also saying that he would be on the night train, as he had cancelled his trip to Switzerland. I felt guilty about spoiling Holmes's holiday, but I was immensely uplifted that I would be seeing my dear friend again so soon.

THE DOCTOR HAD left some chloral as a sleeping draught for Harriet, so she took it and retired early. I sat in the drawing room smoking my pipe and sipping malt whisky, feeling thoroughly dejected. Eventually I went to bed and woke in the morning with a headache and a sour taste in my mouth. Taggart drove me to the station, where I met Martin Ridley and Holmes, and I introduced them to each other. We rode back in silence.

Holmes then showed a side of his nature that I have seldom seen. He was so tender towards Harriet as they walked and talked, that I marveled at it, and was very touched. After a while, Harriet went upstairs to get herself ready for the return journey. Holmes came over to me and said emphatically,

"Watson, we must talk. Perhaps I have been pursuing criminals for so long that I now have an unnaturally suspicious mind, but I would like to know a great deal more about this Reverend Edwin Murray. Tell me everything that you can recall that he said about himself."

It then struck me that he had said remarkably little. He was an excellent listener, and had never interrupted.

"He did not mention his parish," I recollected, with surprise. "We all sort of assumed that he was Church of England, because of the collar that he wore. He had traveled abroad, in fact to many of the places that Harriet and Talbot had also been, but funnily enough they had never met. You have now aroused my suspicions, Holmes. But I cannot understand why anyone would wish to kill a harmless, elderly cleric? Who could want him dead?"

"I presume this mansion has a library, Watson?" Holmes asked.

I nodded in agreement.

"Good. Lead the way, and let us look up our Reverend Mr. Murray in *Crockford's Clerical Directory*."

Holmes quickly spotted the book, next to *Burke's Peerage*, and began thumbing through the pages.

"As I suspected, Watson, our Edwin Murray is no more a cleric than you or I. Did he give any clue where he came from originally? Did he have a Scottish accent?"

I thought for a moment, and then replied, "As far as I can remember, he did say that his grandfather came from just south of the firth that bears his name."

Holmes eyes lit up. "Aha, Watson, perhaps we do our cleric an injustice. Let us look up MORAY, which is of course pronounced the same . . . at least by the Scots!" Holmes thumbed through the pages again.

"As I feared. We draw a blank again. Describe him further, his appearance, his mannerisms, anything of importance you recall."

I struggled in my misery to bring him back to mind. "He was tall, a trifle stooping," I answered. "His greying hair receded a little from his brow. He was scholarly in manner, even ascetic . . . in fact exactly what one would expect of the man he pretended to be."

Holmes was lost in thought for a while. Then he turned to me and said, "Watson, I have had a most sinister and disturbing idea. Get a piece of paper and a pencil, and write out M O R A Y."

I obliged. "Now what, Holmes?"

"Add the letters I R T, in whatever order seems right to you."

Holmes stared at me as I grappled with this unwelcome bit of mental exercise. Suddenly it struck me like a thunderbolt between the eyes, "MORIARTY!" I exclaimed.

"I do not believe that this is a coincidence, Watson. The man you describe is not Professor James, but his brother. I am in no doubt that your dear brother-in-law was murdered, nor by whom, but I am completely stumped as to why!"

It was a shocking and horrible return to an evil which had become all too familiar over the years. I struggled to come to terms with what Holmes had just told me. "You are saying that my brother-in-law was poisoned by that half-bottle of port that was given to him?"

"Quite so, Watson, and our bogus cleric would have been certain that Talbot would not have opened it until later. It is the host's duty to provide, not the guest's. He may be a villain, but he knows his manners! It is quite possible that you, too, my good friend, could have been poisoned, but somehow I think he was gambling on you being more abstemious in your drinking."

I felt slightly humiliated that I should have proven so predictable. "I know the servants have tidied everything up and thrown away the bottle, but don't you . . . " Holmes dismissed my suggestion before I could even finish it.

"The deed is done. The precise details of 'how' will not help us understand 'why.' "

"Come to think of it, Holmes, this whole business of a holiday for us, paid for by a grateful parishioner, seems rather bogus," I said, with some embarrassment at my own gullibility.

"You are right, my friend. And your travel documents being sent to me is no accident. It was to let me know that you were coming here, and perhaps tempt me to come along as well. When I decided that I would not change my plans to go to Switzerland, an event had to be staged that would oblige me to come. Hence, Talbot was murdered—just to get me to this place! It is diabolically cold-blooded, Watson! The stakes must be high to do such a vicious thing—even for Moriarty! I cannot forgive such wanton inflicting of grief upon the totally innocent." He looked profoundly distressed and even in my own pain I could not help a welling up of pity for him.

"My dear, dear friend, you must not—cannot blame yourself for Talbot's death!" I proclaimed, trying to sound convincing, but I knew that Holmes would feel a pang of self-recrimination, whatever I said. "How could you possibly know what evil plan was being hatched?"

"I should have smelled a rat from the beginning," he said bitterly.

"Too late, Holmes. What we must do now is discover why Moriarty wants us here. What is he planning? I cannot see him coming up here just to enjoy the beautiful scenery," I said. "Just pulling in to Ballater Station, with that extra long platform, for the Royal Train, one gets a sense of . . . "

"That's it Watson. You've got it!" Holmes jerked his head up.

"I've got it?" I asked.

"Yes, Watson. The queen is in Balmoral at the moment. Moriarty's plans have something to do with the queen, I know it."

"Do you think he wants to assassinate her?" I ventured.

"Nothing as straightforward as that, Watson. Moriarty does things for money or power. What could he possibly gain by removing an elderly widow, even if it were Queen Victoria?"

"But what if it were done right under your nose, Holmes, and he got away with it, think how it would damage your reputation?" I demanded, certain that we were right.

"You have shed light where there was darkness, Watson, but unfortunately I still do not see the way ahead."

"Could we go and warn them at Balmoral?"

"I think not. They would either dismiss us as cranks, perhaps even lock us up, or just tell us thank you very much and increase their security. That may or may not stop Moriarty's game. We are in a trap, Watson, and we don't really know what sort, nor where it will lead. All we can do is follow, and hope that when the time comes, we can outwit this fiend! Our reputations count for little when it is the life of Her Majesty at stake!"

"What do you suggest we do, Holmes?" I asked.

"Let us call upon Mr. Shakespeare," proclaimed Holmes.

"You've lost me there. Do you mean stirring words from *Henry V,* or soliloquies from *Hamlet?*" I queried.

"Nothing to do with the Bard of Avon, my dear friend, but with Mr. Shakespeare, the maker of the finest fishing rods. Tomorrow we are going angling. Do you have a guidebook as to the best places in this area?"

"Indeed I do, Holmes. Along with the rods, I found this very useful little book entitled *Well-Kept Secrets to Fly Fishing in the Scottish Highlands*. I keep it in my breast pocket. The author boasts that an infallible spot for really big trout is Loch Loch, which is not far from here."

"Then Loch Loch is beckoning us, Watson. Let us make the necessary arrangements with the staff so that we can get there."

"What flies do you think we should use?" I asked.

"Choose the ones that look as though they have been used the most often as they are probably the most successful ones!" Holmes replied with a smile.

"Now why did I not think of that," I said rather plaintively.

"I presume you did not bring your service revolver with you, Watson."

"I did not."

"Never mind. I noticed a rather rusty old Webley and a few rounds of ammunition back there with the fishing tackle. You had better give it a good clean, as I have a nasty feeling that your shooting prowess will be called for! Now we must get Harriet and Martin to the railway station. Tell them nothing about our suspicions. We will make the excuse that we are staying on to sort out administrative details, documents, and so forth. We will join them in time for the funeral."

IT WAS A SAD procession that made its way to the station. The coffin was loaded into the luggage compartment, and Harriet and Martin settled into their first-class seats.

We bade them farewell and returned to the house to prepare ourselves for whatever the following day might bring. I cleaned and oiled the old Webley meticulously, but all the while I had a sense of dread as to what I might be called upon to do with it. My courage or my willingness, I did not doubt, but would I make a fool of myself, act too quickly or too slowly, or with insufficient skill? I had to trust Holmes—as I always did—but he had decided that we should go fishing! We were in a trap, and all we could do was wait. I had a strong sense of apprehension, and I could see that Holmes was no more at ease than I.

Supper was a quiet affair. We did not drink any wine with it, but I could not resist a glass of port after it, just to help me sleep.

"Holmes," I said, "what if we just packed our bags and went home?"

"That might foil Moriarty's plan, Watson, but that means there is no way we can bring Talbot's murderer to justice."

"You are right, Holmes," I acknowledged sadly. "We must play the game as Moriarty dictates it to us, and hope to beat him at the critical moment."

"That's it exactly, Watson. We will have a very demanding day ahead of us. I think I will go to bed."

"I'm off, too, Holmes," I said, and made my way up the stairs, but I knew that I would sleep little.

WE HAD AN UNHURRIED breakfast and then packed our fishing gear into the dogcart. With Angus at the reins, we drove to Loch Loch. I could muster little enthusiasm, but I cast again and again in an effort to catch something, and Holmes was having as little luck as I was. The day was warm and my frustration was mounting when I got a bite, and after a brief battle, I landed one small trout. It lifted my spirits a bit, and then Holmes gave a whoop of joy, as he, too, succeeded. We were too engrossed in what we were doing to notice anyone approach.

"Excuse me, gentlemen, but would I have the pleasure of addressing Mr. Holmes and Dr. Watson?" the man asked. He was in the uniform of an officer in the Household Cavalry, and had left his horse alongside our carriage, with Angus. "Allow me to introduce myself. Captain Urquhart, equerry to Her Majesty the Queen. Tales of your exploits had been brought to Her Majesty's attention, Mr. Holmes, and hearing that you were in the vicinity, she has graciously extended an invitation for you both to join her for a light picnic luncheon. There are not many of us in this entourage, and we are encamped a short distance from here. If you would be so kind as to follow me?"

"We accept, sir," Holmes replied. "Would you allow us a few moments to pack our belongings, and then we will accompany you." Aside to me, he whispered, "The game is afoot, Watson! Are you prepared?"

"As ready as I will ever be, Holmes," I said, and tapped my right-hand jacket pocket where I had put the Webley.

"Good. We must not fail!"

We climbed into the dogcart and the captain led the way on his horse. As we approached the royal party, we could see that the queen had chosen a charming spot for her luncheon. It was set back off the road slightly, and commanded a spectacular view of a loch, with nearby clumps of trees and heather and gorse in bloom. Her staff had set up tables and chairs and all the carriages and horses were assembled out of the way. In the middle was the diminutive seated figure of Her Majesty, dressed in black, as always, since the untimely death of her dear Albert.

We were introduced to the queen, first Holmes and then myself. I felt extremely nervous, and that, on top of my strong sense of apprehension, obliterated my memory. I have no idea what she said to me or what I mumbled in reply, but Holmes was splendid. He duly sat down in the seat offered to him on the queen's left, and I sat on his left, quite happy for him to be in the limelight.

"We have heard such glowing accounts of your exploits, Mr. Holmes, and how you and Dr. Watson have so ably assisted the police in bringing criminals to justice," she said graciously. "It was suggested to us that, since you were temporarily residing nearby, you might be invited to join our little picnic. What takes you away from London and brings you to the peace and tranquility of the Highlands?"

Holmes explained the recent events that had struck my family, without suggesting that poor Talbot had been murdered, of course, and the queen expressed her sincerest condolences. As a widow of many years, she could fully sympathize with my sister. My attention wandered, as I thought to myself, where could the danger be lurking in these beautiful surroundings. Was Holmes making some ghastly mistake that only a man of his supreme intelligence could make, reading into the death of a harmless vicar some sinister machinations of his archenemy, Moriarty? I looked around me and could see trusted ladies in waiting, staff setting out the food, and beyond them, talking to our brave captain from the Household Cavalry, were two strong looking ghillies in full Highland attire—kilts and sporrans, everything—who would no doubt defend Her Majesty to the death. Yet still I felt distinctly uneasy, but did my best to hide it.

The queen continued to talk with Holmes.

"The Highland Scots are amongst the most brave and loyal subjects that we could ever have," she said with deep feeling. "It saddens us that they should have suffered so much in recent years. We are sure that you know of the story of the so-called Massacre at Glen Coe? Mac-Donald was late in pledging his loyalty to the Crown, and the Campbells took this as an excuse to continue their old feud, and rose up at night and attacked them where they slept, killing over ninety of that clan. We do so wish that there could be peace throughout our realm, here and abroad, Mr. Holmes."

"Indeed, ma'am," he agreed.

"We are told that there are two members of the MacDonald clan who have journeyed all the way from Glen Coe," she continued, "in order to present us with a tartan rug that they have woven themselves, as a gift of their devotion. The presentation ceremony will take place very soon, and then we can enjoy some refreshments."

Half listening as I was, the queen's last statement had me fully alert, as I watched Captain Urquhart and the two ghillies approach. I could see that Holmes was getting more and more agitated. I slipped my right hand into my jacket pocket and took hold of my revolver. The captain had already introduced the two ghillies, who had bowed most obediently, and one of them was unwrapping a most impressive tartan rug, when Holmes blurted out to me, "Quick, Watson, he has a gun in there!"

I leapt forwards with my revolver drawn as one of the ghillies drew his revolver out of the rug and pushed Captain Urquhart out of the way with his other hand. I remember firing a shot at the assailant and then a sensation in my chest as if I had been kicked by a mule. I fell flat on my back with tremendous force and after a moment's darkness, opened my eyes to the sound of women screaming and men shouting as they rushed towards Her Majesty.

I tried to sit up but I could not get my breath. I rolled over and clambered onto my hands and knees, and the fishing guidebook that Holmes had assured me would come in useful, fell out of my pocket, neatly plugged by a bullet!

Several yards away one of the ghillies lay motionless on the ground, blood oozing out of his head wound. The second ghillie was locked in mortal combat with Holmes, a wicked blade gleaming in his upraised hand—the sort of knife that the Scot traditionally carries in the top of his sock and called a *skian dhu*. My cry of alarm froze on my lips. It was no time to distract Holmes, not even for a moment.

They swayed back and forth. Holmes was lean of build, and far stronger than many would have imagined, but the ghillie was a big broad-chested fellow with an advantage in weight. Even as I watched in horror, barely aware of men hurrying the queen away and crowding protectively around her, Holmes was about to be overpowered by the ghillie. Captain Urquhart had left the queen's side, and with sword drawn was rushing to Holmes's defense. Just before he could skewer the ghillie with his blade, a rifle shot rang out from somewhere in the nearby bushes, and the ghillie dropped down dead. The sound of a horse galloping away could be heard in the direction from which the shot had come. Captain Urquhart stopped; he must have realized how far away he was from his own horse, and have come to the conclusion that the assailant would be long gone before he or anyone else could give chase. Besides, his duty was here, with Her Majesty, and who knows what immediate danger she might still be in.

Holmes shook himself, as if momentarily dazed by the closeness of his escape. Then with that extraordinary recovery that is characteristic of him, he thanked Urquhart, ignored everyone else, and came striding over to me, his face haggard with concern. He fell to one knee beside me. "Watson!" he said urgently, "are you badly wounded? Stay still!"

I wanted to laugh with relief. I had been every bit as afraid for him, as he now was for me.

"No! No!" I said shakily. "But that fishing guidebook was even more useful than you supposed." I felt on the ground for it, and held it out for him to see.

It was one of those rare moments when he was speechless, but I could read the emotion in his face. Urquhart was coming back towards us, and with Holmes's help I managed to stand upright and get my wits about me. Captain Urquhart declared heartily that it was the bravest act he had ever seen—outside of the military—and that Her Majesty wished to thank both Holmes and myself, in person. Leaning on Holmes for support. I walked over to the queen's carriage and attempted a bow.

"I am indebted to you both beyond words." She looked very composed, but sad. For all her diminutive stature, she was a woman of infinite dignity.

"This is the eighth attempt upon my life, and it distresses me that there are subjects of mine who would wish me dead," she said quietly. "It will only alarm people if they hear that this event took place, and therefore I have decreed that it did not happen. You have the undying gratitude of your sovereign, gentlemen, but I am afraid you will not receive any official recognition. I trust that you will understand." Her imperious expression permitted no argument whatsoever.

Holmes merely bowed his head in acknowledgment.

"Satisfy my curiosity, please, Mr. Holmes. What alerted you to the danger?" she said.

"Well, ma'am, in the first place, the two ghillies were wearing the tartan of MacDonald of the Isles, and not MacDonald of Glen Coe," he answered. "Then when the first ghillie started to unwrap the rug, I could see that that was a Campbell tartan. There was no way that a MacDonald would have woven a Campbell tartan to give as a present to Your Majesty!"

"Your powers of observation are most remarkable," the Queen said, with a slight smile. " I believe that the stories that I have heard about you, complimentary as they are, do not do you justice, Mr. Holmes! I bid you good day and a safe journey back to London." With that there was a gentle wave of her small podgy hand in a lace mitten, and she was gone.

IT OCCURRED TO me that I had every reason to feel elated, and the ache in my chest did not seem so bad after all.

"Do you realize, Holmes, that we have foiled Moriarty!" I exclaimed. "I feel like the boy who has hit a six off the last ball to give his school cricket team victory! All of a sudden I am ravenously hungry, and a glass or two of wine would not go amiss! Let's see what is in that food hamper of ours!"

"You deserve a banquet, my friend," Holmes said as he smiled at me. "You were brilliant, and you are still alive! I could not have done what you did today."

WITHIN FIVE MINUTES of our arrival back at the castle, all the staff had heard from Angus the amazing story of how I had saved the queen's life. They gathered together at the front and formally asked Holmes to give them the real account, which he did with theatrical reenactment, even using my revolver—unloaded, of course. The maids fussed over us and for a short spell at least, the gloom of the previous tragedy was dispelled.

Holmes decided that we should leave tomorrow, in time to catch a daytime train to London. Moriarty was still at large and to travel on the night train would present ourselves as easy targets for his revenge. He would not take kindly to being beaten.

I slept well that night in spite of my grief for Harriet, and awoke the next morning in as good spirits as was possible under the circumstances and caring little about the ache in my chest. We said good-bye to the staff and gave them each a token of our appreciation, and were at Ballater Station in good time. We boarded and were on our way, when ten minutes later the train ground to a halt. The guard came through each carriage announcing that there had been a serious derailment ahead of us, and that we had to wait while it was repaired, which might take hours.

"Not only has Moriarty got access to the queen's ear, and the power to persuade her to ask us to lunch, but he also stops the trains running on time," Holmes remarked. "We shall be on the night train after all, Watson."

In view of this we agreed that we would not use the sleeping compartment, but stay in our seats, keeping watch alternately, one hour on, one hour off. It was a wretched night, and we both felt dog tired but relieved when the train eventually pulled in to King's Cross.

"You must come and have some tea and scones at Baker Street, before you return home, Watson," Holmes said.

"We're safe now, Holmes," I replied thankfully. "Terra firma so to speak. He cannot get us now. Yes, tea and scones sounds excellent. I feel that the worst thing that can happen to us now is that Mrs. Hudson drops the tea tray! You can advise me as to what name I should give to our latest saga."

Seated comfortably in Holmes's apartment, I watched and waited as he filled his pipe and lit it.

"'The Case of the Highland Hoax' is my suggestion, Watson," he said.

I looked puzzled. "What was the hoax?" I asked.

"There was no attempt on the life of Queen Victoria," he replied.

"I know that that is the official version, but . . . "

"No, Watson, I mean there was genuinely no attack on the queen—she was not the intended victim," Holmes insisted.

"You have lost me there, my dear chap." I was now totally confused. "I seem to remember this ghillie pulling out his gun from within the tartan rug and firing at the queen, and I stopped a bullet that was going in her direction! I could not be mistaken about that! And as the other ghillie drew his knife and lunged towards the queen, you wrestled him to the ground! Then that shot came out of the bushes and killed him just as he had the better of you." I recalled it with a sudden vividness. "A bit strange, that. Why, if that shot had been a second earlier, it would have killed you . . .

"Oh my God, Holmes, I see what you mean!" I exclaimed and a cold shudder ran down my spine.

"Precisely, my dear friend, precisely," Holmes continued in a very matter of fact voice. "I was working on the assumption that Moriarty would try to kill the queen in front of us, so that we should both be discredited. The 'great detective' Mr. Sherlock Holmes and his friend Dr. John Watson failed to stop the assassination of Her Majesty! And furthermore were unable to catch the assailants!" He shook his head.

"No, Watson, discredited or not, we would still be able to go about our business of pursuing criminals. Moriarty wanted much more—he wanted me dead, and to accomplish the act right in front of the queen! He would have been quite happy with your departure as well! I hope that I am not placing too high a value upon myself, but I conclude that those bullets were meant for me, not Her Majesty."

"I fear you are right, Holmes," I said. "I also fear that the game is not yet played out."

"My conclusion, too," he agreed, all victory gone out of his voice.

"Those people who repeatedly walked past our compartment last night, and that man who stood for an hour, smoking, right by the door, they were all to keep us on edge, keep us awake and wondering when and how we would be attacked. We arrive back, Watson, thinking we are safe. We are not! I suspect that Moriarty has a yet one more surprise in store for us!"

I looked about the room and could see nothing unusual or out of place.

"What, Holmes? Where?"

Holmes nodded towards the luggage.

"But that was locked up in the luggage compartment!" I assured him.

"Of course. It would be a simple job for Moriarty to bribe the guard and go in there. But to do what, Holmes? Plant a bomb?"

"Those were my thoughts, Watson."

"Then let us hand these suitcases over to the police, or simply hurl them into the Thames!" I demanded. "There is nothing in them that is worth your life or mine!"

"If we hand these cases over to the police, they will only blow themselves up," he said with a dismissive gesture, "And if we throw them into the Thames, somebody will be sure to find them and likewise blow themselves up! We must solve this one ourselves, Watson."

I could feel beads of sweat beginning to stand out on my forehead, and my throat going dry.

"Do not look so alarmed, my dear friend," Holmes said with a smile. "I have taken a precaution. As I was closing the locks on my suitcases, I placed a piece of gray cotton thread over the holes before pressing the catch home. If anyone has been tampering with them, then I would expect the piece of cotton thread to have fallen away. Here, Watson, take one of my magnifying glasses and see if I am right. Oh, and I have done the same with your cases, of course."

Tentatively I picked up a magnifying glass and got down on one knee to examine the locks on my suitcases. Yes, I could see it; not conspicuous to the naked eye, but under each catch there was a thread of cotton.

"So far, so good," I said. "Now let me examine your cases."

I started with the smallest. I could definitely see threads in both locks, and similarly with the next case. With growing apprehension I examined the last and largest suitcase. My hands were getting clammy and my heart was racing. I looked and looked again. There was no mistake—there were no threads of cotton.

"This case, Holmes. It has been tampered with," I said as I stepped backwards.

"Moriarty is the devil incarnate, Watson. I believe he has rigged up a bomb in there that is designed to detonate when I open the lid and thus kill me, or perhaps even worse, blind me and blow my hands off! It might of course, be just another hoax!"

"Be sensible, Holmes. Let's just throw the damned thing away!" I protested.

He raised his eyebrows.

"But then we would never know! We would be frustrated and suspicious of everything, waiting for the next attempt. No, Watson, we must face it now."

"I have an idea. Lay that case flat on the floor, upside down. Now, hand me those scissors over there, and I will unpick the stitching of the back panel, then I can take my clothes out very carefully, and thus, without opening the lid, we can see what little present Moriarty has sent me!"

"Holmes," I protested, "I will do it. You stand well back—no argument! I refused to hand him the scissors, and went to the case myself.

Methodically I cut through the stitching on three sides that held together the bottom panel of the case, and then I peeled it back and cut through the lining. Slowly I removed item by item, socks, trousers, shirts, and placed them on the floor. Then I saw it.

Explosive, wrapped in brown paper, with colored wires coming out of it to an electrical circuit with a battery. Wires led away from it into the lid in such a way that when the lid was opened, the circuit would be completed and the bomb would go off! My hands started to shake.

"Steady, Watson," Holmes instructed. "One by one cut through those wires leading into the explosive."

"Keep well back, Holmes. Here goes." I cut. And breathed a sigh of relief.

"Congratulations, Watson! It seems you have saved my life twice in two days!"

"Think nothing of it, my dear friend," I said with exaggerated abandon, now that it was over. "I was under the impression that I had saved Her Majesty's life yesterday, but I stand corrected!"

"Just as a matter of interest. If it were a question between saving my life or the queen's, which would you choose?" Holmes asked.

"No problem, Holmes. Patriotic chap that I am, I would save yours," I said without hesitation.

"But supposing that Queen Victoria had deceased, and Edward, as King Edward VII were on the throne, would you save his life or mine?"

"Again, no problem. King Edward," I began.

Holmes looked slightly crestfallen, "Your patriotism does you credit, Watson," he said with an effort.

"As I was about to say, Holmes, 'King Edward is eminently dispensable, and I would, of course, choose to save your life.' " I replied with a larger smile than I had intended. "I fear Edward has too many of his parents' vices and too few of their virtues! You must forgive me— it is my turn now for a humble attempt at humor!"

Holmes's look of pride and relief was transparent. "You are a splendid fellow, Watson!" he said, picking up his pipe and fiddling with it.

"I think I hear Mrs. Hudson coming with the tea and scones. If she drops those, it really will be the worst thing that could happen to us, and I think if she sets eyes on this rather nasty device, we can say goodbye to our refreshments!"

As Mrs. Hudson came through the door, Holmes took the tray from her immediately, and not a moment too soon. She spied the mess on the floor, then the bomb, and she put her hands to her face and shrieked, "Mr. Holmes! What is that evil-looking thing?"

"Don't panic, Mrs. Hudson. It is a bomb, but it is quite safe now," I reassured her. "It seems that somebody in Scotland took a dislike to Mr. Holmes, and planted this in his suitcase."

"Well," she said with disgust, "promise me, Mr. Holmes, that you will not go to that country again if there are people that would wish you such ill will! Please choose a country where the English are respected, somewhere like Switzerland."

"As you wish, Mrs. Hudson," Holmes conceded. "In the interests of my health and safety, as you insist, my next vacation will be . . . the Reichenbach Falls, and you, Watson, will accompany me!"

THE RIDDLE OF THE GOLDEN MONKEYS

Loren D. Estleman

IT IS A COMMON misapprehension of old age that the widower is
of necessity a lonely man even in the press of a crowd. In the third
year of the reign of George V, I had been in bereavement for the better part of a decade, and the tragic inroads that had been made upon
the British male population during the wars in South Africa and China
were such that for a solitary gentleman in relatively good fettle to show
himself in society was to trumpet his availability to any number of un-
attached women of a certain age. This situation was exacerbated by
the appearance, since the deaths of our gracious Victoria and that
good-hearted man Edward VII, of a breed of bold, independent
female who would step up and declare her intentions before a teem-
ing ballroom with no more blushes than a tiger stalking a hare.

By the summer of 1913, I had long since abandoned my shock at
such behaviour, but found it wearisome in the extreme. I had reached
that time in life wherein a cigar, a snifter, and a good book quite ful-
fills one's dreams of bliss, but to make such a statement in the presence of one of these daring creatures must needs give offence, and
ultimately lead to the undoing of one's good reputation, which in the
end is all any of us ever has.

"I jumped—it seems," writes Conrad, in *Lord Jim,* and the declaration is appropriate to the action I took that June, when in response

to frequent invitations I bolted London for the South Downs and a holiday from eligibility in the company of my oldest and closest friend.

Those who are familiar with my published recollections may remember that Sherlock Holmes, after a lifetime of unique service to the mighty and humble, had retired to an existence of contemplation and bee farming in Sussex. The setting was isolated, and in lieu of neighbours the modest villa looked out upon the brittle Channel from a crest of severe white cliffs similar to those which are commonly associated with Dover. It was with keen anticipation of this lonely (and unapologetically masculine) stretch of English coastline, as well as the proximity of the man with whom I had shared so many adventures, no two of which resembled each other, that I disembarked from the train at Newhaven and took the hire of a Daimler to convey me along the twenty miles of seacoast that remained. Chugging along at a blistering fifteen miles per hour, I held onto my hat with one hand and the side of the vehicle with the other, remembering when a clattering ride in a horsedrawn hansom towards the scene of some impending tragedy represented the height of excitement for a man of any age.

"Watson—good fellow, is that you? I am only just in receipt of your wire. We are but one more scientific improvement away from outdistancing even the genius of Mr. Morse."

We were slowing for the turn to the villa when I recognized the gaunt figure approaching with the sea at his back. He wore a terry robe only, untied over a bathing costume, which plastered with damp to his skeletal frame testified that retirement from public life had neither increased his appetite nor lessened his distaste for inactivity of any sort. But for the grey in his hair and the thinning at the temples, he did not appear to have aged a day since the attempt was made on his life by the blackguard Count Sylvius ten years before. It was the very last investigation we shared, and my final visit to our dear old digs in Baker Street. (I, meanwhile, had grown absolutely stout, a victim of my comfortable armchair and the bill of fare at Simpson's.)

Years and weight notwithstanding, I alighted eagerly from the passenger's seat and seized his hand, which was iron-cold from his late immersion in the icy Channel. At close range I observed the creases at the corners of his razor-sharp eyes and the deep furrows from his Roman nose to his thin mouth, cut by time and concentration. He put me in mind of a Yankee cigar-store Indian which has been left out in the weather.

"I hope I have not inconvenienced you," I said.

"Not nearly as much as you have inconvenienced your dog. I trust the kennel in Blackheath is a good one."

I was so astounded by the mention of Blackheath that for a moment I could not recall if I'd ever told him I owned a dog.

He laughed in that way which many thought mirthless. "Time has not changed you, nor age sharpened your wit. An old athlete such as yourself cannot resist a visit to the rugby field of his youth, hence that particular dark loam adhering to your left heel. Fullness of age and greatness of girth might prevent a casual excursion, but you would travel that far to board your dog; a bull, if I am any judge of the stray hairs upon your coat."

"It would appear an old detective such as yourself cannot resist the urge to detect."

Again he laughed. "A very palpable hit." Before I could protest, he had paid my driver, relieved him of my Gladstone bag, and started up the path towards the house.

Soon we were in his parlour, he having bathed and put on the somewhat shabby tweeds of a country gentleman. The room was small but commodious, with a bay window overlooking the water and sufficient memorabilia strewn about to create the sensation that we were back at 221B. Here was the dilapidated Oriental slipper, from which he filled his pipe with a portion of his old shag; there the framed photograph of Irene Adler, and she in her grave these twenty years. I recognised the harpoon which had slain Black Peter Carey and the worn old revolver that had saved our lives upon more than one occasion, now demoted to a decoration on the wall above the hearth. A library of tattered beekeeping manuals filled the bookpress which had once contained his commonplace hooks. I asked him how his bees fared.

"Splendidly. Later I shall bring out the congenial mead I've developed from the honey. It may make amends for supper. My housekeeper is deceased, I have not yet replaced her, and my cooking skills are not on a level with my ratiocination. I say, old fellow, would you mind terribly if we have a third at table?"

"A client?" I smiled.

"A man in need of a favour, which in an unprotected moment I agreed to provide. You may find him entertaining company. He's rather in the way of a colleague of yours."

"A physician? I've not practised in years. We shall not be able to converse in the same language."

"A writer; or have you retired from letters as well as medicine? Sax Rohmer is the name." Turning in his armchair, he rummaged among a jumble of books in a case which looked disturbingly like a child's coffin, and tossed a volume across to where I sat facing him upon a sagging divan.

I inspected the book. It was bound cheaply, with a paper slipcover bearing the sensational title *The Mystery of Dr. Fu-Manchu.* Holmes smoked his pipe in silence while I read the opening pages.

I closed the book and laid it in my lap. "I read this story in serial form in a London magazine. I considered bringing suit against the author, but I couldn't decide whether to base it on grounds of invasion of privacy or plagiarism."

"Indeed. I noticed the resemblance myself: a clipped-sounding adventurer with a pipe and a nervous manner and his storytelling companion, an energetic young physician. The late lamented Professor Moriarty might also have brought a case as regards this devil doctor. But the story itself is rather ingenious, and, apart from borrowing your unfortunate practice of leaving out the most important bit of information until the last, his debt to your published memoirs seems negligible. He sent me this inscribed advance copy along with his letter requesting my assistance."

I opened the book to the flyleaf and read: "To Sherlock Holmes, Esq., with admiration. Sax Rohmer."

"I never knew your head to be turned by flattery and a disingenuous gift," I said churlishly.

"Good Watson, it was the problem which turned my head. This old frame is far too brittle to support any further laurels. But here, I believe, is the gentleman himself. You nearly arrived upon the same train, and might have fought your duel on board."

Holmes opened the front door just as another automobile from town pulled away, greeted his visitor, and performed introductions. I was taken aback by the appearance of this straight, trim young fellow, whom I judged to be about thirty years of age; his acquiline features, keen gaze, and general air of self-possession reminded me uncannily of the eager young student of unidentified sciences who first shook my hand in the chemical laboratory at St. Bartholomew's Hospital, three decades and so many adventures ago. So close was the resemblance that I was startled into accepting his handshake. I had intended to be polite but cold and aloof.

"Dr. Watson," he said, "I'm quite as excited to make your acquaintance as I am of Mr. Holmes. You cannot know what an inspiration you have been to me; though you would in the unlikely event you were ever to read my work. I'm a shameless imitator."

This confession—the very last thing I had expected from him—left me with neither speech nor ammunition. I had been prepared to accuse him of that same transgression, and for him to deny having committed it. In one brief, pretty declaration he had managed to turn a contemptible deed into an act of veneration.

I was not, however, disposed to respond to guile. I said, "You might first have sought the opinion of the imitated, to determine whether the honour would be welcome."

He nodded, as if he were considering the matter. "I might have, and I should. I can only state in my defense that I thought you existed on far too lofty a plane to be approached by one of my youth and inexperience. Pray accept my apology, and I shall post the circumstances of my debt to you upon the front page of the *Times*."

This sentiment, and the obvious sincerity with which it was delivered, thoroughly unmasted me. For all his seeming repose, young Rohmer was clearly flummoxed by the celebrated company in which he found himself. This was evident both by his attitude and by his dress; his Norfolk and whipcords, although quite correct to his surroundings, were new almost to the point of gaucherie. He had dressed to please, and his efforts to ingratiate himself touched that which remained of the youth inside me. I told him no public abasement was necessary, and in so doing informed him he was forgiven.

Moments later we were sharing the divan, enjoying the whiskies-and-soda which Holmes had prepared, as carefully as his chemical experiments of old, and with considerably greater success than some. My friend—showing subtle signs of discomfort born of rheumatism—

had assumed his Indian pose of listening, with legs folded and hands steepled beneath his chin.

"Dr. Fu-Manchu, who is the antagonist of my little midnight crawler, is not entirely a creature of fiction," began Mr. Rohmer. "He is based upon a Chinese master criminal known only as 'Mr. King,' who was the principal supplier of opium to the Limehouse district of London at the time I was researching an article on the subject for a magazine. He was a shadowy figure, and though I heard his name whispered everywhere in Chinatown, I never laid eyes upon him until long after I had filed the story, when I chanced to glimpse him crossing the pavement from an automobile into a house. He was as tall and dignified a celestial as you are ever likely to meet, attired in a fur cap and a long overcoat with a fur collar, followed closely by a stunningly beautiful Arab girl wrapped in a grey fur cloak. The girl was a dusky angel, in the company of a man whose face I can only describe as the living embodiment of Satan.

"That, gentlemen," he concluded quietly, "is Dr. Fu-Manchu, as I have come to present him in writing and to picture him in my nightmares."

"Who was the girl?" I heard myself asking; and inwardly jeered at myself for harbouring the interests of a young rake in the body of a sixty-one-year-old retired professional man.

Rohmer, who like Holmes was a pipe smoker, shrugged in the midst of scooping tobacco from an old leather pouch into a crusty brier. "His mistress, perhaps, or merely a transient. In any case I never saw her again."

Holmes intervened. "I take it by that statement that you did see Mr. King subsequent to that occasion."

"Not according to the information I gave to my publicist, or for that matter anyone else, including my wife." He struck a match off his bootheel and puffed the pipe into an orange glow, meeting Holmes's gaze. "But, yes."

"And has he anything to do with the package which you have brought?"

"Again, the answer is yes." His eyes did not stray to the bundle he had placed atop the deal table where our host had once conducted his chemical researches, now a repository for the daily post. Mine, connected as they were to a curious mind, did. The item was roughly the size of a tea cake, wrapped in burlap and tied with a cord. My fingers itched for my old notebook.

"Mr. King is no slouch," said Rohmer, "and like Dr. Watson, recognised himself immediately when he read my description of Fu-Manchu. Beyond this fact, the opium lord and the good doctor have nothing in common. Vexed though he might have been by my little theft, I'm convinced that Dr. Watson would not stoop to kidnap me and threaten my life."

"Good Lord." I exclaimed. In my foolish complacency I had formed the fancy that such incidents had been left behind with the dead century.

Holmes's guest proceeded to exhibit his flair for narrative with a colourful but concise account of his recent adventure. While strolling the twisting streets of Limehouse in quest of literary inspiration, he had been seized and forced into a touring car by two dark-skinned brutes—Bedouins, he thought—in shaggy black beards and ill-fitting European dress, who conveyed him to that selfsame house before which he had first set eyes upon Mr. King. There, in a windowless room decorated only with an ancient Chinese tapestry upon one wall, he was left alone with that weird Satanic creature, attired in a plain yellow robe and mandarin's cap, who interviewed him from behind a homely oak desk about the source of his novel. In precise, unaccented English, Mr. King expressed particular interest in the character of Dr. Fu-Manchu, the wicked Chinese ascetic bent upon world domination by the East.

"He is a creature of my imagination," Rohmer insisted, for he intuited that to profess otherwise would seal his doom.

"Pray do not insult me," Mr. King replied evenly. "I am a law-abiding British resident. Import-export is my trade, and I have no wish to conquer this troubled planet. Beyond these things, your description of me is accurate in every detail. Was it your purpose to malign my character?"

"It was not."

"And yet I find myself incapable of doing business with gentlemen who placed absolute faith in my integrity before your canard appeared. If the situation continues I shall face ruin."

"I sympathise. However, I am not responsible for your sour fortune."

"Will you withdraw the book from circulation?"

"I will not. I am informed its sales are increasing."

Mr. King stroked his great brow. "May I at least extract your word that this ogre who resembles me will not be seen again once the novel is no longer in print?"

"You may not. I am writing a sequel."

"I could bring suit, of course. However, the courts take too long, and in the meantime I shall have no source of income. Shall I threaten you?"

"I rather wish you would. This conversation has become tedious."

At this point I laughed despite myself. Here was an Englishman! Rohmer continued without acknowledging the interruption.

Mr. King's devilish features assumed a saturnine arrangement, he informed us. "I am, as I said, respectful of your laws. This was not always the case. It is difficult for a Chinese to advance himself in business in this society; I was forced to take certain measures, the nature of which I shall not describe. I assume you are aware that if you were never to leave this house, your body would never be recovered?"

Rohmer confided to Holmes and me that he had not been so sanguine as he'd pretended. He knew the house stood before a dock, and that many a weighted corpse lay on the bottom of the Thames with little hope of recovery. The thought that his wife should never learn of his true fate very nearly unmanned him. Yet he held his tongue.

"I shall accept your silence as an affirmative response," said the Chinese. "However, I am not without reason, and I am in the way of a sporting man."

Hereupon he struck a miniature gong which stood upon the desk. It had scarcely finished reverberating when one of the villains who had abducted Rohmer, now draped in the burnoose and robes of the true Bedouin, entered through an opening hidden behind the tapestry, placed a singular object next to the gong, and withdrew.

"This bowl belonged to the Emperor Han, who ruled China from 206 until 220 A.D.," said Mr. King, lifting the ornate object. "It is solid gold. I lend it to you, in the certainty that a clever fellow such as you will succeed in unlocking its riddle. If in Thursday's *Times* I read the answer in the personal columns, the bowl shall be yours, with my compliments. If upon that day the late edition has come and gone and no such item has appeared, you will not live an hour more. You have seen how easily my subordinates may lay hands upon your person. I believe you know I speak the truth."

Rohmer concluded his tale at the moment he finished his pipe. He laid it in his lap to cool.

"I accepted the bowl, for what else could I do? Mr. King then used the gong to summon the Bedouins, both of whom were again costumed as Occidentals, and they returned me to the spot where they had first accosted me. I went home, and puzzled over the thing the night through. Then morning came and I was nowhere nearer the solution than I was yesterday evening, so I sent you the message which resulted in your kind invitation. Tomorrow is Thursday. Can you help me, Mr. Holmes? It is for my wife I am concerned. I've cost her many a sleepless hour with my rash wanderings. To leave her a widow at her tender age would be a mortal sin."

"Your Mr. King is transparent, and hardly inscrutable," said Holmes. "He fears attention and investigation more than the loss of legitimate business, if the résumé you supplied is reliable." He rubbed his hands in the way I remembered from long ago, signifying his eagerness to solve the problem which had been set before him—though he may merely have been massaging his joints. "You were correct to come to me rather than the police. Scotland Yard teems with fresh new faces, behind which churn the same old brains. Let us examine this wondrous bowl."

Rohmer stood, retrieved the bundle he had brought, and placed it in Holmes's hands. A twitch of the cord, and the sun came into the room in the form of a beautiful thing which glistened as if still molten. I rose and bent over my friend, that I might see what he saw at the moment he saw it. It seemed that even in my extremity I remained the same curious creature I had been when I was no older than young Rohmer.

The workmanship was exquisite. The bowl was just large enough to hold in two hands, so bright and gleaming it might have been just struck off. Around the outside of the rim paraded a row of playful monkeys in relief, no two of which wore the same expression, and each so lifelike as to seem poised to leap from its perch and gambol about that staid room. There were thirteen in all, some crouching, some reclining upon their backs, others in the attitude of stalking, rumps in the air and noses nearly touching the ground. One, of more mischievous mien than all the rest, hung from its tail, the tail curling well above the bowl's rim, and stared straight out with arms crossed and lips peeled back into a jeering grin, as though daring the casual handler to unlock the riddle of the golden monkeys.

"This is formidable craftsmanship." Holmes studied the outside, the inside, then turned it over and studied the bottom, which bore no mark. At length he proffered it to me. "What do you make of it, Watson? I confess chinoiserie is far from my long suit."

I hefted it. It weighed, I should have judged, nearly four pounds. "It is twenty-four karat, Holmes. I would stake my life upon it."

"Mr. Rohmer has already staked his. It seems scarcely large enough to support more than one." He took the bowl from me and charged his own pipe. "I commend to you both the sea air. Mind the bees. They are in a petulant humour this season."

I understood this to be a dismissal, and conducted the writer to the outdoors, where we strolled along the chalk cliff listening to the restless Channel coursing along the base. To our left, Holmes's bees swarmed about his city of hives, which reminded me so much of the mosques and minarets of Afghanistan.

"Mr. Holmes is older than I'd suspected," declared my companion. 'Your accounts paint such a youthful and energetic picture that I suppose I thought he was immune to dissipation. Do you think his mental powers sufficient to this challenge?"

"The crown jewels reside in an ancient structure," I replied. "They shine now as they have for four hundred years."

"That is true." He sounded unconvinced.

We spent the remainder of our outing discussing Egypt, which Rohmer was eager to visit, and which I had known intimately long before any tourist with the wherewithal could hire a camel and have his likeness struck before the Sphinx. We took our rest upon a marble bench while he bombarded me with questions. When after two hours we returned to the villa, I was quite drained and looking forward to a whisky-and-soda and silence; the latter a requisite during Holmes's deliberations.

Much to my surprise, we found him quite loquacious. He looked up with sparkling eyes through a veritable "London particular" of tobacco-smoke and bade us be seated. The floor about his feet was piled with books from his shelves, many of which were splayed open upon their spines or stood like tents on the carpet. I noted Lutz's *History of the Chinese Dynasties*, Walker's *Ancient Metalwork*, and Carroll's *World Primates* among the variety of titles. The wonderful golden bowl rested in his lap.

"Dr. Watson can attest that it is a long-held axiom of mine that one cannot make bricks without clay," Holmes informed Rohmer, who unlike me had declined an invitation to make free with the siphon and bottle. "I am to some degree an autodidact, and most of my education regarding arcane subjects has taken place in the pursuit of the solution to problems which at first appeared puerile. When we met, I astounded Watson with the announcement that I was unaware of Copernicus or his theories; however, I have since qualified as an expert. At the end of two hours, the lost-wax process is not lost to me. Similarly, I may converse with some authority upon the Emperor Han's propensity towards painful boils, the origin of the Troy ounce, and some indelicacies in the matter of the posteriors of certain species of gibbon. I am enormously wealthier for the time spent."

"But is my wife any less likely to suffer bereavement?" Rohmer's tone was impatient. He had evidently concluded that Holmes's remarkable mind had commenced to wander. It shames me to confess that I harboured similar doubts. Stapleton and his cursed hound had been mouldering now for a quarter-century, and time was scarcely more kind to the faculties of reason.

"That I cannot say," Holmes declared.

Rohmer's face fell.

"The future is a closed book, even to me," continued the retired detective. "For all I am aware, your driver may become distracted on the way back to Newhaven and precipitate you both over the cliff. However, assuming that your Mr. King is a man of his word, Mrs. Rohmer will not grieve because the golden monkeys have refused to give up their secret. The riddle is solved."

The young are easily read. I saw hope and relief and a dark shadow of doubt upon his face. He leaned forwards to hear Holmes's explanation, Holmes leaned forwards to provide it. Those two hawklike profiles in such close proximity gave me the fancy that Rohmer was gazing into a somewhat clouded mirror.

"I call your attention once again to the graven figures. Does anything about them strike you as remarkable?"

Rohmer accepted the return of the golden bowl and rotated it slowly, scowling in deep concentration. "They are exceptionally lifelike. To think that the Chinese were executing such things when we English were living in mud huts makes one wonder why they do not already rule the world."

"Just so. However, that is material for another conversation, one which will almost certainly not involve this particular piece." Having made this cryptic pronouncement, Holmes plunged ahead without pause. "I direct your young eyes towards the monkeys themselves. Does any one of them stand out from the crowd?"

"The one with its arms folded has claimed my attention since the beginning. Cheeky little fellow, this. He seems just this side of thrusting out his tongue."

"Devilishly clever, these Chinese," said Holmes. "It could be a diversionary tactic to lure the casual observer away from something more informative. Not in this case, however. What do you know of monkeys?"

His guest sought his answer in the ceiling. "According to Professor Darwin, they are related to you and me, and the Americans are of the opinion that they are quite amusing by the barrel. I know a bit more about marmosets, but none is represented here. I'm afraid that's the sum total of my knowledge as regards the species."

"Perhaps you will find Mr. Carroll of assistance." Holmes scooped up *World Primates* from the floor and presented it with his thumb marking the place to which it had lain open. "I would direct your eye to the passage I have underlined."

Rohmer carefully laid the precious bowl beside him on the divan and accepted the book. He read aloud, "'Monkeys occupy two separate and distinct groups, one native to the Old World, the other to the New, in particular Central and South America. Old World monkeys are characterised by their narrow probosci, and are referred to as Catarrhine; none possesses a prehensile tail. Their American cousins are recognised by their flat probosci, and these are designated Playtyrrhine; their tails are prehensile.'"

The young man closed the hook, picked up the bowl once again, and studied each of the golden monkeys in turn. "All the noses appear similar. I believe they are flat, but lacking the other variety for purposes of comparison, I cannot say definitely. How narrow is narrow?"

"A valid observation. As Aristotle said, one requires a place to stand. Disregard, then, the question of monkeys' noses. What do you make of this business of tails?"

"Merely that Old World monkeys are incapable of swinging or hanging by them, while those from the New . . . " Rohmer's voice trailed off. He was staring at the insolent primate with arms folded and tail curled over the lip of the bowl. "Great heavens! And I presume to call myself an Orientalist."

"It is a broad subject. No one man can claim to know it in its entirety. The Chinese were among the first to discover the African continent and to study its flora and fauna. They were privileged to incorporate African motifs into their art. However, for all its advances, even that estimable society could not, in the third century A.D., posit a monkey hanging by its tail twelve hundred years before the discovery of the one continent whose simian population was thus capable. The bowl is a forgery. There is the answer to your riddle."

"Great heavens!" I exclaimed, at the moment unaware that I had echoed Rohmer's words.

Holmes's guest presented a study in conflicting emotions: relief, wonder, and disappointment paraded across his face in a variety nearly as rich as that provided by the thirteen golden monkeys. "When did you suspect?" he asked.

"At the moment the bowl appeared in your narrative. It did not seem likely that Mr. King would threaten you in one breath and in the next offer you an item so tantalising without some promise of benefit to himself. The same rules that govern legitimate commerce also apply to the *demimonde.*

"The crucial factor was the character of the enemy," Holmes continued. "It was not enough to this fellow that you should fear for your life; should you manage to uncover the secret, the solution itself must rob your triumph of its savour. Remember that Mr. King represents a culture that has had two thousand years to refine the punishment of torture. Armed with that intelligence, I proceeded on the assumption that the bowl was counterfeit. Any reputable dealer in antiquities could have done the rest."

"Then the thing is worthless." Rchner gazed disconsolately at the object in his hands.

"Not quite," said Holmes. "Although I should be much surprised if at the point of a pen you should not discover base lead beneath the gold plate. The workmanship is still a thing of beauty. A London pawn-broker might be persuaded to part with ten pounds in order to display it in his shop window."

"Still, I have been cheated. That fraudulent old devil led me to believe I would own something of real value."

"Oh, but you do. He has given you the gift of your life."

Somewhere in the villa a clock chimed the hour. Holmes stirred. "There is a telephone in the hall, which you may use to order an auto to return you to the station. You should have substantial time to place an advertisement announcing the riddle's solution in tomorrow's *Times*."

Sax Rohmer regarded Sherlock Holmes with an expression I had seen many times upon many faces. "You are still the best detective in England."

"Thank you." Holmes closed his eyes, displaying for the first time the weariness which his feat of brilliance had created; he was, when all was said and done, a man in the sixtieth year of an adventurous life suffi-cient for ten of his contemporaries. "One never tires of hearing it."

The Adventure
of the Curious Canary

Barry Day

"**T**ELL ME, HOLMES, do you believe there is any such thing as
the perfect crime?"

We were sitting in our rooms in 221B at a very loose end indeed.
As an indication of the depth of his boredom, the world's most famous
consulting detective was reduced to turning the detritus of the morning's newspapers into paper darts and launching them into the fire
Mrs. Hudson had lit earlier in that morning to ward off autumn's first
chill. More than once I had had reason to fear my friend's somewhat
uncertain aim would end in a conflagration which would be recorded
in the next day's equivalents—"HOLMES AND FRIEND PERISH IN MYSTERY
BLAZE—ARSON SUSPECTED."

When I had almost forgotten the question—which had been asked
more for something to fill the silence than anything else—Holmes
finally answered.

"I am inclined to believe, Watson, that the only crimes that
remain unsolved are the ones that have not been called to my
attention."

As I glanced in his direction, I saw the small twitch of irony catch
the corner of his mouth. It was an expression one had to be quick
to spot and interpret. The next moment the face had regained its

classically sculpted lines, something poised between Roman senator and an American Indian.

"I presume you are thinking of the icicle used as a dagger that subsequently melts?" he continued.

"Yes, or what about the case of the Barchester beekeeper who appeared to have been stung to death, until you proved that his wife had administered a fatal injection before dragging his body next to the hive and inciting the bees to attack. I should say that was a close run thing. If you hadn't been able to prove that the fellow was dead before the bees stung him, she'd have got away with it."

"A simple enough deduction for one versed in the kiss of the needle," Holmes replied, casting me a covert glance in expectation of a reaction. But I am too old a soldier to rise to such an obvious lure. Seeing that his ploy had failed, he continued. "And an insult to such a sophisticated species. One of these days I fully intend to . . ." But then another thought seemed to strike him.

"But, my dear chap, I confess I'm surprised you have failed to mention the infamous Anitnegra Affair—a story for which, like the Giant Rat of Sumatra, I suspect the world is not yet prepared."

"The Anitnegra Affair?" I exclaimed, "But I don't believe you have ever . . ."

"Oh, my dear fellow, how remiss of me. Do forgive me. It must have occurred during one of your many marital sabbaticals. I do declare, now that I think about it, that it comes very close to your definition of the perfect crime."

"Pray tell me the details," I said, reaching for the pad that was never far from my hand, ready for just such a recollection in tranquility.

"It was the rather sordid story of a purveyor of imported meats who became jealous of his partner. One evening in the warehouse there was a passionate altercation and the wretched fellow struck and killed his partner with a frozen steak, which he then proceeded to cook and eat—thus effectively destroying the evidence."

"But, Holmes, how was he brought to justice?"

"Oh, that was simple enough," my friend replied. "The man literally signed his crime. There was a livid mark on the corpse's head which read 'ANITNEGRA.'"

"ANITNEGRA? You mean that was the murderer's name?"

"Oh, no. ANITNEGRA is simply ARGENTINA spelt backwards. The meat had been stamped in its country of origin and had, so to speak, left its mark."

"And that was enough to convict him?"

"There was no need to convict him. The meat happened to be spoiled and the murderer died of food poisoning—along with twenty-three other innocent people. It was one of my least distinguished cases and caused me to give up red meat for at least a week. . . . Oh, my dear fellow, I do wish you could see your face!"

And the wretched man sank back into his chair and gave way to a paroxysm of that silent laughter that has often brought me close to throwing something at him.

It was at that very moment that the doorbell clanged that insistent call to arms that had heralded so many of our adventures. Only some time later did it occur to me that it was impossible for the imprint to have read ANITNEGRA anyway, since the letters E, G and R would have been reversed—but by that time it was too late to go over the whole wretched story again. Holmes was a leading actor with his timing, whereas I was merely a spear carrier.

Nonetheless, I was in the process of planning the form of my retribution when Mrs. Hudson knocked on the door and ushered in a slim, neatly dressed woman somewhere in her mid-thirties. Handsome rather than classically beautiful to my eye, and as Holmes often asserts, "The fair sex is your department, Watson," I consider myself a fair judge.

She was clearly nervous, as many of our first time visitors are, but Holmes is adept at putting women at their ease when he chooses to, solicitous and soft of voice, and it was not long before he had her sitting comfortably in the visitors' chair opposite. I took up my accustomed place in a chair slightly to one side and behind Holmes, my pad ready on my knee.

"Pray do not concern yourself on at least one score, dear lady. You have plenty of time before your return to Lewes."

"But how . . . ?"

"A simple enough deduction, in all conscience. You are clutching tightly a rolled up newspaper of which the letters EWE are visible in the banner. The typography is that used by *The Lewes Examiner* and, while that publication enjoys a wide circulation in its part of Sussex, it is only available in the town itself at the time of day you must have caught the train that brought you here so early. Thus you have come here from Lewes.

"If one needed further corroboration, it is to be found in the numbers you have scribbled on the paper as an aide-memoire. To be sure 1415 could refer to the Battle of Agincourt but I suspect the terse prose of Mr. Bradshaw . . . Watson, would you be so kind?"

I reached to the shelf behind me and passed Holmes that well-thumbed red volume, which he proceeded to flick through with practised fingers.

"Ah, yes—here we are. Fourteen-fifteen London to Brighton, stopping at all stations, including Lewes. It was the first local train you felt you could be sure of catching after you had completed your business here. And by the way, Watson, I see those idle fellows are still engaged in their road works outside Victoria. The young lady has some of their sand on the instep of her shoe."

"Mr. Holmes, everything they say about you is true—you are a wizard." Then, as she reached down somewhat self-consciously to brush the offending sand away, she looked up at him with an expression both fascinated and a little frightened. It was one I was well used to.

"What else do you know about me?"

"Other than that you shop frugally at Gorringe's, are an excellent seamstress, are slightly astigmatic, have a Persian kitten of which you are very fond—and have been crying lately, I know practically nothing. Oh, except that you are a widow and expect to remarry in the near future. . . ."

The young lady's mouth literally dropped open. At which Holmes added—"Oh, and you appear to have no need for the service of a dental surgeon." This last made her laugh aloud and, as Holmes and I joined in, the social ice was effectively broken.

Holmes leaned forward in his chair and I have no doubt there was a distinct twinkle in those deep-set eyes. My department, indeed!

"My little parlour tricks are obvious enough, once explained, Miss—?"

"Lucas—Mary Lucas."

"As Watson knows, they are based on the observation of trifles where one may learn more from a lady's glove or the crease in a man's trouser than from a volume of an encyclopaedia. Take your own. They are obviously new, so much so that in your hurry to get here this morning you did not stay at the shop long enough for the sales assistant to take off the label properly. Only half has been removed, leaving the telltale GOR—. While clearly new, the gloves do not appear expensive and, in fact, were almost certainly a featured item in the shop's annual sale. Indeed, I seem to remember that rather distinctive design in an advertisement in today's *Chronicle*. The same can be said for your shoes."

Miss Lucas looked down at her feet, as though they had just betrayed her, while Holmes continued.

"I deduce that you are a seamstress of some accomplishment from the fact that, although your dress is of the latest style, the slight unevenness of the stitching in places tells me that it is not the work of the original designer. Therefore, you probably made it yourself—also from a Gorringe's pattern, I suspect. Your astigmatism is obvious enough from the two small indentations on either side of your nose, which indicate the use of reading glasses. Once again, they would not be deemed suitable for a visit where you wished to impress on first acquaintance. The Persian kitten? When a lady embraces one of that particular breed—particularly on a regular basis—any item of her clothing will bear some evidence that even regular brushing will never quite eliminate. The colour of the hairs is quite distinctive and since the length is unusually short, it argues for either a very small specimen or—more probably—a kitten."

My friend's last remark produced a rather disconcerting reaction from our visitor. "Oh, Mr. Holmes, what I'd have done without Princess these last few days I cannot imagine . . ."

And Miss Mary Lucas burst into a flood of tears, which caused her to pull a rather crumpled lace handkerchief from the sleeve of her gown and press it to her eyes. As I moved over to give her what comfort I could, Holmes's eyes met mine in an expression that said "Q.E.D."

Then a sudden thought struck her.

"But how did you know about my being a widow and . . . ?"

"The ring finger of your left hand bears the unmistakable mark of a wedding band having been there for some considerable time. You now wear it on your right hand and involuntarily turn it around from time to time. It seems a reasonable assumption, then, that you are no longer married to your first husband but that the idea of marriage is by no means repugnant to you and is presently very much on your mind.

"Now, Miss Lucas, the sooner you tell us of the problem that has brought you here, the sooner we may be able to assist you. You may speak before my friend and associate, Dr. Watson, here with the utmost frankness. Few of my cases would be solved without his invaluable assistance"—and he made a grave nod in my direction, which pleased me greatly—"and none of them would be adequately recorded, were it not for his Boswellian qualities of rapportage.

"Tell us your story in your own words and, I pray you, omit no detail, no matter how insignificant it may appear. It is those details that invariably point the finger of truth." And he settled back in his chair, his lean fingers steepled before his face and his gaze fixed at some indeterminate point on the ceiling.

"Well, Mr. Holmes—Dr. Watson—there really was little to tell until a few weeks ago. I live—as you divined—not far from Lewes where I am housekeeper to Sir Giles Halliford at Halliford Hall. My dear husband died a few years ago quite unexpectedly, leaving me in very straitened financial circumstances. Some family friends were kind enough to recommend me to Sir Giles whose old housekeeper was about to retire after many years of service. I was offered the post and the arrangement has worked out to our mutual satisfaction. He is what one might call a confirmed old bachelor. . . ."

"Sensible fellow," Holmes interrupted, then, not wishing to interrupt her flow, apologetically motioned her to continue.

". . . but underneath a gruff exterior which he puts up to keep the world at bay, he is the kindest and gentlest of men. Over the years we have discovered we have many interests in common and have grown comfortable in each other's company. To cut a long story short, Mr. Holmes, Sir Giles has asked me to become his wife . . . and I have accepted."

"But the problem does not lie there, I fancy?"

"Oh, indeed no. I should add, gentlemen, that this is of very recent occurrence and Sir Giles does not wish to announce our engagement until he has made certain family arrangements."

"But I thought you said Sir Giles was a bachelor?" I could not help interjecting.

"There is no immediate family as such," Miss Lucas continued. "He has a ward, a young lady called Emily Sommersby, not much younger than myself, who lives with him. She is the daughter of some old friends of his from his days in India. When they were killed in a climbing accident there some two years ago, he felt it was his duty to bring the girl back to England and give her a home."

"And how do the two of you get on?"

"To begin with everything was fine," Miss Lucas replied and her hand began to turn the ring around her finger, "but lately I seem to have sensed a change in her. Her manner has been more distant and if I may invoke a woman's intuition . . ."

"Indeed, I wish you would. How often have I not told Watson that a woman's impressions are frequently more valuable than the conclusion of an analytical reasoner."

"Well, then my sense of it is that she felt something in her guardian's behaviour that led her to suspect what he had in mind. . . ."

Looking at her I could not help but think that one woman might just as easily have detected that very same truth from the subtle but telltale conduct and tone of voice of another, but I kept that thought to myself.

Mary Lucas continued. "I am not even certain that she did not overhear the conversation between Sir Giles and myself the other evening, for she entered the room almost immediately afterwards. However, if that were all, I should not be here today taking your time. No, the real trouble began a few weeks ago when a young man arrived out of the blue claiming to be his nephew, Robert . . ."

"When you say 'claiming'?" Holmes interjected.

"Sir Giles had a younger brother who—he told me—had left home under something of a cloud. They had completely lost touch and he had no idea whether his brother had issue or not. It would take a long and costly legal search to ascertain the truth of his 'nephew's' claim—a search, incidentally, which he is about to put in hand."

"I take it that he did not warm to the young man?"

"Quite the opposite. His reaction was almost chemical. There was something about 'Robert Halliford'—for that is the only way I can think of him—that he distrusted on sight. Despite that, he felt obliged to give him board and lodging until the situation could be clarified.

As for Robert, he acted as though he expected to have the fatted calf killed daily on his behalf, which only made matters worse, of course."

"Presumably the young 'Mr. Halliford' was able to provide some sort of credentials?"

"Not entirely. He claimed his effects had yet to arrive—they had been delayed at sea, he claimed—but he certainly knew a great deal about the family and Sir Giles in particular."

"And what had he to say about himself?"

"Not a great deal, now you come to mention it. He seemed to have worked in various parts of the Far East and most recently in India, which is where he learned of Sir Giles's whereabouts. I once asked him about his profession and he answered something about having knocked about doing a bit of this and a bit of that. I didn't like to press the point."

Holmes nodded thoughtfully. Then after a moment he said, "Did you notice his hands?"

Miss Lucas looked surprised, then furrowed her brow, as if conjuring up a vision of the man in question.

"Yes, they were strong hands. Not those of a gentleman. He had earned his living by them, now that I come to think of it. Strange, but I'd never thought of it before. But why . . . ?"

"It is of no immediate matter. Simply that I like to build up a mental picture of someone before I meet them and Mr. Halliford the Younger seems to be a leading character in whatever play you are about to lay out for us. Oh, by the way, how did he and Miss Sommersby get on?"

Miss Lucas thought for a moment.

"To begin with they were very formal with one another. 'Miss Sommersby, Mr. Halliford' sort of thing. Then they appeared to become very friendly, laughing and joking together." She paused, as if recollecting something. "There was one small incident, though, I remember . . ."

Holmes leaned forward.

"Which was . . . ?"

"One day she called him 'Tommy' by mistake and he took it very badly. He told her she must be confusing him with one of her rich friends from the old days. Then he changed the subject and pretended he was only teasing her but one could see another side of him."

"Tell us something of life at Halliford Hall."

Clearly relieved to be back on familiar territory, Mary Lucas continued.

"It is rather a solitary life we lead—but then, that is one of the things we like most about it, the peace and predictability. Sir Giles is what, I suppose, one might call a creature of habit. Even though it is—or has been until recently—only Emily and himself, he insists on dressing for dinner. Then, when the ladies—or, in this case, lady, retires"—she smiled involuntarily at the solecism, and I could perfectly well see the womanly quality that had charmed an old bachelor's heart—"why then Giles would retire himself to the library on the ground floor to smoke his cigars, pass himself the vintage port and—I am perfectly sure—relive the good old days. It is a habit I shall encourage him to continue when we are . . ."

She broke off in some confusion and a blush rose from the collar of her dress. Collecting herself, she continued, "More than once he has fallen asleep in his chair by the fire and I have found him there the following morning. It is something neither of us ever refers to and, frankly, Mr. Holmes, what harm does it do? My only concern is that, since Giles"—I could not help but notice that the "Sir" had been forgotten—"is a chronic asthmatic, the morning chill might prove upsetting."

"And now that there is another man in the house, Robert does not join him after dinner?" Holmes raised an interrogative eyebrow.

"For the first evening or two he did, now that you come to mention it." She spoke reflectively, as if she were trying to conjure up the events from memory. "He would talk about the importance of male tradition and ritual and how the ranking officer—that's how he put it, 'ranking officer'—by which he meant Giles should be in a position to command the field of battle."

"Which meant?"

"Oh, he insisted that Giles's chair be moved next to the fireplace, so that he could survey the room and keep warm at the same time. He seemed most concerned that Giles should not sit in a draft."

"But I take it the smoking room battles did not last long?"

"Not for more than a day or two and then Giles made it perfectly clear that he preferred his own company. A Company of One, I think was how he put it. To make it even more obvious, when he went to the library, one could hear the key turn in the lock."

"So what was different about last night?"

"To begin with—nothing. Dinner was over and we had all said our good nights. I went to my room, played with Princess, and read for a while. Emily was in hers. Giles took himself off to the library as usual and Robert . . . I really don't know what Robert did in the evenings. He talked vaguely of some idea he was working on that would make him a fortune and I suppose he was working on that up in his room."

"Which was?"

"Next to mine in the west wing. I should explain that the house is far too big and many of the rooms, though partly furnished, have been unoccupied for years.

"By the very nature of my duties I am an early riser, Mr. Holmes, and since I had slept but fitfully, I was up and about before it was even light. Something—call it a protective instinct, if you will—drew me to the library and it was then that I heard it. . . ."

"Heard what?" I said.

"A laboured rhythmic sound like someone was breathing as if their life depended on it. I've never heard a sound quite like it—unless it was the old bellows at the local smithy. And then—gentlemen, you're going to think me quite mad. I wouldn't have credited it myself except that Princess, who goes with me everywhere, heard it, too. She was almost out of control . . ."

"Heard what?" I repeated.

"I heard a bird twittering."

"A bird?"

"Yes, Doctor, I know it sounds absurd but that is what it sounded like."

"And then what did you do?" This from Holmes, who was now leaning forward as if to snatch the words from her lips.

"I'm afraid my protective instincts overcame my professional discretion. I feared for Giles and, since I carry a set of keys to all the rooms, I ignored his instructions and invaded the sanctum sanctorum. It was as well I did, I can tell you, Mr. Holmes. He was slumped in his chair, fighting for breath, and scarcely seemed to know where he was. It was as much as I could do to get him out of there and into the hallway. Luckily, as soon as I did, I found Emily there. She had heard noises and come to see what was amiss."

"And Master Robert?"

"Oh, he appeared a moment later at the top of the stairs, saw what was happening and came down to help us get Giles to his room."

"Did you examine the library subsequently?"

"Certainly, but there was nothing misplaced. Giles's chair was where it always was—by the fire—and nothing else appeared to have been moved. Oh, there was one rather strange thing. There was an unusual smell in the room that I cannot recollect noticing there before. . .."

"Can you describe it?"

"It was sweet, pungent—almost like incense, Mr. Holmes. But once I had opened the windows, it soon vanished.

"Mr. Holmes, I realise I may be bothering you unnecessarily. After all, nothing actually happened. All I can tell you is that there was something unbearably evil in that room this morning and I fear for Giles's life. What should I do?"

Holmes appeared to be examining his tented fingers and to address his remarks more to me than to Mary Lucas.

"The case most definitely has certain points of interest and I believe you are right in your sense of something being very wrong at Halliford Hall. My suggestion is that you return there forthwith. Try and act as though nothing untoward has occurred, particularly as far as Robert is concerned. Allow the evening to proceed as normal. Watson and I will arrive on the evening train and come to the house when everyone has gone to bed. Leave the front door on the latch, if you would be so kind. We will keep watch outside the room and see if we cannot determine the origin of these strange sounds and scents. Now, perhaps you will be good enough to draw a map of the ground floor for us . . . and you possess a spare key to the library? Excellent."

A few minutes later a still anxious but distinctly relieved Mary Lucas had dried her eyes, put on her gloves (having removed the offending label), and departed for the railway station.

"And what do you think of it all, Watson?" my friend asked, leaning back in his chair.

"For my money it's the nephew," I said. "Sees himself being cut out of the old man's inheritance; but how . . . ?"

"Yes, yes, Watson," Holmes interrupted impatiently. "Mr. Robert Halliford is clearly trying to secure what he thinks of as his—always supposing he is who he says he is—but, as you rightly ask, how? Not in this case, who—but how?

"This afternoon we shall make our pilgrimage to Lewes. Oh, and slip your service revolver into your pocket, would you, Watson? There's a good fellow. I always feel that Mr. Webley's No. 2 makes such a comfortable travelling companion. He can be so persuasive."

IN THE END WE reached Lewes with ample time to spare and were able to enjoy an evening stroll around the Sussex county town before keeping our rendezvous. I have always been partial to country air, but to Holmes there is something almost sinister about the great outdoors. Where I see air and space, he perceives isolation and the privacy to perform all manner of secret wickedness. "In the lowest part of a big city, Watson, there is always someone to hear the cry for help and perhaps even to provide it but here . . . If Miss Lucas lived here in this bustling little town, I would have less to fear for her than in some brick mausoleum even a few miles distant."

As dusk began to fall we hired a pony and trap and drove to the small group of houses that passed for Halliford village. Since one of them was inevitably the village pub, we were able to make ourselves popular by buying drinks for the regulars and steering them—no great feat—into local gossip. They were able to confirm most of the facts of Miss Lucas's narrative. The squire, as they referred to Sir Giles, was irascible but well liked, as befitted one of the "old uns." For the "young un" they had no time at all. "A bit above 'isself" was the general verdict. "It'll be a sad day for Halliford if that one gets to be squire," said an old man in the chimney corner.

"Have you noticed, old fellow, that one often learns as much from the locals as from the protagonists in a case?" said Holmes, as we returned to our corner table. "They frequently do not know what they know."

We whiled away the evening pleasantly enough in this fashion until, consulting his watch, Holmes finished his drink. "What do you say to a visit to the library now, Watson?"

Our entry to Halliford Hall passed off without incident. The heavy front door opened to the touch and as we passed through the silent marbled hallway, a dark figure glided up to us.

"Thank heavens you're here, gentlemen," Mary Lucas whispered. "Everyone is in their rooms, except Giles"—and she indicated the door of what we now knew to be the famous library. "But there was a dreadful row over dinner between Giles and Robert and it was as though Robert was already the master of the house, the way he talked to Giles. Something is in the air, I know it."

"My best advice to you, Miss Lucas, is to take yourself off to bed now. Watson and I will stand guard from the room opposite." A moment later her ghostly presence could be seen flitting up the wide central staircase and Holmes and I were alone in our vigil.

We have been obliged to stay awake through the small hours on more than one occasion in the past but truth to tell, I have never found it easy. The mind is an easy prey to idle fancies and every noise carries too many disturbing possibilities. The creak of an old house settling can be a footstep approaching one with evil intent and, of course, Miss Lucas's premonitions did not exactly help matters. My only consolation was the reassuring presence of my two old friends— Mr. Holmes and Mr. Webley.

From time to time one or other of us would tiptoe across the hall and listen at the door. Each time the result was the same. There was the crackling of the fire—a sound which gradually diminished as the night wore on—and a regular, rather congested breathing, presumably the result of Sir Giles's asthma.

Then at around five, when I happened to be listening, there was a sudden staccato sound, as though one last ember was stubbornly giving up the ghost. It was over in a moment. Half an hour or so later the wheezing began. By this time we were both at the door.

It was rhythmic but erratic. The noise would build up and then suddenly stop. A minute or so later it would start up again. I looked at Holmes and mouthed, "What?" but he raised a finger to his lips in warning.

Now the noise had stopped altogether as suddenly as it had started. We looked at one another and I could see indecision written on Holmes's face. A moment later it had been replaced by determination as a new sound from inside the room came to our ears.

It was the sound of a small bird chirruping.

"Come along, Watson," Holmes shouted, "there isn't a moment to lose. Fool that I am, we may already be too late!" The key was ready in his hand.

Without ceremony we burst into the room. Before I could take in any of the detail, something bright yellow and in movement caught my eye. Flying around the room, briefly perching here and there and singing its heart out, was a small yellow canary.

Seeing that there was no immediate possibility of catching the little fellow, I turned my attention to Holmes. He was bending over the figure of a man slumped in a club armchair next to the open fireplace. His face as he rose told me the entire story.

"We are too late, Watson. I blame myself for this."

I went over and examined the corpse. As Holmes had indicated, there was no sign of a pulse. Sir Giles's face was flushed and the pupils dilated. At a guess, I would say that he had been dead no more than a few minutes.

"Heart attack, I would imagine," I offered, "probably brought on by his asthma."

"That, I am sure, is precisely what the murderer would like us to think, Watson. In fact, I venture to suggest that an autopsy would reveal nothing other than that. Technically, yes, he died because his heart stopped beating. The question is—what stopped it?"

By this time he was on his hands and knees by the grate in that trufflehound position I knew so well. He was busily sifting through the still warm ashes.

"Murder? How can this be murder? No one entered or left the room or we would have seen them. And as you can see, the room is sealed as tight as a drum."

"Exactly so, my dear fellow, and that is precisely what the murderer was counting on. Ah, Miss Lucas. I'm afraid we have failed you signally in your hour of need. You have my humblest apologies. . . ." Mary Lucas stood in the doorway. Behind her was a dark, rather plain young woman, presumably Emily Sommersby, whose eyes never left the housekeeper for an instant.

"I grossly underestimated the urgency of the situation. I confess I did not take your concerns seriously enough—or rather, I failed to appreciate the sense of urgency motivating the other party . . . or parties."

There was a pause before the significance of Holmes's words sank in and then Mary was clutching the frame of the door to prevent herself from falling. I went across and with Miss Sommersby's assistance helped her to a chair. I thought I saw the other woman flinch at Holmes's final words.

"Tell me it was a quick death, Mr. Holmes, and that he felt no pain. He was fond of joking that, as an old soldier, he didn't expect to die but only to fade away—preferably in his favourite chair with a glass of something by his side. At least he had that. But, oh!" And then she gave way to her grief.

As she spoke, Holmes continued to prowl around the periphery of the room. When he came to the large double French windows, he paused and ran his fingers around the frame.

"Come and take a look at this, old fellow."

As I joined him, I could see that attached to the original wooden frame was an additional construction of wood and metal which appeared to act as an extra seal.

"Oh, Mr. Holmes," a tearful Mary Lucas said, clearly relieved to have something to distract her, "that was Robert's idea. Giles had been complaining about the 'infernal draft,' as he put it, and Robert said 'Don't you worry about that. I'll take care of everything.' And he did the job himself only a day or two ago. I don't think a professional could have made a better job of it."

As she spoke, a glint of metal caught my eye. Some small object had fallen to the floor and been hidden by the heavy curtains Holmes had disarranged in his inspection. I bent down and retrieved it.

"Good heavens, Holmes," I heard myself exclaim, "I haven't seen one of these since my Army days."

In the palm of my hand lay a small multipurpose spannerlike tool that had seen a good deal of wear. Partly worn away was an engraving which I tried to decipher.

"The property of Her Majesty's Royal Engineers, I think you'll find, Watson." Holmes spoke so that only I could hear. "I believe we have found the previous occupation of the would-be Young Master."

"Of course, that would account for the 'ranking officer' talk. Old habits die hard. Why, I know myself . . ."

"And does it not strike you as odd that at a moment like this the young man who is so very caring of his elders is noticeable by his absence?"

"You're right, Holmes. Why don't I go and . . . ?"

At that moment a sudden flash of yellow distracted us once more.

The canary, which had been perched on a high bookshelf and eyeing our doings beadily, now swooped down and landed on Miss Sommersby's shoulder. She reached up and patted it in an abstracted fashion.

Holmes continued as though nothing had occurred. "Yes, indeed, Miss Lucas—leaving a totally sealed environment. Would you be kind enough to come over here to the fireplace, please? Watson, perhaps you will assist her?" With obvious nervousness she did so. "Do you notice any unusual smell?"

She wrinkled her nose and frowned. "Well, now that you mention it, I do—just as I have for the last couple of days. A sort of sweet, sickly smell. I must have a word with our coal merchant."

"I don't think that will be necessary," Holmes said gently. "The source comes from somewhere a good deal south of Sussex. Now, since I presume you are the one to lay and clear the fire, what do you make of this?" And he opened a hand to reveal the results of his researches in the grate. On his palm was a small pile of what looked like grit.

She looked at it for a moment, then took a pinch of it between her finger and thumb.

"That's strange. I noticed the same stuff yesterday morning and that was the first time I'd seen it. If I didn't know any better, I'd say it looked like—bird seed. But how ever did a bird get in here?"

"Just what we are about to ascertain." Holmes carefully placed the pile of dust in an ashtray on a side table.

"You will, of course, have observed, Watson, that Sir Giles's chair is firmly bolted to the floor next to the fireplace. He would have been unable to change his position, had he wished to do so. Our indefatigable engineer at work again, I fancy. Miss Lucas, who occupies the room immediately above this one?"

"No one at present. As I told you, much of the house is unoccupied. But, Mr. Holmes, what do you think happened?"

"The foulest of foul play, dear lady. The locus invariably speaks for itself and this one shrieks its own story. Had I been here to listen to it twenty-four hours earlier, I could have prevented this tragic dénouement. As it is, the events of last night are emerging with great clarity and only a few pieces remain to be put into place. But, as Watson knows, I refuse to hypothesize until I have all those pieces in my possession. Ladies, shall we?"

NOT SURPRISINGLY, THE upstairs room was considerably smaller than the library, but the configuration was clearly similar. Dominating one side of it was the brick extension of the chimney. Immediately opposite were a set of mullioned windows. The room itself was entirely bare of furniture and it was apparent that it did not normally benefit from Miss Lucas's domestic attentions, for there was a distinct layer of dust everywhere except the floor area immediately next to the chimney embrasure and the central window. There were signs visible even to my eye of considerable activity.

"As I told you, gentlemen, this room is unused and normally kept locked," Miss Lucas said, looking around it in some surprise. Holmes and I followed her inside, though I noticed Miss Sommersby lingered in the doorway.

"And yet the key turned in the lock with surprising ease," Holmes remarked, moving purposefully over to the chimney, where he proceeded to tap with his fingernail at the brickwork.

"Ah, as I thought." His long fingers prised away a section of the brickwork exposing the chimney opening. Producing a lens from his inside pocket, Holmes examined the top edge of the exposed bricks with great care, before handing the lens to me to verify his findings.

"I think you will find clear indications that the brick has been scratched by a metal link chain, Watson. There are minute shavings of new metal embedded in the old brick and here and here are clear imprints of where the links have rested. And now . . ."

And with that—in the catlike manner that he invariably adopted when he was hot on the trail—he darted over to the window.

"And yes—although the rest of the windows are firmly shut and warped with age, this one "—and he demonstrated by opening and closing it—"has clearly been used very recently. And here again the metallic scratches . . . Now, let me see, somewhere near the chimney we should find . . ."

He dropped disconcertingly to his hands and knees and peered closely at the floorboards near the chimney aperture. Then, seeming to find what he was looking for, he gave a satisfied grunt, pulled two envelopes from the jacket pocket which was their invariable resting place, and carefully brushed the twin heaps of dust he had accumulated into them.

"What do you have there, Mr. Holmes?" It was Miss Lucas, riveted as anyone must be watching Holmes at work for the first time.

"The final pieces of our little puzzle, unless I am very much mistaken," Holmes replied. "Now, why don't we all repair to the morning room—I believe the local constabulary will require the library in due course—and I will attempt to explain the series of events."

"Don't you think I should ask Robert to join us?" Miss Lucas asked, looking around her as if she had suddenly mislaid him. "I don't know where he can be."

"I hardly think that would prove a very profitable request," Holmes replied, studying his watch. "I would estimate that Master Robert, realising that the game was up, and that a little bird would soon be telling us all we need to know, will have caught the—let me see—the 9:05 train to town. Watson, you might like to telephone our old friend Inspector Lestrade and ask him to have the gentleman in question met on his arrival. Main line stations can be so impersonal, especially to people who have been wandering the wild blue yonder and may even now be contemplating doing so again. Oh dear, Miss Sommersby appears to have fainted."

"IT WAS OBVIOUS that Robert Halliford had to find some means of disposing of Sir Giles that appeared to be entirely natural." Holmes was sitting in an armchair covered in colourful chintz—a far cry from the battered Baker Street equivalent. Mary Lucas and I were opposite him on a sofa with Miss Sommersby propped among cushions on another. We had moved to the conservatory to allow the local constabulary I had called earlier to do their routine work in the library.

"Sir Giles' asthma gave him the idea. That, together with the fact that he invariably fell asleep in his usual chair conveniently placed by the log fire. At Robert's insistence, by the way. After that—like all good ideas—it was simple enough.

"First, he had to make sure the room was completely insulated. It wasn't, strictly speaking, a locked room. For his purposes it was better—it was a completely sealed room.

"I would be prepared to wager a small amount that we shall find 'Master Robert' or 'Tommy'—or whatever his real name turns out to be—was cashiered from the Royal Engineers for conduct unbecoming—though I somehow doubt he was either an officer or a gentleman—and thrown on his own dubious devices.

"So here we have a trained engineer who is also familiar with the strange and exotic ways of the Far East—even as my friend Watson is . . ." And he gave me an ambiguous little smile. "Many's the time he has regaled me with stories of how his more rakish friends were inclined to experiment with the inhalation of—shall we say—somewhat outré substances. This particular potion crossed my path during some rather extensive researches into perfumes and their origins. It is a particularly potent derivative of a species of the coriander, known to have an hallucinogenic effect on certain subjects. Its odour is particularly distinctive.

"I think we may assume that the young man brought a quantity of it back with him in powdered form for his personal use. But then it occurred to him that here at Halliford Hall he might find another and more deadly use for it.

"What a strong young constitution might tolerate in moderation might have a very different effect when administered in excess to a man in Sir Giles's condition, sitting captive in an alcohol-induced slumber. Literally a sitting target. It was certainly worth the experiment."

"But, Mr. Holmes, why wasn't I overcome with the same fumes when I went into the room the next morning?" Miss Lucas cried.

"You were witness to what turned out to be a failed test, my dear Miss Lucas. Halliford wasn't entirely sure that his mechanism would prove effective and did not use enough of the powder on that first occasion to have the desired effect. What it did prove was that the insulation worked. None of the fumes escaped and when you entered the room, all you detected was a faint residual odour, almost like a perfume."

"But how had he introduced the powder when, as you say, there was no one else in the room?" I asked.

"Simple. He had waited until Sir Giles was safely asleep and the fire down to its ashes, then poured it down the chimney from the room above—probably using a rubber tube. Traces of it remain in the room above and can easily be analysed. The heat from the embers created the fumes and Sir Giles, being in such close proximity, was the unknowing recipient. The first night he survived. The second, unfortunately, he did not.

"Robert Halliford's principal problem," Holmes continued, "was to remove the evidence—the poisonous smoke. And this is where his engineer's training came into play. For such a man it was child's play to obtain a simple bellows pump and convert it, so that instead of pumping air out—it would suck it in. With a simple hose attachment he could hope to drain the heavier, fume-laden air back up the chimney."

"And out of the open window," I cried.

"Precisely, Watson. So the evidence literally vanished into thin air. We find an ailing old man dead in his favourite chair in a room where he had palpably been alone. Who would think to analyse the ashes from the dead fire?"

"The perfect murder, Holmes?" I asked almost innocently, only to be rewarded by what I can only describe as an old-fashioned look.

"But what about the canary?" This from Miss Lucas. Every eye turned to where the small yellow bird sat once again on Emily Sommersby's shoulder. She seemed to find its presence curiously comforting, for she was stroking it in an abstracted manner. Her eyes looked as though she, too, might be drugged. From the time we had first met her she had said not a word.

"Ah, yes, our little feathered friend. The unwitting accomplice who let him down badly. When the police drag the lake I noticed at the bottom of the garden—as I strongly suggest they do so without delay—they will undoubtedly find, in addition to the aforementioned and unpatented pumping device, a small bird cage. On the base, unless

I am very much mistaken you will undoubtedly find the legend 'T. WILSON BERMONDSEY.'"

"Wilson the notorious canary trainer?"

"The very same, old fellow. Remind me one day to recount the full story of our earlier encounter. Yes, friend Halliford had clearly remembered the traditional coal miner's device of taking a caged canary down into the mine to ensure that the air below ground was pure enough to breathe. Why a canary rather than any other species, I have not the faintest idea but a canary it was.

"Having purchased a number of them, no doubt, from the disreputable Wilson, he adapted the practice for his own purposes. Once the fumes had been pumped out of the room, he would lower the bird in its gilded cage down the chimney, leave it there for several minutes and then retrieve it. The bird's continued good health would be an indication that the room was now clear. Unfortunately for him, on this occasion he had neglected to fasten the door of the cage securely. Seizing the opportunity, his bird literally flew the nest and there was nothing Halliford could do about it.

"Incidentally, there was one other factor he overlooked . . ."

"Which was . . . ?"

"The best laid plans of mice and men should not include the canary. Anyone who has ever owned one will tell you that they insist on spilling their food with unconfined abandon. In lowering the cage Halliford was actually introducing alternative evidence."

"Ridiculous! The whole thing is ridiculous! You're making up a fairy tale!" Emily Sommersby was sitting up rigidly on the sofa, her face as white as parchment. These were the first words she had spoken. The bird fluttered around her head for a moment before settling again. It had never left her side from the moment she arrived at the scene of the crime.

"Ah, Miss Sommersby, I was wondering when we should hear from you." Holmes's voice had a flat and final tone that struck a chill even in that sunlit room.

As all eyes turned on her, he continued. "Fairy tales are designed to have happy endings. This one, I fear, will not. It seemed to me obvious that the soi-disant Robert Halliford must have an accomplice inside Halliford House, if he was to proceed with his plan without excessive risk of detection and you, I'm afraid, were the only candidate. I believe we shall find that you knew one another in India and perhaps had—shall we say?—some sort of 'understanding,' which was upset by your parents' death and his perpetual 'lack of funds.'

"Then circumstances—and Sir Giles's generosity—brought you back to England and landed you on your feet, as it seemed. Sir Giles was an old man and clearly ailing. Who else was there to inherit? But then you learned of his plan to remarry and instead of feeling happy that your benefactor had found a partner to brighten his last years, you felt cheated. Then, when you heard from your former lover of his own 'misfortune' in life, a sordid little plan began to take shape to destroy one of the people who had shown you kindness and defraud the other."

There was a gasp from Mary Lucas, who sat there ashen-faced.

"I suspect you were the one who actually poured the powder. Dust, my dear young lady, is a powerful medium and the shoe an equally fine expression of it. There were marks in the upstairs room of a man's footprint and also those of a woman of about your height. Since Miss Lucas has already told us that she is not in the habit of visiting the room in her professional capacity, it should prove a simple matter to make the necessary identification. Perhaps you have read my trifling monograph on *The Tracing of Footprints*—a seminal work? Ah, I see not."

Emily Sommersby was shrinking as far back in the sofa as she could and I felt fleetingly sorry for her, until I thought of the deed in which she had conspired. Holmes clearly shared the sentiment, for his voice was calmer when he resumed.

"I prefer to think that you had qualms when the theory turned to reality but your lover was determined. He could feel that the inheritance that would come to him one way or another. For with Sir Giles dead, who would spend further time and money on a legal search? He became the driving force and you, perforce, went along with it. For, after all, Master Robert had promised to marry you, had he not? It would have been a union to rival the Borgias. Who would have been next—Miss Lucas? Or would you have been content to dismiss her without benefit of reference?

"You were the one who handled the canary. When you entered the room, the bird clearly recognised you and came to you, as it was trained to do. In a very real sense, it identified the murderer. Watson, I do believe Miss Sommersby has fainted again. Would you be so kind . . . ?"

AN HOUR OR SO later we were on the train back to London. The local police had taken Emily Sommersby into custody and informed us that Robert Halliford had been apprehended as he stepped off the train at Victoria. Mary Lucas—her grief fighting with her gratitude— had thanked us with such simple dignity and grace that Holmes had exhibited signs of rare embarrassment.

"Mr. Holmes, I see now that some greater power must have intended that Sir Giles and I were not to be allowed a life together. Perhaps the differences between us were too great after all. All I know is that I am grateful for the few happy months we were given and more grateful to you than I can say for ensuring that his death will not go unavenged. He was a good man and so are you, Mr. Sherlock Holmes, and the world is a better place for your being in it."

As the train sped along, though, I could not forbear to ask my friend how she would manage.

"One thing the privileged classes understand, Watson, is the oblig-ation of privilege. Having committed himself to the lady in question and being aware of his own fragile mortality, I think we shall find that Sir Giles had already taken care to make adequate provision for her, without ever saying a word to her. No, my dear fellow, money will not be Miss Lucas's chief concern."

"And what will be?"

"Persuading the cat and the canary to live together in reasonable accord."

And with that he slumped in his opposite corner of the carriage and proceeded to brood over what he considered his relative failure. I offered him a penny for his thoughts.

"About all they are worth, old fellow. I was thinking about that damned bird."

"What about it?"

"I should have asked her for a more explicit description of its song. Had I been able to identify it sooner as a canary, the game would have been ours. Watson, remind me to prepare a small monograph on *Bird*

Song and Its Application to the Solving of Crime. It might prove quite invaluable."

Then a more pleasant thought struck him.

"We should be back in town just in time for lunch. What do you say to a decent steak at Simpson's-in-the-Strand?"

"It depends."

"On what, pray?"

"It depends on whether the steak has ANITNEGRA written on it. And by the way, Holmes, you do realise, don't you, that . . ."

BEFORE THE ADVENTURES

Lenore Carroll

Mr. H. Greenhough Smith   May 6, 1881
Editor, *The Strand Magazine*
Burleigh Street, The Strand,
London

Dear Mr. Greenhough Smith:

Many thanks for your kind letter. Your warm response to the story I submitted to your magazine is indeed heartening. I have had two short novels about my detective character published, one in *Beeton's* and one in *Lippincott's*. But they were met by only a very small response, and I feared this "scandalous" orphan might find no home. So I am delighted that you see a series of these stories, and am greatly encouraged to continue.

Let me assure you that the principal characters (aside from the detective and his friend) have no counterparts in real life to my knowledge. I created them by stitching together bits and pieces of real life into a patchwork fiction. I trust the results are seamless.

It is true, however, as you suggest, that there are actual people who inspired the story's protagonist and his narrator friend. And it is flattering for you to ask how I came to write these tales. I must confess that I, like my narrator, am a trained physician; and at one time I had no thought at all of ever becoming an author. I entered the Army Medical Department after receiving my degree, and eventually found myself in India as an Army surgeon. I had determined to make my career in Her Majesty's service, and had looked forward to making a good start.

My career was cut short, however, when I was gravely wounded during service in the Afghan war. And when I was invalided out of the Army, I found the rain-soaked greenery of my native island, for which I had longed heartily while residing in the brown desert, only aggravated the wounds I had sustained. An irony to add to the irony of a surgeon sent to heal being hurt in the fray. I had taken one Jezail bullet in the shoulder and another penetrated my leg at the fatal battle of Maiwand.

I began limping about despite the pain, as soon as I was able, thinking that improved circulation of blood to the region would aid its healing. At first I ventured in the immediate vicinity of the hotel where I had taken lodgings. As I regained my health, I roamed further afield to escape the dreary hotel. On the streets of the great Metropolis of London I found human beings of every description—prosperous businessmen, ladies of fashion, street Arabs, gin-sodden bawds, stevedores from the docks, Roman clergy like so many ring-necked blackbirds, well-dressed children accompanied by uniformed nannies. When my distress at having my career in India cut short got me in the dumps, I would take to the streets, learning each avenue, lane, and mews as I once learned the arteries of the body while studying medicine at the University of London. I learned the texture and humour of the city as I spent day after day stumping the streets, my stout cane in hand. I walked through drizzle and fog, some days from midmorning until the lamps were lighted at dusk.

My legs and eyes were well occupied and my self-prescribed cure worked very satisfactorily, but I cast about for some similarly healthy occupation for my brain. I am not a person of great imagination, nor am I prone to be in exceedingly high spirits or low, but when left with no occupation, memory returned again and again to the horror of battle. Over and over my thoughts recalled the heathen cries of the attackers, dust obscuring the charge, red blood soaking redcoats, pounding hooves, and the piteous cries of the wounded. I would not have escaped but for the action of my orderly, who threw me across a packhorse and brought me safely to the British lines.

Thus I revived my youthful habit of composing verse in my head. My Bohemian proclivities (which had nearly prevented my taking a degree) came to the surface in aid of my practicality. As I walked, I occupied my mind with rhyme, meter, form, and syntax. Nothing equals verse in its demands on the writer. After several hours I would return to my hotel and transcribe the lines into my journal, another therapeutic aid to maintaining sanity. I passed several months and regained my health to a large extent, although my shaken nerves would not bear disruptions or rows.

I continued to walk as if in the streets of my beloved London I would find direction for my future. I had neither kith nor kin in England and no money, my wastrel brother having squandered the little our father had left him. I needed to rouse myself to recommence the practice of medicine, or resign myself to a limited existence on half-pay. But when the weather turned cold and rain poured down daily, the soot-coloured fog seemed to penetrate even my lodgings. I would prop my bad leg on a cushioned chair and sink into a brown study. Although my wound did not prevent me from walking, it ached wearily at the change in the weather. The thoughts that filled those grey days in my rooms were of money—how could a surgeon on half-pay find the capital to buy a London practice? I had proceeded to Netley after taking my degree and went through the course prescribed for Army surgeons. To what use could I put that knowledge in London?

And what girl, or rather, woman, would ever condescend to share my life under these circumstances? What woman could look upon my wounds, though fading from scarlet to a politer pink, without repugnance? I was still in my twenties, and while I counted myself not bad looking in a sandy, freckled way with my imposing new mustache, I could not rely on charm or dash to carry my suit. Rather, common sense, respectability, and application were my virtues. I had no fear that my Bohemian penchant would interfere with married life. My mentor at university, Dr. Averill, described it a response to boredom. Loyalty and not so many brains as to be likely to get myself in trouble was his estimation of me.

It was on one of my rambles near the Thames that I made the acquaintance of Budger.

I was negotiating the cobblestones outside the saloon bar of the George & Dragon when my cane slipped on the muddy surface. My bad leg gave way when the unexpected weight of my body fell upon it. I lay on the stones for a moment to catch my breath and ensure no serious damage had been done. Before I could right myself, however, I felt a helping hand reach over my shoulder and help me up.

"This ain't Afghanistan, Doc," said a man's voice as he heaved me to my feet. I turned to thank him and beheld a minuscule Cockney, whose strength belied his size, a bowler tilted to a raffish angle and hands already back in his pockets.

"How did you know I was a doctor?" I asked.

"Are ye, now? Why a lucky guess, I'm certain." (I will not try to set down his Cockney dialect exactly. The transliteration is tedious for the writer and even more tiresome for the reader to decipher. I will try only to capture some slight indication of his colourful manner of speaking.)

I rummaged in my now-muddy trousers for a coin with which to reward him.

"No charge, Doc, glad to oblige."

"Would you do me the favour of sharing a pint with me?" I indicated the George which I had just quitted.

"Don't mind if I do," he replied, and took my elbow as if he feared I might come a cropper again. He steered me into the public bar and I ordered our pints. We introduced ourselves and he told me his name was Budger.

Again I asked, "How did you know I was a doctor? And that I had been in Afghanistan? Do you refer to everyone as Doc? Surely a lucky guess would not have been so accurate."

"To tell yer the truth, Doc, I *know* what I know, but damme if I can learn *how* I know it. Fer instance, take that man at the window table. He's a railroad worker, probably a ticket agent, who works at Waterloo. He's stopped in here for a pint afore he goes home. He's got to stop and pick up sothin' fer dinner and take it home to the missus."

I gaped in astonishment.

"Now it wouldn't do, would it, Doc, to disturb the man's privacy and ask if it was true, but we can follow him out and after he runs his errand, ask him for directions and say he looks like a ticket agent of our acquaintance from Waterloo. Are ye game, Doc?"

"Yes, certainly. But try to think of how you knew I was a physician."

"There's yer mustardy-colour complexion, if you'll fergive my mentionin' it. That says you've been in Hindia or Afghanistan or one of them places probably, most likely with the Army, as you don't have the look of the sugar merchant about you. More military-like in the way you walk, despite yer limp. Now if you was a gentleman, you would be exercising on horseback; if you was a foot soldier, you'd rather be drawn and quartered than walk. Since yer neither fish nor fowl, I'd taken you for an Army doctor. With yer limp and the faded look of yer skin I'd say yer were invalided out three month ago, give er take a week. 'Ows that?"

"That's remarkable!" I exclaimed. "You guessed within a week of how long I had been back."

"Well, now, I *can* study as to how I know these things," he said with a touch of surprised pride.

At that moment, the man arose from the window table and left the George. We followed him from a slight distance and, true to Budger's prophecy, saw him stop at a greengrocer and come out in a few minutes with a parcel. "He's getting on fer 'ome," said Budger after a few blocks. We picked up our pace and overtook him at the next corner.

"Pardon me, guv'nor," said Budger, in his engagingly cheeky manner. "Is this the way to Nelson Square?"

"Why no," our quarry responded. "You must go in the opposite direction to find it."

"Sir, you put me in mind of an agent I've boughten tickets off of," said Budger.

"That may be true," said our anonymous friend, "I have a cage at Waterloo, although I hope I shan't offend you if I say I do not recognize you."

"Notter tall, sir," said Budger, "and thankee for the directions." He winked as he rejoined me, pleased with his success. We waited until the ticket agent had turned down the street, then I besought Budger to explain his "lucky guess" this time.

"Well, got a whiff of him as we came in and he 'ad the smell of the coke they use for steam engines. If you spend much time at a train station, it gets into yer clothes and hair. There were a worn place on the front of his waistcoat where he must rub against the edge of the counter and red stamp-pad ink on his fingers from stamping the tickets." He cocked his head to see if I followed his drift. I nodded him to continue. "Then Waterloo was a guess. Victoria's on the other side of the river and if he lives hereabouts, why the George is halfway between it and where he's headed 'ome, and handy fer a nip. He was scowling at a piece of paper, probably a note from the missus. What should it be but sothin' he fergot she wants him to fetch and he ain't too happy, neither."

I gaped at him, astonished. Truly, he *knew* better than he could explain.

When weather permitted, I found myself drawn by curiosity to the George, where Budger could usually be found at midday for tiffin and a pint. He continued to announce his speculations on his fellow tipplers with surprising accuracy, occasionally winning a bet from doubting persons not yet familiar with his peculiar gift.

We became friends in a way. I sadly lack a firm sense of class consciousness. I frequently wonder who I am and who I presume to be, and to which class I would most familiarly fit. I am a physician by training and inclination, but the rigid restrictions of my time and place frequently weigh heavy on me. Often I wish for the camaraderie of the officers' mess, the openly sensuous women of the East who are not bound by convention, as exemplified by our beloved sovereign. Every woman I saw in London was encased in that cage of whalebone which symbolised these conventions. It was deemed necessary for beauty, but was nearly disastrous for muscle tone and adequate breathing (although it did aid some back disorders and those of posture). The frequency of fainting could probably be laid at the door of the corsets necessary for fashion.

Budger, with the delightful cheerfulness of his rank and class, was also a maverick, in his own way. He treated me like an old chum from the docks rather than as a proper professional man. My rather shabby though genteel clothes and penchant for unconventional experiences gave him leave to take what liberties he might.

Budger seemed always to have enough money to while away his afternoons at the George. If my powers of observation had been as acute as his, I would have made note of his coming and going there. He moved from his own table and talked briefly first to this man, then another. So expert was his sleight of hand, scarcely ever did I note money and information changing hands.

One brisk day as the winter sun endeavoured to pierce the yellow pall of fog that hung over Bankside where we strolled, I put it to him. "How," I asked, "do you make your living, Budger? Now tell me straight. We've known each other several months and I have yet to see you short of funds, yet you are daily at the George. No common labourer, office clerk, or delivery man could spend his time so freely. Tell me, what is it you do to support yourself?"

We had stopped and Budger gave me a sharp look from under the rim of his bowler. He was so short and I so tall that it was better to converse while sitting. He had once remarked as we strolled out of the George together that he looked like my pet that I was walking off the lead, so vast was the difference in our respective sizes. He did not answer at once, but turned his glance from me and began strolling again. "Well, Doc," he said at length, "I know there's no malice in yer intention, but it's for the best yer don't know too much. Wotcher don't know can't hurt ye, don't yer know."

"But surely you have some visible means of support," I remonstrated.

"Doc, ye must take this much and not worry me fer more: I'm in the way of being a private accountant. I hold money while my foolish friends bet, taking a percentage for my profit. I'm apt to run errands for solicitors and other toffs who don't wish to be seen digging for information for their cases among the low life. If a gentleman is looking for a coachman, likely I can find an out-of-work chap who'd fill the bill. I do a bit o' this and a bit o' that, and one way and another I make enough to stay ahead of me creditors. If you must, call me a private agent, but an agent of what, I couldn't say."

I mused over this information for a bit, and then commented, "You are putting to use your remarkable gifts of judging people."

"Coo! I guess I am," he replied in amazement. "I never thought of it like that, Doc. It must be good for sothin'."

We turned away from London Bridge and retraced our steps to the George, and after a bit I ventured, "It occurs to me that you could make yourself wealthy, putting this gift to great use."

"Wadder yer mean, Doc?"

"Why, you could go upon the musical comedy stage and astound the audience with your divinations, or, with a little backing, go into a business where your knowledge of human nature could be turned to profit."

"Aye, yer on the track, Doc. But there's sich a thing as telling people more than they want to hear, isn't there? A little bit of it now and again is fun, and people says 'How amazing!' and 'Wadder yer know!' But tell a man he'd 'ad a fight with his missus that morning, that he must have got dressed in a rush because his socks don't match, and his boots ain't been cleaned nor his hat brushed, and he won't thankee for it." We walked in silence for a bit as I slowly recognized the truth of what he had said, and then he continued: "Tell a lady she takes belladonna at night, laces her stays too tight because her figger ain't wot it uster be and uses powder to cover the circles under her eyes, and she won't thankee. Lucky you'll be if she doesn't throw a 'ysterical fit and pretend to faint. Add to that that she not only knows what a mattress is for but has enjoyed the time spent there, and she'll fall into a brain fever and take three month to recover. Too much o' the truth is frightenin' to folks."

"I fear you are correct, Budger, and my suggestion was ill-put. I was only trying to find recompense in measure equal to your gifts."

"I know that, Doc, and think the world o' ye fer it."

"I dare say you could have told me more about myself that first day you hauled me from the kerb, had you less diplomacy. Of course, I feel an open book to you now."

"Yes, Doc, I could. I could've told ye yer were in a bad way for occupation, and getting low on money."

"Really, now!"

"'Tis true, 'tisn't it?"

"Yes, I must admit you are accurate as usual. I do not like to burden my acquaintances with my own troubles, but rather to deal with my problems in private. I do not wish to appear a weeping sister to my friends," I replied, somewhat stiffly.

"Come offen it, Doc. Yer livin' on half-pay and there's not a situation in sight. Yer leg's 'most healed, as well as it ever will, and ye haven't had a woman since ye left Hindia."

I started to draw myself up and remonstrate with Budger for his liberties. But I knew in my heart that he read me accurately and that any objections on my part would only further prove his statement that people didn't want too much truth. "Alas, Budger, you are correct," I replied. "Now, pray tell me, what am I to do about my circumstances? And don't tell me any more about myself for the time; I've heard as much as I can bear."

"Doc, I can only indicate. It's yer life to lead and I'd like to give you a leg up, if I could. Yer going back to doctorin', I suppose?" He raised his voice to indicate there might be some doubt, but it was a statement of fact, not a question. Yes, I would return to work as a physician, by some means or another. But I told him that I lacked the capital at present to buy a practice in London, and hesitated to ask for a situation at a hospital where the staff physicians worked long days for little remuneration.

"Wotcher need is an old doc who's getting on in years and thinkin' about retiring. One who's got a good practice now, hasn't let it slip too much, and who's got a little put by for a rainy day."

I admitted that that was the kind of situation I should like to acquire.

"Then I'll keep me eyes peeled, won't I now?" he said.

"But now . . . where . . . can you . . . ?" I sputtered.

"Never you mind, Doc, just leave me at it," he said with a wink, and we parted company for the day.

Inclement weather kept me indoors for several days. When next I sought the George, I found Budger fairly bursting with excitement. After a hasty pint, he led me out and we repaired immediately to Harley Street.

"I think I've found ye a likely situation," he boasted, as we hurried along the street.

"Surely I could be counted on to know that all the best doctors reside in Harley Street," I answered with impatience.

"Just yer wait, Doc, and we'll see what we'll see, won't we now?"

Budger drew to a halt in front of a prosperous residence-*cum*-surgery. A brass plate with the name Morestone was reflecting the midday sun.

"There she is, Doc," he said proudly.

"There what is? Now, see here, Budger, what is this all about? Why drag me along here to see another doctor's prosperity? Have I not enough to plague me?"

"Now, now, Doctor, take it easy. First, I said to myself, we needs to find a older doc, one that'd take kindly to some assistance (that's you). So's I spent a little time hereabouts chattin' up the drivers and butlers and some of the prettiest parlourmaids in London. This bloke"—he indicated Morestone—"seems the likeliest prospect."

"But how do you know?" said I, ever the naïf where the machinations of Budger's mind were concerned.

"First, there's his steps. The stoops hereabouts was laid when the houses was built, but this one is more worn than many another. Tells me he does a thrivin' practice. He keeps a brougham and driver, three maids, a butler, a cook, a scullery maid, and a page, all just for him and his daughter, Mary. Not bad at all!"

"And just how did you learn all this, this . . . intelligence?"

"Same way I pick up stuff for the solicitor toffs. Hanging about, liftin' a few at the nearest pubs, keeping me eyes open and puttin' two an' two together. You know better'n I how I do it. You studied it; I just do it."

Lest he think me unappreciative of his efforts, I murmured, "Carry on."

"Morestone's got rheumatiz pritty bad. And he don't do much surgery no more, on account of his 'ands is all crippled up. His brain's as sharp as ever, but the old machine is wearin' out. He looks like a man who could use a rest, but he's probably giving a thought to his daughter, isn't he? He needs to stay active until she's taken care of, married or provided for, one way or another. . . . One more bit I found out, Doc," said Budger, his pale eyes dancing with secret amusement. "He put in some time as a Army surgeon when he was a young 'un. He might take a shine to ye."

I told Budger that I appreciated his efforts on my behalf, and despite his disappointment, I hurried away from Harley Street determined to forget his presumptuous arrangements for me.

However, my resolution did not withstand my curiosity. After a day or so, I began casual inquiries of my own and discovered Budger had made an excellent choice, by his lights. I repaired to the George and

apologized for my brusque treatment of him. He took it well and
allowed as how people didn't like to have their lives arranged for them
by an outsider. I did, however, have a question for him. Assuming I
decided the situation was desirable, how was I to go about ingratiat-
ing myself to Dr. Morestone? This put Budger at a loss, but he said to
leave it to him, he'd think of something, hadn't he always?

In the meantime, I arranged a proper introduction to Dr. Morestone through my former mentor, Dr. Averill. It was at a reception for
the new director of Lambeth Hospital, with the cream of London
medical society present. I doubt I impressed him very strongly as there
were many young doctors there, ready to make themselves agreeable
in hopes of future notice by their betters.

One morning as I sat over a cooling pot of breakfast tea, I received
a note from Budger. His writing was not educated, but the message
was clear: I was to meet him at Dr. Morestone's address in Harley
Street at 12:20 promptly.

I wondered what adventure was afoot as I dressed with more than
usual care.

I appeared at the corner at 12:15 and started toward the doctor's
address. Budger's bowler-topped head appeared from behind the
steps of the house opposite and he waved me back. I stopped at the
corner and looked around for a few minutes, wondering what Budger
wanted of me. I checked my watch, and found that the appointed
hour had arrived. I looked up as I slid it into my waistcoat pocket to
see Budger's arm motion me forward. As I started toward the address,
a young lady came down Morestone's steps and entered a brougham
which had been waiting, apparently for her. My brief glance had told
me the woman was comely and well dressed. I assumed her to be one
of Dr. Morestone's patients.

No sooner had the carriage pulled into the street that I noticed
Budger's signal again from the corner of my eye. I looked about me
wondering what I was supposed to do, when a boy with a handcart
darted in front of the brougham. The driver reined in the horses to
avoid collision and the horses shied. The urchin escaped, but a loud
noise from across the street alarmed the horses further and they
began galloping in my direction. The driver could not control them
and they were gaining speed as they approached me. I limped des-

perately toward the horses, grabbed the harness of the one nearest me, and pulled with all my weight. With the aid of the driver we stopped the animals and brought the brougham to a halt.

My next thought was for the lovely occupant. I pulled open the door and found her sitting bolt upright, her face pale and her hands gripping the seat so that the knuckles showed white from the strain. She took one look at me and her eyes slid up as she fainted. I hoped it was from the shock and not from my appearance. I propped her up in the seat and called to the driver that I was a doctor, that she had fainted, and that I wished to take her home. He answered that she was Miss Morestone and that she had just come from her residence. Rather than wait until he had turned the vehicle around, I swept her into my arms and carried her down the street to her father's house.

The door opened as I climbed the steps. A maid evidently had seen what had happened and was waiting for us. She showed me into a parlour, and I laid the still insensible Miss Morestone on a horsehair sofa. Her father hurried in, his stethoscope still dangling from his neck. He pushed me aside (I had been beside Miss Morestone, taking her pulse), and examined her himself. I sat on my heels and waited. He held smelling salts under her nose and presently she came around.

"Oh, Papa," she said, "The most dreadful thing happened!" She then looked about her and noticed that she was in her own parlour and that I was present. She gasped and said, "This gentleman rescued me when the horses bolted. How did I get home?"

"There, there, now, you've had a fright," the old physician replied. "You're safe and sound."

As if to prove his words, Miss Morestone sat upright and looked at me. "And you, sir, is it to you I owe my thanks?"

So abashed was I in the presence of her beauty, I merely nodded my head, not trusting myself to speak normally. I realized that I had held her in my arms in a moment of need, and would never again have that privilege.

"So I, too, have you to thank," said Dr. Morestone. He extended his hand and we rose (me helping him slightly) and shook. "Who are you, sir? And how did you happen to be in Harley Street today?"

"I, too, am a doctor, and was coming to meet a friend." In the excitement I had totally forgotten about Budger.

"In that case, perhaps we should not impose any further upon your time," he responded. But a glance from Miss Morestone told me that she did not wish me to depart.

"My friend had not arrived," I temporized, "so I am completely at your disposal."

Tea was ordered and the doctor took a few minutes from his surgery to make my acquaintance again. I mentioned that we had met, and at his urging told him a little about myself. He then left me with Miss Morestone. Our conversation was commonplace—weather, health, and the current debate in Parliament. If eyes could speak, mine would have poured out the entire sonnet series of Shakespeare, so smitten was I with Miss Morestone's charms. She seemed not immune to whatever charms I may have displayed. Before I left, I had secured an invitation to tea two days hence.

I scarcely remembered leaving and was halfway down the block on my way back to my lodgings when a familiar voice reached my ears. "Dropped yer stick, Doc." Budger! I had completely put him out of my mind. It was now over an hour past our appointed time!

"Oh, Budger, my friend! I have completely forgotten you in the excitement! Did you see me take the lady into Dr. Morestone's house? That was Miss Morestone, and a lovelier lady I have yet to meet. What were you doing by those steps? And what happened to the boy with the cart?"

Budger looked up at me quizzically and did not reply. Slowly the realization came over me! Budger had arranged my "heroic" rescue of Miss Morestone!

"Budger, did you have anything to do with what happened today?"

"Now, how could I have anything to do wif an Act of God, like an accident?" he said with a twinkle in his eye. I gave him a hard look and he gave me a cheeky grin and nothing more was said.

My visits to the George became more infrequent in the following weeks. I called on Miss Morestone as often as she would allow. I had progressed to dinner invitations and then to driving out with her (in her father's brougham, alas). The old doctor took to me, and my fondest wish was granted on the evening he took me into his private study.

"You wish to marry my daugher?" he asked bluntly.

"More than anything in the world," I replied.

"And what will you live on?"

"I receive half-pay from the Army and hope to find a suitable situation, perhaps with a hospital as a resident physician, so that I can support her."

"I see. What would you think of coming here as my assistant?"

My mouth fell open and I did not trust myself to reply.

"The hours would be easier and I could use some help," he continued. "If you're not completely an idiot, you should be able to take over my practice so I can retire in a few years and enjoy my grandchildren."

I could think of no suitable reply, but simply grabbed his arthritic hand and shook it until he winced. My problems were solved and my life better arranged than I had dared hope, and all thanks to Budger.

The ensuing months sped by. Miss Morestone and I were soon married, and I moved into the house in Harley Street. I began by taking overflow patients, and after a few months was seeing all but a few of his oldest patients, whom he reserved for himself for old time's sake. In a year, I could scarcely remember the trying time when I stamped the streets of London, wondering bleakly what the future would be.

I retained, however, my friendship with Budger. He had declined to be my best man, saying it would not be seemly, and I'm sure Mary was relieved when I sorrowfully told her his admittedly garish checked suit would not stand up with us. He did sit in a place of honour, grinning like a cat who swallowed a complete aviary of canaries, remembering his part in my happiness. We met almost weekly after that at the George for a pint and a "natter," as he put it. It felt good to escape my stuffy surgery and the busy round of patients for an hour or so. He continued to astound me with his gifts of acute observation. He, in turn, was fascinated by my tales of experiences in India. At his suggestion, I wrote some of them down and submitted them to the weekly magazines, but with little luck.

One afternoon, Budger asked what was sticking out of my coat pocket. It happened to be a story returned by an editor with polite regrets. He read it through slowly, then sat staring out of the windows of the George, lost in thought. "Wotcher need," he said at last, "is some interesting blokes in yer story. You've got the action right enough, but the people don't come through."

I was astonished that an unlettered Cockney would have the temerity to criticize my literary efforts, but as he continued I realized he had a good idea. I borrowed his stub of a pencil and made notes in the margins incorporating his suggestions. He added touches of behavior that illuminated the characters in a way I would never have thought of. I put aside my wounded pride as a neophyte author and revised the story along the lines he suggested. The tale was accepted, and I shared the modest payment with Budger when we met. As time went on, our weekly meetings were spent working on other stories I had written. We had a certain indifferent success, until one fateful day when Budger said: "We're too smart by half, I fancy."

"What do you mean, Budger?" I asked.

"Instead of bein' God and tellin' all there is to tell, have the derteck-tive tell 'em," he replied. I had observed that Budger had a goodly share of mother wit, and while he was unlettered, in the sense of formal education, he was not unread. "Why, folks don't want yer to be too subtle wif 'em, do they now?" he continued. I hadn't been aware that he knew the word.

"What do you mean?" I asked.

"Like sayin' the man who ruined the girls was handsome. People like their villains to look bad. And the dertecktive studying who done it—you gotter give the readers a little show-off stuff, show 'em how 'is mind works, so's they can see how 'e does it, not just spring the answer on the last page."

"Carry on. I think I see what you're getting at."

"Like that jewel thief. He collects art, he dresses well, and the ladies like him. When yer finds out he's the crook, yer disappointed. Better make him despicable in some way. Or the boxer in t'other story. You'n me know that the bigger the fellow, the gentler he is. A big bruiser knows his strength and isn't so apt to throw his weight around as some feisty little chump like me. In real life an ugly man can have a heart of gold, but it's confusing in a story, isn't it? But people expects the bad 'un ter be nasty and pushy.

"And take the lady in the story who lied about the jewels. We both know that people can lie without turnin' a hair, like the patients who come to yer surgery and don't tell you everything, but expects yer to cure 'em in spite of what they're holding back. Best let her give herself away a bit, or the end don't seem ter hang right."

I acknowledged the truth of that.

"In a story there's got ter be sothin' to give 'em away, so that yer reader feels good when the dertecktive solves the crime. Like me, I can't tell a body too much about hisself or he'll be up in arms and I'll never get anywhere. But give 'em a bit to attract their curiosity, and they're eating' outer my hand."

I nodded with increasing excitement.

"Can ye fathom my meaning, Doc?"

"That I can, Budger! Let me mull this over, and I'll bring you a story every editor in London will want to publish!"

True to my word, I returned in a fortnight with a new tale for Budger to look at. We altered some few lines together on my foolscap draft, then pronounced it finished. We drank a pint of mild to celebrate. "Doc, I think yer on the way to bein' a spellbinder." Better praise I never earned.

The story was accepted by *Beeton's Christmas Annual,* and it opened a new chapter in my life. It began with a brief description of the narrator, then picked up a character Budger and I had put together. He had polish and education and a different physical appearance, but he had Budger's gift of reading a person from slight clues. A show-off, but in an agreeable way with enough quirks of personality to be interesting. We created him without interest in money or women so as to be incorruptible. The narrator, who somewhat resembled myself, was self-effacing in the extreme and nearly colourless, but the protagonist achieved some popularity.

His first words were similar to the first I heard from Budger: "You have been in Afghanistan, I perceive."

"How on earth did you know that?" asks the narrator in astonishment, ever the naive but willing foil for the genius with whom fate had cast him.

It was all really elementary.

HOLMES AND WATSON, THE HEAD AND THE HEART

Philip A. Shreffler

I N ALL OF ENGLISH literature, there are few more celebrated
friendships than that between Sherlock Holmes and Dr. John H.
Watson—even if the two men sometimes seem to be diametric oppo-
sites. Over the years, due to frequent misreadings of the Holmes
adventures, and chiefly to a number of theatrical misinterpretations,
Watson has often mistakenly been seen as either a mere foil for
Holmes's brilliance or else as a complete bumbler. It's almost impossible, for example, to imagine how Basil Rathbone's famous Sherlock
Holmes in the old Universal films could have the slightest interest in
Nigel Bruce's huffing, moronic Dr. Watson, much less a true friendship. Yet this error-filled popular view fails to take into account the
many facets of Watson's character that demonstrate him to be not only
an intelligent and powerful storyteller (it is Watson, after all, who nar-
rates most of the Holmes tales), but also the perfect complement to
Holmes's more dynamic and eccentric personality. This is particularly
so in Watson's role as an emotional balance to Holmes's often cold scientific attitude.

Certainly on the simplest social level, Sherlock Holmes and Dr. Watson are well suited to one another. In few of the Holmes stories is there
real tension among members of different social classes; Holmes and
Watson, at any rate, seem to spring from the English middle class. The

social tension that does exist, however, is that between Official Man, usually represented by a police officer, and the unofficially creative and rational man who is, of course, Holmes. The tension, therefore, is between the conformist and the nonconformist—in Holmes's case, an outrageously unconventional bohemian. As Hugh Eames wrote in *Sleuths, Inc.* (Lippincott, 1978),

> Sherlock Holmes and his fellow problem solvers are restricted to criminal problems rather than problems in more respectable fields, because Poe [in his groundbreaking Dupin detective stories] placed originality in opposition to social control and, as he did so, created the archetypal problem solver, the genius who is smarter than the cops.

When Holmes and Watson meet in 1881, each looking to share a flat with another gentleman, Watson is able to adapt to Holmes's peculiarities because he has just returned from a rough-and-tumble life in the Afghan war: friendless, living on a small military pension, "free as the air," and "leading a comfortless, meaningless existence." In short, Watson, too, at this point is an unofficial man, representing no agency but himself. Apprised by Holmes of some of the detective's strange forms of behavior, Watson replies in kind, saying that he "keeps a bull pup," objects to "rows," gets up "at all sorts of ungodly hours," and is "extremely lazy." Elsewhere, Watson refers to his "natural Bohemianism of disposition."

So at the outset, the Holmes stories offer a unique unity of character: the bohemian Watson becomes the chronicler of the bohemian Holmes. But to carry these similarities too far would be to belie the special quality of their relationship. Watson possesses a set of solidly conventional British characteristics, as observed by Conan Doyle biographer Charles Higham (*The Adventures of Conan Doyle*, Norton, 1876):

> Watson was kindly, sensible, outwardly genial and composed. He enjoyed sea stories, and was only casual about studying medicine. He liked sport, and played Rugby and billiards expertly. . . . He had a kind of wild courage, and tended to be romantic and gullible. He was loyal, a patriot, faithful to his friends and wife.

> Self-effacing and considerate, though capable of being rash and
> head strong, he was the perfect Boswell for Holmes.

As accurate a listing of Watson's personality traits as this is, it's still
not the whole reason that the doctor is "the perfect Boswell for
Holmes." It does form, though, one of the most popular common per-
ceptions of Watson—that of a rather dull, conservative bulwark of the
British Empire, infinitely Holmes's intellectual inferior. And the image
is not much improved upon by Watson's own comments in "The
Adventure of the Creeping Man" about his relationship with Holmes:

> I was a whetstone for his mind. I stimulated him. He liked to think
> aloud in my presence. . . . If I irritated him by a certain method-
> ical slowness in my mentality, that irritation served only to make
> his own flame-like intuitions and impressions flash up the more
> vividly and swiftly. Such was my humble role in our alliance.

This is certainly a "self-effacing" enough statement, but it's hard to
see how this modest fellow with a "methodically slow mind" could ever
serve to stimulate Sherlock Holmes, or, for that matter, compose the
fifty-six short stories and four novels of the Holmes Canon with the
rare insight and perceptivity with which Watson is clearly gifted.

The solution to this dilemma does not lie in Watson's being a common man whose very lack of Holmes's intellectual abilities (a negative
quality) makes him a foil for Holmes. Instead, it lies in his psychological inclination toward the irrational (a positive quality in Watson)
that supplements Holmes's apparent cold reason. The result is that
the reader is presented with a coherent vision of a world carefully
balanced between the rigorous logic of the head and the passion of
the heart.

Nowhere in the Sherlockian Canon is this dichotomy clearer than
in those numerous remarks about Holmes's antipathy toward
women. In *The Sign of the Four,* in which Watson takes a wife for the first
time, and in which the doctor boasts of "an experience of women
which extends over many nations and three separate continents,"
Holmes comments, "Love is an emotional thing, and whatever is emotional is opposed to that true, cold reason which I place above all

things. I should never marry myself lest I bias my judgment." And he adds his darkly cynical assurance that "the most winning woman I ever knew was hanged for poisoning three children for their insurance money."

This last comment is typical of Holmes's rather perverse delight in needling Watson with unseemly statements and behavior. Here one thinks of Watson's shock when he learns that Holmes has beaten cadavers in a medical school to discover how long after death bruises may be produced, or later at Holmes's appearing in Baker Street after having strolled about London carrying a harpoon, and certainly of his casually inquiring as to whether Watson would care to partake in a few cubic centimeters of the detective's cocaine. Such occurrences surely seem to place Watson at the awkward disadvantage that Holmes so enjoys, and yet at the same time they betray Holmes's own emotion—his deriving pleasure at Watson's expense. So Holmes isn't as intractably emotionless as he pretends, and it is Watson's very emotionalism that often draws such behavior from Holmes.

Watson, though, does have his moments of cool logic. Again in *The Sign of the Four,* Holmes proclaims that "there is no great mystery in this matter," at which point he expounds his theory about the case. But upon Watson's raising a series of very sound objections to that theory, Holmes must pensively admit: "There are difficulties; there are certainly difficulties."

But just as we can't make Watson too much like Holmes, we can't pretend that Holmes is a seething cauldron of hidden emotion either. This has been a major difficulty with many Sherlock Holmes pastiches. In books such as Nicholas Meyer's *The Seven-Per-Cent Solution* (Dutton, 1974) and motion pictures such as *Murder by Decree,* there is a strong inclination to try to "humanize" Holmes by drawing from the caverns of his psyche an impossible progression of traumatic emotions. What this does is disrupt the balance between doctor and detective. In *The Seven-Per-Cent Solution,* Watson must become the rationalist in order to deal with Holmes's drug addiction, whereas in *Murder by Decree,* in which Holmes (played by Christopher Plummer) actually weeps big glycerine tears, poor James Mason's Watson has the look of a lost cocker spaniel precisely because Holmes the rationalist takes over Watson's emotional role as well.

As the subtle interplay of the Holmes-Watson relationship unfolds in the original Holmes stories, it becomes clear that even Holmes and Watson's professions relate to how their personalities dovetail. Sherlock Holmes is the rational man of science with an understated inclination toward the emotional; Dr. Watson acts principally as a romantic author who tends toward the world of science because of his moderately successful medical practice.

In fact, it is as the narrator and presumptive author of the Holmes stories that Watson puts his emotionalism to work, in the process revealing something of the great detective's thoughts and even his feelings. To refer to Watson merely as the chronicler of Holmes's cases is misleading, for it is Watson as author who *chooses* the details of his friend's life and career that he will use in his stories. If Watson's bent were simply toward a well-paced adventure yarn, he would not take the time that he does to enrich the tapestry of life at 221B Baker Street for his readers, by including those many private glimpses into the detective's home and his heart.

A classic example of the latter is Watson's quoting Holmes's mournful thoughts upon meeting Josiah Amberley in "The Adventure of the Retired Colourman": "Is not all life pathetic and futile? Is not his story a microcosm of the whole? We reach. We grasp. And what is left in our hands at the end? A shadow. Or worse than a shadow—misery." There are many other moments in Watson's tales during which Holmes is caught by the doctor with a chink in his rational armor, and it's Watson's sensitivity that reveals them to the reader.

Watson, therefore, exercises his options in constructing a narrative that is balanced. He is not, heaven forbid, greedily trying to find weaknesses in Holmes in order to expose them and justify his own emotionalism. Instead, he is motivated to report these moments because of his own emotional passion—and by his realization that a Holmes without emotion is an automaton, as much as a Watson without insight cannot be a writer.

This doesn't stop Holmes, though, from upbraiding Watson on a number of occasions for investing his stories with too much emotionalism, too much romance. Says Holmes in *The Sign of the Four:*

Detection is, or ought to be, an exact science, and should be treated in the same cold and unemotional manner. You have attempted to tinge it with romanticism, which produces much the same effect as if you worked a love story into the fifth proposition of Euclid.

In "The Adventure of the Retired Colourman," Watson attempts to report the results of an investigation carried out at Holmes's request: "Right in the middle of [the weary suburban highways] lies this old home, surrounded by a high sun-baked wall mottled with lichens and topped with moss, the sort of wall—" To this Holmes responds sharply: "Cut out the poetry, Watson. . . . I note that it was a high brick wall."

These examples are typical of Holmes's impatience with Watson's writing style, of the scientist's impatience with the novelist's techniques. Yet even in the midst of this apparent resentment, it is Holmes in "A Case of Identity" who, by commenting on truth versus fiction, suggests, perhaps without knowing it, that even truth may demand Watson's particular narrative skills:

> My dear fellow, life is infinitely stranger than anything the mind of man could invent. We would not dare to conceive the things which are really mere commonplaces of existence. If we could fly out of that window hand in hand, hover over this great city, gently remove the roofs, and peep in at the queer things which are going on . . . it would make all fiction with its conventionalities and foreseen conclusions most stale and unprofitable.

To remark that truth is stranger than fiction may seem insipid on Holmes's part, but when coupled with his strong objection to Watson's treatment of his cases, the irreconcilable contradiction of Holmes's position becomes clear. Holmes himself suggests that the cold, hard truth is more like fiction than fiction itself.

He suggests this, in fact, not only by implication but in actual practice. Toward the end of his association with Watson, Holmes finds it necessary to record a story himself since Watson had not been present. In "The Adventure of the Blanched Soldier," Holmes writes:

... I have often had occasion to point out to [Watson] how super-
ficial are his own accounts and to accuse him of pandering to the
popular taste instead of confining himself rigidly to facts and figures. . . . I am compelled to admit that, having taken my pen in
hand, I do begin to realize that the matter must be presented in
such a way as may interest the reader.

He goes on to tell a very Watsonian tale, and the same thing happens in "The Adventure of the Lion's Mane" in which the style is again
Watson's but the narrator is Holmes. It should be small surprise that
Holmes is able to adopt Watson's writing style when he needs to, as
he is obviously well-versed in literature generally, and more than familiar with Watson's writing in particular. Despite Watson's initial observation in *A Study in Scarlet* that Holmes's knowledge of literature is
"nil," Holmes quotes or paraphrases from literature in a majority of
the stories—from Horace and Hafiz to Shakespeare and Sand. It's just
that on the most ideal level, the scientific logician—which Holmes
always *strives* to be—must find the emotional element of storytelling
repugnant.

So it's almost always left to Watson to record the most galvanic
moments of emotional stress, for to have Holmes do so would be to
compromise his rational facade. Probably the best example in all of
the stories is Watson's relating the horrors that he and Holmes experience when they come under the effects of the Devil's Foot drug:

A thick, black cloud swirled before my eyes, and my mind told me
that within this cloud, unseen as yet, but about to spring out upon
my appalled senses, lurked all that was vaguely horrible, all that
was monstrous and inconceivably wicked in the universe. Vague
shapes swirled and swam amid the dark cloud-bank, each a men-
ace and a warning of something coming, the advent of some
unspeakable dweller upon the threshold, whose very shadow
would blast my soul.

Though Holmes may disapprove of the way Watson describes the
event, he certainly cannot deny its emotional intensity. This instant of
"freezing horror" is the most eloquent emblem of the Holmes-Watson
friendship. Holmes, with his typical cool scientific curiosity, suggests

that he and Watson experiment with the drug, which is suspected in a murder case. Because of his fraternal loyalty, Watson agrees. Bound by these archetypal motives, the two men plunge together into a pit of horror, and together are subject to its terrors. But at this moment of ultimate hellishness, it is Watson, not Holmes, who rouses himself to sanity enough to drag himself and Holmes into fresh air where they are able to recover. And it is Holmes who softens his aloofness enough to apologize to his friend: "Upon my word, Watson!" says Holmes. "I owe you both my thanks and an apology. It was an unjustifiable experiment even for one's self, and doubly so for a friend. I am really very sorry."

So the balance between the heart and the head in this deep friendship—between what Holmes calls the love story and the fifth proposition of Euclid—is not in a rigid opposition between an unperceptive bumbler and a logician who always sets things right. Nor is it, as some pastiche writers have suggested, between a Holmes who is incapable of controlling his emotions and a Watson capable of asserting Holmesian logic when it becomes necessary. If that were the case, either Holmes or Watson would be expendable at any given moment.

No, it is between a very human logician and a very insightful physician who represent different means of interpreting life—but who, reaching toward one another, provide a cohesive quality to the Sherlockian Canon that has unified its sixty stories in the reading public's fond eye for more than seventy years.

And if ever there were any doubt as to the profound depth of Holmes and Watson's friendship, it must utterly vanish in witnessing the scene in "The Adventure of the Three Garridebs" when Watson takes a bullet in the leg from the pistol of the vicious Killer Evans. Grabbed up in Holmes's "wiry arms" after Evans is subdued, Watson is helped to a chair, the detective fairly shouting: "You're not hurt, Watson? For God's sake, say that you are not hurt!" And turning to Evans, he adds chillingly: "If you had killed Watson, you would not have left this room alive."

SHERLOCK HOLMES ON THE INTERNET

Christopher Redmond

THE CHAMPION LETTER-WRITER of the Baker Street Irregulars, the late John Bennett Shaw, was not a user of the Internet. His typewritten letters, rich with character, would not have translated well into E-mail format. Then again, who knows what he might have made of this new medium if he had been with us longer? Today it seems a requirement that the Sherlockian's bookshelf, laden with volumes Shaw recommended in a list of one hundred "basic" books about Sherlock Holmes, must be accompanied by a connection to the wires that circle the world, wires that distribute a whole new form of Sherlockian literature.

Today's Sherlockians live with one foot in the computer age and the other in the Victorian age. For those of us who love Sherlock Holmes, our heads, and frequently our typing fingers, are firmly in the world of computers and networks, but our hearts and our inward eyes are in the age of gaslight and telegrams.

Take a look at one of those one hundred best books, the *Encyclopaedia Sherlockiana* of Jack Tracy, published in 1977 and unlikely ever to be surpassed as an essential reference book about the Holmes stories. The introduction is one of the finest pieces of Sherlockian writing ever, eloquent and thought provoking. However, I think it's also wrong. Tracy asserts that everything has changed since the late

Victorians, that modern readers can't be expected to understand the olden days—not just the details of daily life, the gasogenes and post office pens and shillings, but larger matters of scientific optimism, psychological unsophistication, and ethnocentric confidence. But we are still the product of Victorian thinking. We may be more cynical than the Victorians, but our lives are governed by mass media, corporations, and statistics—all essentially Victorian inventions.

It's startling to realize that the invention of the computer came closer to 1895 than to 2001. Various candidates to be the first were developed in the 1940s. And although there were military needs for computing devices, the real impulse for the development of data processing equipment was the need to deal with masses of census information, largely a product of the Victorian urge to count, measure, and control. Those early computers were what are called mainframes. Desktop computers are more familiar to most people now, joined by laptops and palmtops, and the action is not so much in inventing individual computers as in hooking them together.

In 1983, I helped to put together an issue of the little magazine *Canadian Holmes* about Sherlock Holmes and the computer. One can't read those articles now without smiling. We all saw computers as nothing but big calculators. One article assessed how useful a computer might be in calculating a train's speed based on how fast the telegraph poles fly past, as Holmes did in the story "Silver Blaze." There was some recognition of the computer for manipulating words. (Watson using WordPerfect to record Holmes's adventures.) The possibility of databases from which Holmes might retrieve information when needed was seen as far-fetched. There was no inkling of the computer in its central use these days as a communications device. The killer application, E-mail, never crossed anybody's mind.

Sherlock Holmes himself welcomed technology. The first time we glimpse him, in *A Study in Scarlet*, he is devising a chemical test for blood, and later he seems current about typewriters, microscopes, and gramophones. Later still, he installs a telephone at Baker Street. And if Holmes enjoys technology, unquestionably Sherlockians do, and use computers lavishly, especially as the access point to networks—that is, the Internet.

Internet users are very often looking at Web sites and interacting with them. However, the Internet also includes E-mail, and other

forms of communication such as newsgroups and chatrooms. As software becomes more sophisticated, these channels are becoming more
or less unified; a user can click from a Web site to send E-mail, or from
an E-mail message to go to a Web site. And pretty much anything on
the Internet can also be captured and distributed on a CD-ROM. The
important differences have to do with convenience (CD-ROMs are
faster and don't require wires) and cost (usually the user pays to
acquire them, whereas the Internet is more or less free). So most of
what can be said about the Internet is potentially true about those
shiny round disks as well.

When anyone looks for Sherlock Holmes on the Internet, the first
thing to expect would be the texts of the stories. The sixty stories are
available on sites all over the Web, in English and in several transla-
tions, although it's not quite clear who first put them onto a Web site,
or when. In 1999 *The Adventures of Sherlock Holmes* appeared in the
repertoire of Project Gutenberg, the most extensive site for literary
texts, and other parts of the Canon are being added. But the final volume, *The Case-Book of Sherlock Holmes,* is not there, because American
copyright law still covers the *Case-Book* stories. Those last dozen tales
are, however, available—even to American users—from sites in several
other countries.

The same questions come up that Sherlockians raise when they
look at a printed copy of the tales: What text is this, and how good is
it? Even casual readers know about some variations from one printed
edition to another: the passage that appears in both "The Cardboard
Box" and "The Resident Patient" in many editions, the famous "crows"
(rather than "crowds") at the Lyceum Theatre in *The Sign of the Four,*
and so on. Any edition is better than none, and adequate to captivate
a twelve year old. But the experienced reader wants a good text, especially if thinking of basing a research paper on the information in the
printed pages.

Most texts available on the Internet are apparently derived from a
scanning done by Robert Stek twenty years ago. He originally distributed the scanned text on diskettes, and today's texts on the Web and
CD-ROM are generally copies of copies of his. Computer-literate Sherlockians are hugely indebted to Stek, but what he produced contains
a number of errors, as most scanned texts do. Both Stek's and Guten-

berg's versions come from the Doubleday *Complete Sherlock Holmes,* still the most common printed edition in America despite its weaknesses. Indeed, most readers may not know that there are alternatives; for example, the *Annotated Sherlock Holmes,* edited by W. S. Baring-Gould, uses the British text published by John Murray, with no duplication between "The Cardboard Box" and "The Resident Patient."

Good text or bad, the next question is: Who wants to read Sherlock Holmes from a computer screen? The stories are readily available in print, more comfortable to read than the best computer screen. Researchers are trying to develop screens as thin and versatile as paper, but for now, whether in my armchair or the bathtub, I'd rather read a book than a Web page.

However, electronic texts are searchable. If you want to know which story mentions a picnic, an electronic text will let you find out quickly. Similarly, you can compare various versions of Holmes's famous dictum about eliminating the impossible—"Once you have eliminated the impossible, whatever remains, however improbable, must be the truth"—without flipping pages and dog-earing your book. Last year I wrote something alluding to various colors of light as they appear in the tales, and an electronic search helped me quickly find red light, yellow light, green light, and so on.

So much for texts. There are other Sherlockian resources on the Internet, and an important one is a society, the Hounds of the Internet—a "listserv" that delivers E-mail messages to everybody signed up to receive them. If a member addresses something to the Hounds, all the three hundred members of the list receive it. Because Sherlockians seem to be as enthusiastic in this form of communication as they are in print publications, not to mention face to face, the result is an electronic conversation that goes on almost continuously.

The Hounds have become an important element of Sherlockian culture. Some serious literary discussion goes on there; the Hounds are particularly strong at elaborating and explaining details of Victorian life and background. But the Hounds list is important for other reasons, too. It's now the chief way that news spreads in the Sherlockian world. If an article with Sherlockian implications is published in a major newspaper, it'll be mentioned in a Hounds posting while the paper is still on the newsstand. What makes the Hounds a society are the personal interactions, the intermittent teasing and bad jokes, and the periodic flareups of angry words; that's how people behave, online as well as face to face. And the Hounds have other characteristics of a Sherlockian society, the special customs, private jokes, and adopted names that borrow phrases from the original stories.

There are other Sherlockian "gathering-places" on the Internet. People who have never met, or live far apart and meet only occasionally, converse electronically as though they were all in a room together. And unlike other Sherlockian societies, electronic ones continue twenty-four hours a day, every day of the year. Naturally, individual conversations develop "off-line," that is, in E-mail not sent to the whole group. Private E-mail between Sherlockians is largely replacing the typed letters that used to be the standard means of keeping in touch.

There are other E-mail lists, one or two of them started by people who got fed up with something or other on the Hounds and decided to create their own. There is also a Conan Doyle list that maintains a less frivolous tone. Sherlockians can communicate over the Internet in other ways: on "bulletin boards," for example, or instant messaging, or so-called "chatrooms." There is at least one group on the Yahoo bulletin board system, and a Sherlockian "talkroom" on the A&E Network Web site from the days when it broadcasted episodes of Jeremy Brett as Sherlock Holmes.

It would be easy to extract the worthwhile postings from the torrent of material and collect it on CD-ROM for later use, or print it out to be copied. Indeed, the archives of the Hounds of the Internet are available and can be searched by keyword, an underexploited resource. A collection of the best of the Hounds postings, with some editorial judgment applied, would soon look very much like a Sherlockian magazine or scholarly journal, of the kind that already exists in purely print form.

But there is one difficulty: Electronic communication is not congenial to extended thought, elaborate argument, and deep ideas. Readers have a limited attention span when looking at a screen—and it's so easy to dash off a few quick words that it becomes a struggle to think and polish and revise, rather than leap into worldwide communication with a wisecrack. Books about Internet communication advise a special style of writing: keep sentences short, paragraphs short, articles short; use lists and bullets, and words that get people personally involved—good advice any time, but doubly so when readers are in an uncomfortable position in front of bright glaring screens. Note what happens when you encounter text on the Internet more than a couple of screens long: you print it out, and set it aside to read on paper when you have time (if you ever do).

Accumulate enough printed pieces, and you begin to have a collection. List all you collect, things that don't interest you as well as things that do, and it becomes hard to resist the word "library" to describe what's available over the Internet. Traditionally a library is a collection of books. The University of Minnesota Library's vast Sherlock Holmes collections extend to other kinds of material as well, such as journals and manuscripts. Now imagine a collection of electronic documents, housed not in a building but under the metaphorical roof of a Web site or database.

One great thinker about libraries was S. R. Ranganathan, who in the 1920s offered "five laws of library science." The first says simply: "Books are for use." Books have to be available, not locked up where nobody can get at them. It also follows that they have to be cataloged in some way so they can be found. The same is true of electronic texts, of course.

Ranganathan's second law says beautifully: "Every reader his book." If I want *The Valley of Fear*, then *The Sign of the Four* will not do; and if I want a volume that will tell me what was the phase of the moon the night when "The Abbey Grange" took place, I need *Whitaker's Almanack* for 1897, not 1896 or 1898. Similarly, if only one Web site indexes Sherlockian imitations according to the characters in them, that's the electronic help I need when I want to track down Winston Churchill's supposed encounters with Sherlock Holmes, and I want no substitutes.

Ranganathan's third law is the converse of that one: "Every book its reader." Every conceivable book, or information in any form, will be useful to somebody sooner or later. So we cherish the enormous collections at Minnesota and at the Toronto Reference Library. But we recognize that a library is not merely its massive collection of material. A library also provides tools for finding the right book—or right page—from thousands and millions of choices, with helpful professionals to guide users when they need guiding.

Most of us grew up using card catalogs, the *Reader's Guide,* and similar printed tools. Sherlockians are accustomed to working with Ronald De Waal's bibliographies and the notes in the *Annotated Sherlock Holmes* and *Oxford Sherlock Holmes* editions. Faced with a proliferating universe of electronic information, though, we may be somewhat at a loss. Beginning Web users quickly learn about two or three search engines, such as Yahoo and Google, and are lucky if they learn enough about query language to get the most out of them, let alone become familiar with many other tools for exploiting the Internet. One of the biggest challenges librarians face is to persuade potential users that they have help to offer in electronic research as well as in the use of old-fashioned printed resources.

Those old-fashioned resources had to be cataloged and indexed before they could be found through the card catalog and *Reader's Guide.* A library of even a few thousand books is just about useless unless it's cataloged, and the incredible riches of a major research library are little better than rubbish unless they have been past a librarian's scrutiny. The same is true for CD-ROMs and Web sites. A search engine may add a site to its huge database as the result of a chance visit by a piece of software called a spider, but information collected by spiders is nowhere near as useful as information classified by human experts. (Ask Google about "The Yellow Face," and it will come back with several Web sites about a yellow-faced parrot. Ask for "The Priory School," and it will offer information about modern-day schools in Britain, Jamaica, and the United States.) Some libraries have begun cataloging Web sites almost exactly as they catalog books: title, author, subject, and so on, in an electronic file, the modern equivalent of a card catalog. (A proper catalog record for a Web site needs to include the date when it was listed as well, because a site can change in small ways day by day or even hour by hour, and sometimes in big ways as well. One Sherlockian site, changing owners, was suddenly reborn as a seller of pornographic videotapes.)

These resources have brought an amazing democratization to the Sherlockian world. There are still rare books that collectors long to own, and resources that cannot be found electronically—but the most naive beginner has access now to more Sherlockian information than John Bennett Shaw himself, unchallenged as the greatest of collectors, had thirty years ago. And because Internet access is cheap, a poor Sherlockian scholar is more nearly on an equal footing with a rich Sherlockian than ever before. This new world puts new emphasis on ideas, now that everyone has access to facts. It is no accident that two kinds of conversation are characteristic of the Hounds of the Internet. One is the request for very obscure information, which someone almost always instantly can and does provide. The other is the imaginative, carefully elaborated analysis of a Sherlock Holmes story, demonstrating for example that Holmes got the solution of the mystery wrong, or that Watson isn't telling the whole story. Ingenious thinkers are free from any handicaps of location or wealth or even species. On the Internet, no one knows you're a dog, as long as you don't bark in the nighttime.

It's hard to realize that eight years ago hardly anyone had surfed the Web; now we turn to our browsers routinely, and take what we find very much for granted. It's easy to forget that "Web page" is a metaphor, and, unlike printed pages, can be of any size, can contain multiple media, and can be changed by the owner without warning. Still, these analogies to pages make up analogies to books, and it can be useful to think of Web sites as the electronic equivalent of books. A future list of Sherlockian "books" might well include such Web sites as Hounds of the Internet and my own Sherlockian.net.

Sherlockian.net reached just about two hundred pages this year. When I created the site in 1994, I called it the Sherlockian Holmepage, and it was nothing more than a list of links to what little Sherlockian and Victorian material existed on the brand-new Worldwide Web at that time. It grew bit by bit, until two years ago when I realized that it needed some work. I broke it into multiple pages, gave it a new graphic design, acquired a domain name for it (www.sherlockian.net), and began to add new material. Now the site includes substantial blocks of text, as well as links with the occasional sentence of background information. I persuaded Rosemary Michaud, who had been leading the weekly Hounds of the Internet discussions, to let me include her sixty brief essays introducing the original stories. Other kinds of information followed, and several Sherlockians made articles or stories available.

Sherlockian.net now reaches off in many directions, from pastiche to erotica to advice on how to write term papers about Sherlock Holmes. But the site's backbone is its pages of reference information, and I plan to strengthen that backbone—not to include everything, but to provide a starting point for things Sherlockian that the user can rely on. It's turning into the online equivalent of my printed book *A Sherlock Holmes Handbook,* now unfortunately out of print, the one volume that a new Sherlockian should turn to first.

But it's an "equivalent" of that book, not identical. There are limits to how much anyone is prepared to read from a screen, and, even more important, the technology of the Web gives the user the expectation that he or she can jump from one spot to another, using hyperlinks to pursue a specific idea or fragment of information. A Web page that doesn't will either drive users away or bore them to sleep.

It seems that Web pages are a whole new genre of publication, not the same as books, journals, or television programs, not the same as anything we have seen before. Web pages have rewritten most of the rules of communication, or at least presented us with new rules in parallel with the old ones. This change is disorienting, and among its many effects is resentment on the part of people who maintain that all knowledge exists on the printed page. I have some sympathy with that. At least I agree that a vast amount of knowledge exists only in print and is unlikely to be moved to any other medium in our lifetime. Still, that doesn't diminish the value of electronic communication, especially if we use it imaginatively.

Similar media transitions have happened before—most recently the arrival of cheap printing and photocopying in the 1960s. Many middle-aged people now remember the first time they used a Xerox machine. It was an extraordinary experience, and it gave new power to practically everybody. With the new technology, everyone could publish and distribute ideas—the results might not look as elegant as books and magazines from professional publishers, but they could appear. Every Sherlockian could start a newsletter, and for a time it seemed that every Sherlockian did, with or without anything to say. The proliferation of cheap publications helped fuel the Sherlockian boom of the 1970s, in which so many books were published and societies founded. Web sites have not so far fueled a comparable boom, but the potential is there. The ability of the Internet to link people with common interests, over long distances, seems to be leading to important social changes, discussed ad infinitum in every news-magazine and television program.

The Internet gives Sherlockians a universal reach. My Web site can be read by anyone who understands English, anywhere in the world that the wires reach, and any of those people can E-mail me with their comments or questions, or create their own sites with the capacity of responding to mine. There's also another significant way in which the Web provides universal reach: on a Web page, I can use the simple computer code that creates a hyperlink, and direct my readers' attention to sites created by other people, much more immediately than footnotes and other traditional devices.

The concept of hyperlinking makes the Web powerful. Click on a word or phrase in a Web page and be transported to some other Web page with information applicable to your needs or desires. With the Web, at least in theory, no one need "make a long arm" for the encyclopedia, as Holmes once told Watson to do. The knowledge of the human race can be immediately available, and the only real limitation is temporary, the limit on how much information has been formatted and uploaded onto Web pages. The contents of Holmes's commonplace books would have been immensely more useful to him if they had been stored in this format. And because it is searchable, Holmes would never have risked losing data through the notorious eccentricities of his filing system, such as classifying "venomous lizard or gila" under V.

We do not yet have much Sherlockian hypertext, but chances are we soon will. A model is the Web files that Leslie Klinger has made available as he works on his (printed) *Sherlock Holmes Reference Library*, the successor of Baring-Gould's *Annotated Sherlock Holmes*. Both sets of books—Baring-Gould's two omnibus volumes from a generation ago, the four individual volumes of Klinger's published so far—consist of the full text of the Sherlock Holmes tales with appended notes. The Web pages I refer to have turned Klinger's notes into hyperlinks that could—if their creator had more time to work on them—lead to other pieces of online data, background knowledge, illustrations, and so on. All knowledge is connected, and there seems no field of study that a Sherlockian can not make relevant. So hyperlinks can go on forever.

Unlike a spider's web, the electronic Web does not have a single center. Practically any piece of it can be the center, with all other extant pages connected to it (more than a billion, with more being created every second). For a Sherlockian, it might seem logical to want a properly annotated text of the tales such as Klinger's as the center. But there are large parts of Sherlockiana not directly related to the stories, such as pastiches, films, cartoons, societies, and so on. I like to think of my own site, Sherlockian.net, as being the center to which everything else is attached, but perhaps the ultimate center for the Sherlockian Web would be a properly annotated version of De Waal's bibliography, *The Universal Sherlock Holmes.* It does exist on the Internet, thanks to the University of Minnesota. But so far it is a bare text, without hyperlinks. The possibilities all lie ahead.

There has been talk of creating a CD-ROM using hyperlinks to connect De Waal's bibliography, the *Annotated Sherlock Holmes,* and other central Sherlockian works, such as Tracy's *Encyclopaedia.* I do not know if someone will make the dream come true in our lifetime, and I certainly don't know how well it will be done. The one prediction I can make is that there will continue to be other Sherlockian works to which it will need to be linked. *The Baker Street Journal,* fifty years of it, is now available on CD-ROM, as are Conan Doyle's other works. Other CD-ROMs are certain to follow. The possibilities are endless, and any hyperlink that is even a possibility becomes a desire and then a need.

However, I doubt that any hyperlinked Canon will eliminate traditional books and journals. It will change the way certain kinds of research are done, replacing page flipping with electronic searching, but the connections offered in any hypertext site are unlikely to be a match for the whimsical and creative connections made in the human user's mind. Here is an unanswerable question: Will such a site look most like a book, a journal, or a library? Remember that a hyperlink does not have to be aimed at text. It can be aimed at a picture, a movie, a sound clip, or electronic mail to a live human being; a comprehensive Sherlockian hypertext site might resemble a society meeting more than print.

That observation about the expanding scope of hypertext—not just hypertext but, increasingly, hyperlife—leads to a final thought. Could the Internet be a way to escape into the London of Holmes's day? Sherlockians are talented escapists already, and as technology advances, we will be able to make the escape come almost literally true. I am thinking of the convergence of two computer technologies: databases and virtual reality.

Already there are computer games in which the player's character moves about Holmes's London. "The Case of the Rose Tattoo" is no longer available, but continues to intrigue users. Its London is greatly simplified, but increasingly powerful computers could base an authentic Victorian London on the details of Ordnance Survey maps. Today's Internet user can take a "virtual tour" of the campus where I work, or of St. Peter's Basilica in the Vatican. A computerized walk through Victorian London will soon be possible, and tomorrow's gamer will not merely click on a polygon labeled "Scotland Yard," but see the building, with little constables like the figures in SimCity streaming out of it. From there, it will be a very small step to travels through London in the company of Sherlock Holmes and his Watson—a Sherlockian escape into virtual reality from which it will be tempting not to return. Making this convincing will require detailed graphics and masses of data, but there can be few human settlements better documented than London during the Victorian era. The only obstacle is cost, and cost continues to go down as computers steadily become more powerful. If the program is powerful enough, and fully interactive, we may one day stroll down a Regent Street that will never exist in reality again, or ride out to Norwood, or spy on the sordid occupants of Mitre Square.

Until then, which may be sooner than we think, the Internet already has much to offer. Amazing as it is, it will soon be even more disorienting for those whose mental model of the world is not so very different from Watson's or Conan Doyle's. A good many of us may wither before its blast, as Holmes said in a somewhat different context. But I firmly believe that the Internet has the paradoxical ability to move us not just into the golden future, but into the golden past where we have already chosen to keep our hearts. I can hardly wait until my next chance to log on.

Some Essential Web sites

www.Sherlockian.net
(the author's Web site)

www.special.lib.umn.edu/rare/holmes.html
(University of Minnesota Library's Sherlock Holmes Collections)

www.bakerstreetjournal.com
(The Baker Street Journal [Baker Street Irregulars])

www.bcpl.net/~lmoskowi/hounds/hounds.html
(Hounds of the Internet)

www.ash-tree.bc.ca/acdsocy.html
(Arthur Conan Doyle Society)

www.acdfriends.org
(Friends of the Arthur Conan Doyle Collection [Toronto Public Library])

www.sherlock-holmes.org.uk
(Sherlock Holmes Society of London)

www.westminster.gov.uk/libraries/services/special/sherlock/
index.cfm
(Sherlock Holmes Collection, Marylebone Library [London])

A SHERLOCKIAN LIBRARY

Jon Lellenberg and Daniel Stashower

THE AMOUNT OF material that has been published about Sherlock Holmes, just in the English language alone, is immense. In 1979, John Bennett Shaw of Santa Fe, New Mexico, a prominent Baker Street Irregular and bibliophile, compiled the list of one hundred basic books about Sherlock Holmes mentioned by Christopher Redmond in his preceding essay "Sherlock Holmes and the Internet." Shaw revised and updated this list periodically; the last update was in 1993, a year before his death.

We have chosen to compile a new list of our own here, for a number of reasons. Some items listed by Shaw have since been eclipsed by newer ones better fulfilling the promise of their particular subject matter. Others on Shaw's list were notable as rarities, hard to find and expensive to purchase. Some were so arcane, or so closely associated with the local chapters ("scion societies") of the BSI that were publishing them, that they can only be truly appreciated after having been initiated into the mysteries of Sherlockiana.

We give you here fifty book and periodical titles written or edited by members or close friends of the Baker Street Irregulars, men and women who know and love Sherlock Holmes and Dr. Watson best. Editions noted, unless otherwise stated, are the first U.S. editions. Although many of them are out of print today, they are often available from used book dealers. So the game is afoot, and the persistent book sleuth has a great deal of good reading ahead.

THE CANON

As Redmond notes, most commonly found editions of Sherlock Holmes contain textual flaws that argue against them for anyone with more than casual entertainment in mind. Recommended here are three especially reliable (if still slightly different) editions of the text, the first of them richly introduced by leaders of the Baker Street Irregulars in its golden age, and the other two newly annotated for the edification and pleasure of readers.

1. *The Adventures, Later Adventures,* and *Final Adventures of Sherlock Holmes* (3 vols., Easton Press, 1995): The classic BSI edition published originally in the 1950s, with essays by Vincent Starrett, Edgar W. Smith, Christopher Morley, Elmer Davis, Rex Stout, Fletcher Pratt, and Anthony Boucher.
2. *The Oxford Sherlock Holmes* (9 vols., Oxford University Press, 1993): An edition annotated by some of Britain's best Sherlock Holmes and Conan Doyle scholars, under the editorial direction of Owen Dudley Edwards of Edinburgh University.
3. *The Sherlock Holmes Reference Library* (Gasogene Books, 1998 and since): A new American annotation of the Canon edited by Leslie Klinger. Five volumes to date: *The Adventures, The Memoirs, A Study in Scarlet, The Hound of the Baskervilles,* and *The Return.*
4. *The Baker Street Dozen,* edited by Pj Doyle and E. W. McDiarmid (Congdon & Weed, 1987): The thirteen Sherlock Holmes stories that Conan Doyle thought best, with commentary on each by Baker Street Irregulars.

APOCRYPHA

In addition to the four novels and fifty-six short stories of the Canon, A. Conan Doyle also wrote parodies and plays about Sherlock Holmes, and a considerable amount of auctorial comment about the Great Detective.

5. *The Uncollected Sherlock Holmes,* edited by Richard Lancelyn Green (Penguin, 1983): Parodies, plays, prefaces, and miscellanea by Conan Doyle and one or two others.

6. *Angels of Darkness,* by A. Conan Doyle (Baker Street Irregulars, 2001): The previously unpublished play about Dr. Watson, based on the American section of *A Study in Scarlet.*

GENERAL WRITINGS

The "Writings about the Writings," by Baker Street Irregulars and others, are truly vast. The titles below cover the scope of the scholarship, the changing perspectives of students of the Canon over time, and the public's response to Sherlock Holmes over more than a century.

7. *Sherlock Holmes of Baker Street,* by William S. Baring-Gould (Clarkson N. Potter, 1962): A fanciful "Biography of the World's First Consulting Detective" by the editor of *The Annotated Sherlock Holmes,* the first annotation of the entire Sherlock Holmes canon.

8. *Sherlock Holmes in America,* by Bill Blackbeard (Harry Abrams, 1981): A visually spectacular look at the Sherlock Holmes phenomenon in America over its first century.

9. *A Sherlock Holmes Commentary,* by Martin Dakin (Drake, 1972): Thought-provoking examination of the events in all sixty tales, by a prominent late member of The Sherlock Holmes Society of London.

10. *The Sherlock Holmes Letters,* edited by Richard Lancelyn Green (London: Secker & Warburg, 1986): A fascinating compilation of public reaction to Sherlock Holmes from 1887 on, through nearly a century's worth of letters to newspapers over the years.

11. *The Sherlock Holmes Scrapbook,* edited by Peter Haining (Clarkson N. Potter, 1974): A breezy and visually pleasing whirl through the world of Anglo-American Sherlockiana.

12. *In the Footsteps of Sherlock Holmes,* by Michael Harrison (London: Cassell, 1958): Classic examination of the stories' Victorian settings in London and the English countryside. A revised edition was published in 1971 by David & Charles (U.K.).

13. *Sherlock Holmes in Portrait and Profile,* by Walter Klinefelter (Syracuse University Press, 1963): A profusely illustrated history of how

Sherlock Holmes has been depicted, and the stories illustrated, over the years.

14. *The Sherlock Holmes Handbook,* by Christopher Redmond (Toronto: Simon & Pierre, 1995): Wide-ranging and in-depth coverage of the cultural phenomenon that is Sherlockiana in the English-speaking and reading world.

15. *In Bed with Sherlock Holmes,* by Christopher Redmond (Toronto: Simon & Pierre, 1984): Freudian psychological analysis of Conan Doyle's Sherlock Holmes stories, with much to provoke both thought and indignation.

16. *The Standard Doyle Company,* edited by Steven Rothman (Fordham University Press, 1990): The complete published writings about Sherlock Holmes by Christopher Morley, the American author and critic who founded the Baker Street Irregulars.

17. *The Baker Street Reader,* edited by Philip A. Shreffler (Greenwood Press, 1984): "Cornerstone Writings about Sherlock Holmes," and the best one-volume introduction to the scope and breadth of Sherlockian scholarship.

18. *Profile by Gaslight,* edited by Edgar W. Smith (Simon & Schuster, 1944): Classic "Writings about the Writings" from the golden age of the BSI, compiled by its Buttons-cum-Commissionaire and the founding editor (in 1946) of the *Baker Street Journal.*

19. *The Private Life of Sherlock Holmes,* by Vincent Starrett (Macmillan, 1933): The *magnum opus* of the best-loved student of Sherlock Holmes. An expanded edition, recommended, was published by the University of Chicago Press in 1960.

20. *Encyclopaedia Sherlockiana,* by Jack Tracy (Doubleday, 1977): A fine readable reference guide to practically everything mentioned in the Sherlock Holmes stories. An expanded paperback edition was published by Avon in 1979.

BIBLIOGRAPHY

Looking for more after reading the fifty books and periodicals in this list? Ronald De Waal may have missed a few items about Sherlock Holmes, and John Gibson and Richard Lancelyn Green a few by and about Conan Doyle, but no one in a lifetime could possibly find and read everything that they have cataloged.

21. *The Universal Sherlock Holmes,* by Ronald B. De Waal (Toronto: Metropolitan Toronto Reference Library, 1994): The third edition of the work that began in 1974 with De Waal's *World Bibliography of Sherlock Holmes and Dr. Watson* (New York Graphic Society).

22. *A Bibliography of A. Conan Doyle,* edited by John Michael Gibson & Richard Lancelyn Green (Oxford: Clarendon Press, 1983): A valuable guide to Conan Doyle's work, with a foreword by Graham Greene.

PERFORMING ARTS
Others turned Sherlock Holmes into plays in the 1890s, while the first stories were still appearing, and into movies as early as 1900. In more recent decades, many people first discovered Sherlock Holmes on a movie or television screen. These books provide the history of Sherlock Holmes in those forms, and the impact upon the public.

23. *Sherlock Holmes,* by William Gillette (Doubleday Doran, 1935): The legendary and often revived play, by the great American actor-playwright who performed it between 1899 and 1932, in the edition prepared by Vincent Starrett.

24. *Sherlock Holmes on Screen,* by Alan Barnes (United Kingdom: Reynolds & Hearn, 2002): A new, up-to-date, and excellent guide to Sherlock Holmes on the movie screen and on television.

25. *The Pictorial History of Sherlock Holmes,* by Michael Pointer (Mallard Press, 1991): A profusely illustrated guide to Sherlock Holmes on stage, movies, and television, up to date through Jeremy Brett.

JUVENALIA
Sherlock Holmes has often been abridged for children, or turned into new formats to entertain or instruct the young. Here are two of the best.

26. *Basil of Baker Street,* by Eve Titus (Washington Square Press, 1958): First of a series, beautifully illustrated by Paul Galdone, about a mouse who lives at 221B Baker Street. (Filmed by Walt Disney as *The Great Mouse Detective.*)

27. *Match Wits with Sherlock Holmes,* by Murray Shaw (8 vols., Carol-rhoda Press, 1990 and later): Simplified versions of the stories (two to a book), strikingly illustrated by George Overlie, challenging young readers to solve the mysteries themselves.

PARODY AND PASTICHE

Who has not wanted to write a Sherlock Holmes story of his or her own? These books are some of the best and most imaginative attempts.

28. *Sherlock Holmes through Time and Space,* edited by Isaac Asimov et al. (Bluejay Books, 1984): Best of several collections of Sherlock Holmes pastiches with a science fiction twist.

29. *The Case of the Baker Street Irregulars,* by Anthony Boucher (Simon & Schuster, 1940): A mystery, by a professional writer and critic, in which a Hollywood movie writer's not unwelcome murder is investigated by the Baker Street Irregulars.

30. *The Exploits of Sherlock Holmes,* by John Dickson Carr and Adrian Conan Doyle (Random House, 1954): A collection of new tales by the famous mystery writer and one of Arthur Conan Doyle's sons.

31. *In Re: Sherlock Holmes,* by August Derleth (Mycroft & Moran, 1945): First in a long series of loving pastiches about Solar Pons of Praed Street, by the prolific American writer.

32. *The Incredible Schlock Homes,* by Robert L. Fish (Simon & Schuster, 1966): First of two hilariously punnish collections of parodies by an American mystery writer and Baker Street Irregular.

33. *The Return of Moriarty,* by John Gardner (Putnam, 1974): What happened when Holmes's nemesis, Professor Moriarty, also returned from the dead, written by a British novelist and crime writer.

34. *The New Adventures of Sherlock Holmes,* edited by Martin Greenberg et al. (Carroll & Graf, 1999): Second expanded edition of a 1987 collection of new Sherlock Holmes stories by famous mystery writers, including Stephen King.

35. *Holmes for the Holidays,* edited by Martin Greenberg et al. (Berkley, 1996): First of two collections of new Sherlock Holmes stories set at Christmas time, by famous mystery writers.

36. *A Taste for Honey*, by H. F. Heard (Vanguard Press, 1941): A classic tale in which the great detective in retirement, without his name ever being mentioned, foils an ingenious murderer.

37. *The Seven-Per-Cent Solution*, by Nicholas Meyer (Dutton, 1974): The modern best-seller about Sherlock Holmes, in which Holmes and Sigmund Freud join forces to foil an international conspiracy.

38. *The Misadventures of Sherlock Holmes*, edited by Ellery Queen (Little, Brown, 1944): An historical collection of early Sherlock Holmes parodies and pastiches, edited and introduced by the dean of American mystery writers.

ABOUT ARTHUR CONAN DOYLE

Although Baker Street Irregulars like to call Conan Doyle Dr. Watson's literary agent, he was a fascinating and versatile figure—author, sportsman, adventurer, war correspondent and historian, champion of the underdog, social reformer, psychic investigator, and spiritualist missionary.

39. *Memories and Adventures*, by A. Conan Doyle (Little, Brown, 1924; rev. ed., London: John Murray, 1930): The autobiography; most recently reprinted by Greenhill Books (London) in 1988, with a new foreword by Richard Lancelyn Green.

40. *The Life of Sir Arthur Conan Doyle*, by John Dickson Carr (Harper & Row, 1949): The exciting authorized biography by the famous American mystery writer, and the major influence on the public perception of Conan Doyle.

41. *Conan Doyle*, by Pierre Nordon (Rinehart & Winston, 1967): A valuable literary biography of the creator of Sherlock Holmes, by a French professor of British literature.

42. *The Quest for Sir Arthur Conan Doyle*, edited by Jon Lellenberg (Southern Illinois University Press, 1987): American, British, and Canadian scholars examine how Conan Doyle's life has been treated autobiographically by himself and biographically by others.

43. *Teller of Tales,* by Daniel Stashower (Holt, 1999): The most recent biography of Conan Doyle, with unprecedented attention to his interest in psychic investigation and spiritualism.

44. *The Works of Sir Arthur Conan Doyle* (E-Codex Publications, 1997): A CD-ROM containing nearly all Conan Doyle's published works, plus an expanded second edition of no. 42 above.

BY ARTHUR CONAN DOYLE

Conan Doyle was the author of much besides the Sherlock Holmes stories. Here are the most comprehensive collections of his best fiction:

45. *Professor Challenger Adventures* (Chronicle Books, 1989, 1990): Two volumes containing his pioneer science fiction stories about Professor Challenger, including the often-filmed 1912 classic *The Lost World,* inspiration for *Jurassic Park.* (For the scholar: *The Annotated Lost World,* edited by Roy Pilot & Alvin Roden [Indianapolis: Wessex Press, 1996].)

46. *The Historical Novels* (United Kingdom: New Orchard Books, 1986): Two volumes containing Conan Doyle's superb Brigadier Gerard stories, his novels of knighthood *The White Company* and *Sir Nigel,* and several other historical novels.

47. *The Conan Doyle Stories* (United Kingdom: Galley Press, 1988): Seventy-six other examples of master short-story telling from other collections by Conan Doyle—tales of adventure and of the sea, of sport, of mystery and terror, of medical life, and of ancient times.

PERIODICALS

Many are the serious and amateur journals, past and present, about Sherlock Holmes. These three are the mainstays, and available from the sponsoring societies whose web sites appear at the end of Christopher Redmond's essay in this book.

48. *The Baker Street Journal:* Scholarship, commentary, and society news, quarterly since 1946, by the Baker Street Irregulars. The first fifty years of the *BSJ* are now available on CD-ROM.

49. *The Sherlock Holmes Journal:* Published twice a year since 1951 by the equally redoubtable Sherlock Holmes Society of London.
50. *A.C.D.*: The annual journal of the Arthur Conan Doyle Society, since 1989; a must for anyone interested in the creator of Sherlock Holmes.

CONTRIBUTORS

Colin Bruce is the author of *The Einstein Paradox and Other Science Mysteries Solved by Sherlock Holmes,* and *Conned Again, Watson! Cautionary Tales Of Logic, Math, and Probability,* both published by Perseus Books.

Bill Crider is the author of the Sheriff Dan Rhodes series, the first book of which won the Anthony Award in 1987. Crider's short stories have appeared in numerous anthologies, including *Holmes for the Holidays* and all the books in the celebrated Cat Crimes series.

Sharyn McCrumb, an award-winning Appalachian writer, is best known for her "Ballad" novels, set in the North Carolina/Tennessee mountains. Her novels include *New York Times* best-sellers *She Walks These Hills* and *The Rosewood Casket,* which deal with the issue of the vanishing wilderness.

Other Ballad novels include the *New York Times* Notable Books: *If I Ever Return Pretty Peggy-O, The Hangman's Beautiful Daughter* and *The Ballad of Frankie Silver,* a novel based on the true story of a young mountain woman hanged for murder in 1833, and *The Song Catcher,* which traces a ballad through a frontier family from colonial times to the present.

McCrumb's honors include: Outstanding Contribution to Appalachian Literature Award; Chaffin Award for Achievement in Southern Literature; Plattner Award for Short Story; Virginia Book of the Year nomination; Best Appalachian Novel; SEBA Best Novel nomination; St. Andrews' Flora MacDonald Award for Achievement in the Arts by a Woman of Scots Heritage; and the Sherwood Anderson Short Story Award. Her works, published in more than ten languages, are studied in both the United States and abroad, and she was the first writer-in-residence at King College in Tennessee. In 2001 she served as fiction writer-in-residence at the WICE Conference in Paris.

Jon L. Breen is the author of six novels, more than eighty short stories, and two Edgar Award–winning critical volumes. His most recent books are *The Drowning Icecube and Other Stories* (Five Star), the second edition of *Novel Verdicts: A Guide to Courtroom Fiction* (Scarecrow), and the anthology *Sleuths of the Century* (Carroll & Graf), edited with Ed Gorman. He also contributes "The Jury Box" review column to *Ellery Queen's Mystery Magazine.*

Carolyn Wheat is known for her series of legal mysteries involving Cass Jameson, although recently she has turned her hand to editing short-story collections, including the recent anthology *Women before the Bench.* She has taught mystery writing at the New School in New York City, and legal writing at the Brooklyn Law School. An Adventuress of Sherlock Holmes, her investiture is *The Penang Lawyer* (Hound).

Daniel Stashower is the author of the Edgar-winning *Teller of Tales: The Life of Arthur Conan Doyle,* and a member of the Baker Street Irregulars.

Anne Perry writes, "I was born in Blackheath, London, in 1938. From an early age, I enjoyed reading and two of my favorite authors were Lewis Carroll and Charles Kingsley. It was always my desire to write, but it took twenty years before I produced a book which was accepted for publication. That was *The Cater Street Hangman,* which came out in 1979. I chose the Victorian era by accident, but I am happy to stay with it, because it was a remarkable time in British history, full of extremes, of poverty and wealth, social change, expansion of empire, and challenging ideas. In all levels of society there were the good and the bad, the happy and the miserable."

Malachi Saxon was born in 1944 in London, England, and studied medicine, as well as philosophy and psychology, in Oxford. He went to Rhodesia in Africa and after serving in the Army, worked at a variety of medical posts, including lecturing on anatomy at the university. Now retired, he lives in the Scottish Highlands with his wife and children. His principal sport is rifle shooting, having won the top prize, the President's Medal, in Zimbabwe. Lately, however, he spends more time playing golf, to keep his son, a budding Tiger Woods, company.

Loren D. Estleman is the author of fifty books, including the Amos Walker detective series, several westerns, and the Detroit historical mystery series, including *Whiskey River, Motown, King of the Corner,* and *Edsel.* His first Sherlock Holmes pastiche, *Sherlock Holmes vs. Dracula,* has been in print for twenty-four years.

Barry Day is the author of books on Noël Coward, Oscar Wilde, and P. G. Wodehouse. He was one of the original team that rebuilt Shakespeare's Globe Playhouse on London's Bankside. He has published five Sherlock Holmes pastiche novels.

Lenore Carroll has published five novels and over a score of short stories, usually set in the historical American west. Her last novel, *One Hundred Girls' Mother,* told the story of Thomasina McIntire, who was a missionary to women in nineteenth-century Chinatown of San Francisco. She teaches writing and composition in Kansas City area colleges. Her 1988 novel, *Annie Chambers,* based on the life of a Kansas City madam during the Victorian era, was nominated for a Spur Award by Western Writers of America. She currently works for an environmental nonprofit organization.

Philip A. Shreffler, a former editor of *The Baker Street Journal,* and author of two mystery novels about the Baker Street Irregulars (*The War of the Worlds Mystery* and *The Twentieth Century Limited Mystery*), lives in Connecticut.

Christopher Redmond works at the University of Waterloo, Ontario. He is author of *In Bed with Sherlock Holmes* and *A Sherlock Holmes Handbook*, and Web master of Sherlockian.net.

Jon Lellenberg is the Baker Street Irregulars historian and the U.S agent for the Estate of Dame Jean Conan Doyle.